USING LIFE

A NOVEL

EMERGING VOICES FROM THE MIDDLE EAST

SERIES EDITOR
Tarek El-Ariss

Other titles in the series include
I Want to Get Married!, *A Bit of Air*, and *Limbo Beirut*.

USING LIFE

A NOVEL

Ahmed Naji

ILLUSTRATED BY
Ayman Al Zorkany

TRANSLATED BY
Benjamin Koerber

CENTER FOR MIDDLE EASTERN STUDIES
THE UNIVERSITY OF TEXAS AT AUSTIN

Cover image: Cover illustration © Ayman Al Zorkany. Courtesy of the artist.

Library of Congress Control Number: 2017953586
ISBN: 978-1-4773-1480-7

Originally published in Arabic as *Istikhdam al-haya*, in 2014

The Center gratefully acknowledges financial support for the publication of *Using Life* from the National Endowment for the Arts in Washington, D.C.

CONTENTS

TRANSLATOR'S NOTE

Using Life (*Istikhdam al-haya* in Arabic) has been the victim of some infamous misinterpretations. In late 2015, its author, Ahmed Naji, was referred to a Cairo criminal court after an earlier version of two chapters appeared in the prestigious Egyptian literary journal *Akhbar al-Adab* (pp. 117–126 of this translation). The charge of "harming public morals" was based, ostensibly, on the testimony of a private citizen who suffered a "drop in blood pressure" after encountering the text's sexually explicit language. There is, in reality, nothing remarkable about the obscenities in *Using Life*, and language far more explicit has appeared often in both contemporary and classical Arabic literature. Most observers considered the case absurd, all the more so when the prosecution appeared to have mistaken this work of fiction for a personal confession of acts committed by the author. Nonetheless, after an earlier acquittal, a higher court sentenced Ahmed Naji to the maximum of two years in prison. This marks the first time in modern Egypt that an author has been jailed for a work of fiction. After ten months in prison, and an international campaign of solidarity, Naji was released pending an appeal. The original sentence was finally overturned in May 2017. At the time of writing, his case is awaiting retrial.

Perhaps ironically, such direct and draconian displays of state power are largely peripheral to the novel's core critical concerns. Instead, *Using Life* directs the reader's gaze at the more subtle mechanisms of repression and constraint at work in contemporary Egypt: the perfidy of friends and lovers, the "kitschification" of culture, and, most importantly, conspiracies wrought in the realm of architecture and urban planning. The book is a response, in the first place, to the utterly unlivable state of today's Cairo—"a miserable, hideous, filthy, rotten, dark, oppressive, besieged, lifeless, enervating, polluted, overcrowded, impoverished, angry, smoke-filled, simmering, humid, trashy, shitty, choleric, anemic mess of a city," according to the protagonist, Bassam Bahgat. Let the reader be aware that among the city's current residents, Bassam's feelings are far from unusual. Cairo's decades-old crises in housing, electricity, waste management, and traffic (to name a few) have left the city both physically and psychologically scarred, and have remained unresolved amidst the waves of revolution and counterrevolution unleashed since January 25, 2011. The intervention of the security services into urban planning has disfigured the city even further: unbreachable metal sidewalk fences, forcibly depopulated public spaces, and huge concrete block walls constructed in the middle of major streets are now familiar sights around the capital.

Yet as parts of Cairo have shut down, new aesthetic practices have emerged over the last decade to open new spaces for expression, as well as to repurpose old ones. Graffiti artists have laid claim to the city's walls and barriers. Comedians and cartoonists have attracted cult followings through YouTube, and bloggers have emerged from the obscurity of their bedrooms to pioneer new literary genres (see, for example, Ghada Abdel Aal's *I Want to Get Married!* [2008; trans. Eltahawy, 2010]). In fashion, advertising, and graphic design, independent artists have made spectacular interventions in fields typically dominated by foreign brands.

In *Using Life*, Naji, together with illustrator Ayman Al Zorkany, has managed to synthesize many elements of this resurgent urban culture into something that is more than just a novel. Its publication in November 2014 was followed by the sale of t-shirts, coffee mugs, and a variety of accessories featuring Al Zorkany's illustrations, which the artist has also developed into a short film entitled "The Last Dance of the Blue Anus-Fly." As a book, *Using Life* follows a number of recent experiments in graphic fiction in Egypt and the wider Arab world, such as *Metro* (El-Shafee, 2008;

trans. Rossetti, 2012) and *Fi Shaqqat Bab al-Luq* (The apartment in Bab al-Louq) (Maher, Ganzeer, and Nady, 2014); as a literary-graphic hybrid, it resembles most closely Hilal Chouman's *Limbo Beirut* (2013; trans. Stanton, 2016). In spite of these affinities, it remains a highly idiosyncratic work, whose style and content can best be understood as the product of its author's and illustrator's aesthetic sensibilities and professional backgrounds. Naji, whose former digital avatar "Bisu" was a renowned trickster and collector of oddities in the early years of Egypt's blogosphere (2004–2009), has since become known for his assorted creative and critical works, including his novel *Rogers* (2007), his "history" of Egypt's blogger subculture (2010), and his contributions as editor of the prestigious literary review *Akhbar al-Adab.* Ayman Al Zorkany's background in illustration, costume design, and advertising places him outside the jealously guarded borders of Egypt's literary establishment, and thus pushes *Using Life* well beyond reigning definitions of the Arabic novel.

Portions of *Using Life* are indeed "graphic" in both senses of the word, and this presents the reader and the translator with special challenges. While it is hoped that the English reader will approach the depictions of sexuality, drug use, and urban rot with greater forbearance than the Cairene prosecutor, it is inevitable that certain images or expressions may not fit comfortably with everyone's tastes. In this respect, the reader is urged to bear in mind that certain words in the novel's vocabulary—e.g., "balls" (*bidan*), "ass-kissing" (*ta'ris*), and "cocksuckery" (*khawlana*)—have a different sort of currency, and inhabit a somewhat different web of associations, in the Arabic original. Moreover, while such words are certainly marks of an "attitude," their transposition into a foreign idiom will make it difficult to draw wholly accurate assumptions about a speaker's social status, intelligence, or political leanings. These qualifications apply equally to the novel's illustrations. Sometimes, an image's local significance will be grasped easily enough: to paraphrase William S. Burroughs, a rat is a rat is a rat is a rat, is a police officer (see p. 82). At other times, one will have to be thoroughly immersed in Egyptian popular culture to know that a scientific description of cockroaches, for example, is a jab at the mercurial public intellectual Mustafa Mahmoud (see p. 75).

All footnotes in *Using Life* belong to the narrator. Though literally marginal, they are part of the story, complementing the main text much like the illustrations. While I was often tempted to augment the text further with my own explanatory footnotes and back matter, I place faith in the reader that she or he may resolve—whether through intuition, imagination, or further research—whatever mysteries or mayhem the text conjures up. Moreover, in this day and age, a quick online search will provide sufficient background information on quite a number of the persons and places mentioned in the novel. To facilitate these connections, I have, when possible, rendered Arabic names as they occur in the Wikipedia entries (e.g., Maadi, Zamalek, Natacha Atlas, Mohamed Hassanein Heikal), rather than subscribe to a particular system of phonetic transcription.

I owe a tremendous amount of gratitude to those many who have assisted in the present translation. Special thanks are due to Wendy Moore, publications editor for the Center for Middle Eastern Studies at the University of Texas, for her tireless efforts and support at all hours and stages of the project. Dena Afrasiabi, publications editor for CMES, performed extraordinary and brilliant work in guiding the book through the intense final stretch. Series editor Tarek El-Ariss was, long ago, the first to recommend this book to me and recognize the importance of its translation. I thank Marcia Lynx Qualey (ArabLit.org) for providing many helpful comments and suggestions on the offending Chapter Six, and generously promoting *Using Life* and the work of Ahmed Naji on a truly global scale. For his brilliant insights into the finer points of Arabic-English translation, many illuminating conversations on the worlds summoned in this novel, and support and sustenance along the way, I offer my utmost gratitude, thanks, and cat memes to Ehab Elshazly. I owe an unpayable debt to the anonymous reviewer who went above and beyond the ordinary duties of that role to offer very helpful and much needed guidance on nearly every aspect of this translation; while any remaining faults are my own, this reviewer's insights and suggestions have had a significant impact on the final product.

Most of all, I would like to thank Ahmed Naji and Ayman Al Zorkany for welcoming me into the worlds they have created, helping me adapt, and not minding when I run off to play on my own.

#FreeNaji

#ضد_محاكمة_الخيال

Forever is one thing born from another; life is given to none to own, but to all to use
—LUCRETIUS,[1] 96–55 BCE

---

1. I came upon Lucretius by pure coincidence while rummaging through the Society's archives. He was the first, I discovered, to dedicate himself to a truly monastic lifestyle. Steeped in Pythagorean notions about the world and "zero state," he strove to attain a scientifically balanced level of existence. Through his knowledge of mathematical and astrological formulas, he crafted an ingenious defense of Epicureanism—a philosophy that, among other things, allows man to transcend the trivial flaws of his nature and overcome the temptations of hesitation and regret.

USING LIFE

A NOVEL

CHAPTER ONE

. . .

The *khamaseen* winds blew gently over Cairo that year. Dust storms swirled for just two days in early April. A heat wave passed through the country for about a week, and soon things were back to normal. Then, one day in July, the residents of Cairo awoke to find themselves buried under a mountain of sand.

It wasn't just winds, or humidity, or a heat wave. It was all these things together, with the added flavor of smoke and an unseasonal burst of the *khamaseen*. A disaster beyond imagination, later to be known as the "Tsunami of the Desert." Days and nights. Nights and days. Ten days, fifteen days. Cases of asphyxiation. Eye inflammations and respiratory fits. People retreated into their air-conditioned buildings and boxes, hoping to escape the cursed hell that had enveloped their great and historic city. But this hell would slowly creep inside their fortresses. Air conditioners malfunctioned due to the increased temperatures and the particles of smut and smoke that seeped into their parts. Visibility on the roads was more or less compromised, and traffic accidents multiplied. Infant mortality rates increased, as did heart attacks among the elderly.

The increased temperatures, together with the gusts of sand and earth, all but paralyzed the electricity and communication grids. The government treated the situation as if there were no cause for concern. By the twentieth day, the sands had covered the streets of Cairo. We're talking about a quite specific area: the disaster zone stretched from Nasr City in the east to the Pyramids of Giza in the west, and from Maadi in the south to the edges of Shubra in the north. Layers upon layers of muck and murk, going deeper than half a meter in some neighborhoods. The sidewalks all but disappeared along main roads, which filled up with stalled automobiles, their passengers trapped inside. If you so happened to be taking a stroll under one of the city's famous bridges, you'd see avalanches of sand pouring down on either side of you. Then came the earthquake—or, to be precise, an unbroken series of earthquakes and seismic tremors. The dust storms intensified. Pain and agony covered everything.

Recovery of any kind seemed a near total impossibility. The losses, in both human and financial terms, were just too great to fathom. Yet rescue operations began apace, followed by eager campaigns of solidarity. "Adversity Shows Egypt at Its Best," one of them was called. In September, as the city's residents were just beginning to recover from the most traumatic summer of their lives, there came a series of tremors and earthquakes that would be known as "The Great Quake." It resulted in the destruction of nearly half the city. Then there was an eruption of sinkholes that swallowed entire streets and distorted the flow of the Nile. Whole islands disappeared, including the bourgeois enclave of Zamalek. The sinkholes did not spare even the pyramids, and nothing could be done for the Great Pyramid itself, which was reduced to a simple pile of rubble. All that was left of our great heritage—our civilization, our architecture, our poetry and prose—would soon meet a fate even worse than that of the pyramids. Everything collapsed into the earth or was buried under oceans of sand.

The wrath of God. A curse from the heavens. The Lord had decided to give the Egyptians another Seven Plagues. The destruction couldn't be compared to any of the bombings, wars, revolutions, coups, celebrations, and carnivals that the city had witnessed in the past. What happened couldn't be compared to anything in the future, either, for the city no longer had a future. Cairo was no more. The capital was moved to New Cairo. The details have now been thoroughly documented. Dozens of books and films have attempted to record what happened. The dust storms continued for years; entire areas of Fatimid and Khedivite Cairo vanished into the desert. A tremendous loss; a scandal for human history. The real tragedy, however, was the millions who lost their lives, and even more, the additional millions who survived to bear the pain of loss.

That all seems like such a long time ago. Yet I do not write here in an attempt to remind us of what was, or to analyze what happened. What you're reading is no more than a collection of papers and memories gathered in secret, over a number of years, by a lonely old man. It is a lengthy epistle addressed to the past, an act of narrative trickery in the form of a travel guide. There's no real justification for this writing, either because I've never found any, or because no such justification has ever existed.

You're looking for paradise, but paradise is all around

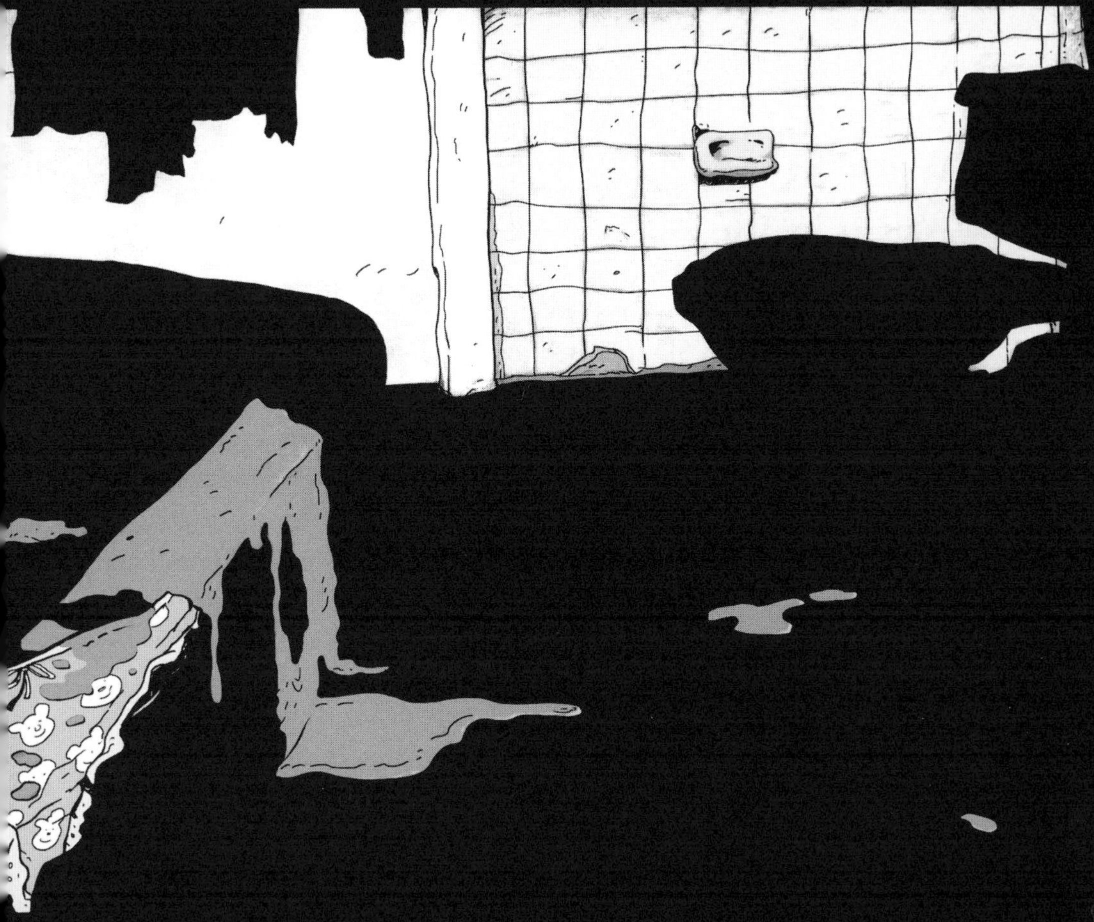

—NATACHA ATLAS

. . .

WHERE IS THE GRAVEYARD OF MUSIC?

"I'm cold," she said, turning around to grab a t-shirt draped over the side of the bed. She put it on and went back to rolling the joint, twisting one end into a little hat. She took out her lighter and set the little hat on fire. Watching the slow, dark burn gave me a tingle on my cock, which I put out with a scratch. I smiled as she passed me the joint and stretched out in front of me. Her nipples stood out from under her t-shirt, and her soft-spoken thighs spread apart, giving off wafts of a pungent perfume.

I probably cracked some joke or snapped a gag. She laughed and told me a little story that had happened to one of her friends. We both laughed, and went on smoking. Before the joint went out, we argued about some trivial little thing, and traded smacks. As usual, I ended up conceding the point, and drew her into my arms with some whispered nothings before falling asleep. When I opened my eyes, feeling thirsty, I found her absent from my side.

A faint stream of light trickled in through the window. *Did I fall asleep?* My phone told me it wasn't even six a.m. I reached for the bottle of water I had left by the bed, but it had disappeared. My eyelids were pasted shut under a film of yellow fatigue. My mind was in disarray, its gears requiring more water in order to function properly. I left the room completely naked, not knowing whether I was looking for her, or for the bottle of water. I found her in the hallway sleeping on a sofa, next to the dog. In order to get to the bottled water, I'd have to pass by them without waking up the dog—a feat that I deemed unlikely. I'd always been afraid of confronting this dog when naked; I was afraid of all animals when naked. So I thought it better to go to the bathroom and stick my mouth under the faucet. I wet my hands and wiped my face. I rubbed my eyelids with water and washed away the thicket of sleep. Even if my other organs were slow to wake up, I needed my eyes to start working, that I might see the *here* and the *now*. Here and now, where everything shall begin. I looked at my face in the mirror, and asked myself a serious question:

What am I doing here?

If I could put up with her arrogance, her stupidity, her hallucinations, her midlife crisis . . . what should I expect in return? At the very least, if I loved her, was still obsessed with her, then there was no reason for me to be here, since my presence clearly caused some kind of disturbance in her world. Why else would she have left me to sleep alone on the sofa?

I went back into the bedroom and put on my clothes, careful not to make a sound. I put my phone in my pocket and made sure I had my wallet. I remember clearly that a gentle breeze passed through the room at that moment, carrying the scent of the mint she had planted in her window. I wasn't angry or upset. But despite my stealth, as soon as I opened the door, the dog woke up, let out a little yelp, and bolted toward me, so I shut the door quickly and left.

I resolved never to return, but the labyrinths of fate and fortune tricked me into coming back again. It was on this return visit that I had her in front of a camera. A moment of truth: no dogs or cigarettes, just Reem, wearing a hijab. She shot me a look of such doom, I couldn't help notice this was a sinking ship.

Our relationship did not end. Friendship and a certain tenderness remained. Love smoked like the *ringa* fish.

Sometimes I read everything in my life as the direct consequence of my father's pressure. "I wanna see you come out on top" was the mantra he raised me by. Putting my life in perspective, I feel I've had a raw deal. Why don't I feel happy like everyone else?

A better question might be: Does everyone else feel happy, in general?

Let me just say that the particular reflects the general. Then the general screws the particular, and why don't the two of them go straight to hell.

But sometimes I see a couple in a public place, or a mother hugging her child, or two friends looking into a store window while sharing a joke. I find that others are enjoying happiness, and when I consider my own situation, I ask, Why me?

And why not?

Those lucky others look at you and ask why you aren't happy like they are. Someday, when God resolves to reward man for his misery in this life, He will strip away his vision and foresight, and return him to blithe happiness and spiritual clarity: a blind beast grazing among verdant gardens, knowing nothing of feelings or emotions save for the fulfilling of his basic needs and cravings. Such is paradise.

Contrast this with life on earth. We're a pitiful bunch, wandering in the desert under a thorny sun, imagining ourselves to be chasing after things that are actually chasing after us. Reem, for example, was someone I had absolutely no feelings for. I would see her at the human rights organization where I worked after graduation, when she stopped by to help with translation. After only a few months there, I lost all belief in this line of work. Frankly, I was only working there because I wasn't accepted at the Ministry of Foreign Affairs and decided, like most of my fellow fanatics for liberalism, to join civil society. When the opportunity arrived to work as an assistant in making documentary films, and then as an artistic producer with a salary I couldn't have dreamed of, I said good-bye to social work. I left the apartment I had been sharing with two friends from college and moved into another in what was known at the time as 6th of October City.[1] When we needed to translate one of our films into English, I looked for her phone number and initiated our first direct contact.

A few days after our first formal meeting, I got a text message from her.

It was two in the morning, and she was inviting me for a beer at the Odeon Hotel downtown. Two days later, we were sinking our teeth into each other on her sofa.

The day after that, under the cover of night, I left her place for good. We traded insults over the phone, before she hung up on me for no goddamn reason. I was just as loud and incoherent back at

---

1. At the time, 6th of October had not yet become its own province, let alone the bustling port city of today. October was still a suckling child feeding off the sperm, smoke, and fire of Cairo's sizzling teat.

her, and couldn't care less about the consequences. As far as I was concerned, let the buck go fuck the duck. I determined not to return her calls, and to help myself stick to this plan, I changed her name to "X3" on my phone.

I spent the rest of the day trying to understand what had happened. I could put up with her inanities; I could put up with that motherly affection she exuded in taps and tickles. But this was a warning signal, a yellow card. She was reminding me that she was seven years older than me, but this is precisely what attracted me to her in the first place. The girl's a dried-out crock of bull, a chewed-up stick of gum. She's a slice of shrimp withering in lard. Still, I'm prepared to take any of this, but not to wake up and find she's left my side. Especially if I'm at her place—that's just rude, and she knows it. I know that she knows that I know. (What a sentence!) And so, I have to leave her house, her place, to herself. All this rudeness called for a pause. It was she who decided this pause should last forever.

Our last night together, we were listening to some sixties rock, something by Led Zeppelin, Morrison, one of those old rhinos. As usual, she dragged us into an argument over music that she concluded by saying, "You've gotta understand something, Bisou: music died in the seventies."

"Like hell it did," I shot back. "Can you show me its grave? Where's the graveyard of music? Where's the holy shrine of music that houses its goddamn holy corpse? Answer me this, O cruel diva: *Where* is the graveyard of music?"

She put out her joint and flashed me a smile as raw as a raincloud about to urinate over a city in Europe. "Just take a look outside," she whispered, before adding with a sigh, "Just look at this dump."

After the breakup call, I thought that maybe this was all because I'd asked, amidst the clouds of hash, about the graveyard of music.

All that looks pretty silly now; I'm not sure why I chose to begin there. If this weren't the real beginning of my story, however, it would certainly be two weeks later, when Reem received a short text message from someone claiming to be me. I would later find out that this fake message was the first contact between her and "the Saviors"—the name she would give to all the members of "the Society." Since it was my name they used to initiate contact with Reem, I was sure they knew all about our relationship.

The message read, "Need 400 bucks, urgent. Resto called Magou's, Champollion[2] St. Tomorrow 1pm."

. . .

THE QUARTETS OF IBN ARUS

Once, when I was younger, I became aware that my general understanding of the universe was beset by a singular impairment.[3] Someone had given me some mistaken bit of information, or perhaps it had been transmitted the wrong way. Previously, I was under the impression that Ibn Arus was the stage name of the late folk singer Shawqi Qinawi.[4] As a result, while I'd developed an al-

---

2. Curious about the name, I did some searching through the portions of the Society's archive that I've managed to obtain copies of. I found it interesting to know that Brother Champollion was one of the chief proponents of Saint-Simonianism.

3. An impairment of this kind may be the result of something more than just an individual's confusion of the facts, or the substitution of one name for another. In many cases, it can be explained in terms of the imperfections that beset humanity's transmission of knowledge from one generation to the next. The transmission of knowledge has never been a totally secure operation; we have been left to hang forever above an abyss of unfathomable depths.

4. Unfortunately, Qinawi was not a member of the Society, and would never know about the events that would transpire. I made sure to confirm this fact more than once. There were, certainly, other musicians—and even folk performers like Qinawi—who played both major and minor roles in the history of urban planning. Here I recall the musician Félicien David, who used his tour through Germany and Austria in 1846 to promote the construction of the Suez Canal, one of the Society's most important projects in the nineteenth century. But Shawqi had no such role. According to the Doctor, the so-called Guardian

most spiritual devotion to Qinawi and his music, I hadn't really read anything about the real Ibn Arus. It's true that most of Qinawi's lyrics were originally quartets by Ibn Arus that appeared in the Hilali Epic. However, Qinawi has others songs as well, and is several centuries removed from Ibn Arus.

The accumulation of mistaken facts about both men led me to another set of assumptions and false impressions. I imagined that Shawqi Qinawi's life was split into two distinct phases: first, that of the sixty-something highway bandit, imposing his will through brute force and demanding loyalty payments from terrorized victims; and second, that of a love-struck poet, whose fifteen-year-old bride ran away with another man on their wedding day, turning his world upside-down and leaving him with nothing but his woeful songs about the wiles of women and the treachery of fate. Shawqi / Ibn Arus, the long-necked man cradling a fiddle, was both men. Fixated on this image and carried away by his music, I thought it likely, too, that his bride and her lover had ended up renting a cheap basement apartment on Faisal Street.[5] What a miserable life!

---

of Cairo, Shawqi belonged to that group of mortals whom the Society's musicians considered worthy of close attention. This group could even on occasion provide valuable insight about life and its mysteries, and should thus be dealt with mercifully.

5. I have a special hatred for this street, and even now I get disgusted by the mere mention of its name. It's exactly like the human appendix: at some point in human evolution it probably helped with something important like the digestion of the cellulose found in plants. That was back when all was still young and green—catch my drift? In any case, the appendix used to store such substances and digest them patiently, but today our diets have changed. The fancy young women of Cairo now follow nutritional regimes based largely on the consumption of grains. If one of them ever dared to go down to Faisal Street, it's quite likely she'd pass out from a mere whiff of the liver carts. We have evolved beyond Faisal Street. It remains only to remind this city that parts of it lie in permanent waste. Faisal threatens Cairo like a silver dagger shoved against your aorta. And of course nobody cared, but then . . . then all this happened. Dear God, how I detest Faisal Street.

CHAPTER TWO

• • •

Love let up . . . the gnats went their way
—SHAWQI QINAWI (IBN ARUS)

Reem stepped into Magou's. In the entryway there stood an older sort of gentleman with a thick mustache, who greeted her with a rather uncomfortable smile. Before she could get a word out, the man motioned toward a narrow wooden staircase in the back. Going up in her short black dress, she imagined the lumpy old dope could see her thighs from the bottom of the stairs, but didn't care. She didn't care either that her breasts pressed against her t-shirt like a pair of lemons, or that her curly hair overflowed from her sky-blue bandanna.

Her odor is that of something callous and cruel, but she's fragile to the touch. When kissing her neck or licking her like a hungry dog, I sometimes was afraid she'd snap like a twig.

Upstairs, it smelled of hamburgers burning in grease. There she encountered another old rooster, but this one was thin. A plumage of white hair ringed his otherwise bald head, and he smiled at her from behind a pair of minute spectacles. With his full suit and bow tie, it wouldn't be far off to call the man eccentric. He opened a red door in the wall, revealing a dimly lit corridor.

It's strange how we, the denizens of this great city, treat our relationships with others. Your close friend becomes a stranger. Your friend becomes your enemy. Yet the past remains a part of your relationship, and a part of you as well. Then there are those deep-seated beliefs that stick to you wherever you go.

For example, Reem made the decision that her relationship with Bassam was "over and done with." As a mature and experienced woman, she was fully aware of the consequences of her decision. True, she would have liked for them to remain friends, but she also believed that any sort of lingering ties between them would fundamentally destabilize her.

Don't look behind you, lest you turn into a pillar of salt. So the legend tells us, and so Reem tells herself. But with one simple text message, all of this turns to sand in the wind.

At first, she tried calling him, but: "The number you have dialed may be disconnected." In the end, all she could do was follow the instructions in the message and go to Magou's at the appointed time.

In the dark, the corridor seemed rather long for what was supposed to be just a cozy little eatery. But just thirteen steps later she found herself standing in front of a thick metal door, flushed in the red of an emergency light. The thin, old rooster stepped past her and nudged it open, letting out a draft of cool air that carried the echoes of some pretty smelly jazz. He closed the door behind her as she entered.

Inside was a small movie theater, with red seats and walls covered in blue velvet. In the front of the theater sat a blond-haired girl who glanced at them as they entered. In the back there sat an old man, next to a boy who couldn't have been more than fourteen. Taking her seat in the middle, she kept her eyes fixed on the old man, who wore sunglasses in the dark of the theater, and whose hair was parted to the side like the actor Mahmoud Yassine. He struck her as more interesting than the movie itself, probably because his fly was open and the boy next to him was giving his member a nice little whirl like sugar in a glass of lemonade.

The screen flared up with a series of ads for some cheap porno flicks, all pretty much the same. Washed up bimbos pretending to have a good time. Dark, gaping holes and eyes pretending to swoon. Unidentifiable lumps of flesh quivering in orgasm. Stiff, veiny penises about to explode. Sighs and groans. The boy's eyes stayed fixed on the screen as his hand worked the old man's half-erect phallus in a mechanical up-and-down motion.

"Damn you and your whole family, Bassam. Where the hell are you?"

She spread out in her seat, pretending to ignore the screen. "Bassam will show up any minute and explain everything." Suddenly, the cheap American porn ads came to an end, to be followed by an advertisement for aiding refugees from Darfur. Pictures of children covered in flies in classic scenes of poverty and misery, with George Clooney's smile shining over a bleak African landscape. Then silence. The blond girl in the front row burst into applause.

"THE LAST DANCE OF THE BLUE ANUS-FLY"

The man of the future obtained knowledge. In his arrogance, he defied his Maker, and created a fly.

I am the "smart fly." My mind is electronic, and my mission is eternal. I clean my maker's behind after he defecates.

My maker is of a tribe that knows not of the bidet. He refuses to use toilet paper in order to conserve the environment. He made me that I may wipe his ass.

The leftover particles of shit that stuck to our bodies resulted in certain deformities. Marital relations suffered, and many died.

. . . .

"Don't leave me, Johann! I'm dying . . . I love you, I love you, I love you!"

"Nooooooooo!!!"

The battle was fierce . . .

. . . and much blood was spilled.

But the era of man had to end, in order to save the flies, and planet Earth.

And now we are depressed. For there are no longer any asses to clean.

.   .   .

PORTRAIT OF AN OLD MAN
IN 6TH OF OCTOBER

As I recollect all these events, I try to recapture the perspective I had back in my twenties, forgetting everything I've come to know since. Perhaps that is why I began to write this report.

I remember the moment I started writing the report entitled "Using Life." I was winding down my daily routine, which consisted of a series of exercises to help me feel my loneliness and work my way into nostalgia. Suddenly I noticed the day's date. Tomorrow would be my forty-sixth birthday. The number itself gave me a jolt: 46. I turned off the phone, and started thinking about *Love Letter for Frogs*, the art exhibition I had seen the other day.

What's with all this green? Did we ever even have this color here? If not, then what's all this greenish nostalgia that's firing up our city's artists and urban planners? Even the avant-gardists—those who have always stuck up their noses at nostalgia and kitsch, and who were mostly breast-feeding infants at the time of the *naksa*[1]—can't seem to get enough of it. It would seem that green is more a symbol than just a color. As such, it gestures not only toward the future, but also toward a certain past, attempting to construct a civilizational patrimony grounded not only in Egyptian national identity, but in a broader global cultural movement. All this was taking place at the same time that the National Campaign to Greenify the Desert was touting its new slogan, "Together, Egypt Fights Yellowism"—a variation on its older slogan, "Let's Go Green!"

We never saw any of this green before the Catastrophe. It only got started in the second half of the twentieth century—part of a

---

1. Or the "Setback," the term used to refer to Cairo's burial beneath the sands. An older generation might think it refers to Egypt's 1967 war with Israel.

new, melancholic religion that was born of man's ability to monitor significant changes in his environment.

Like any other religion, the adherents of this new faith believe in an omnipotent higher power—in this case, Mother Nature. They believe man to be Her errant son, who must repent his sins and trespasses lest he suffer Her maternal wrath. The disasters that have beset Cairo and other cities in the past few years have been interpreted along these lines, as retribution from an angry green goddess, Mother of mankind.

The reality is that nature never remains in stasis. Climate change isn't the exception, it's the rule—without it, the human race and all other species on this planet wouldn't have existed. And another thing: nature isn't just green. The desert, with its range of yellows and reds, is a fundamental part of it as well. This whole idea of "fighting yellowism" under the pretense of appeasing the great green goddess is therefore nothing but a savage transgression against the natural order of things.

But who'd listen? These nature fanatics can be real pricks.

Even now, a full twenty years later, we haven't managed to grasp the true scale of the disaster.

In the aftermath of the great earthquakes and tsunamis of sand, an alliance of new construction companies introduced "green" as a catchword in their promotions and advertising. Within the space of a few years, the adjective had become a verb, and from the verb were derived diverse neologisms, which in turn came to form the contours of a veritable discourse. From this discourse sprang forth yet more discourses, which gave rise to a whole new meta-phenomenon that expressed itself in numerous art forms and socio-cultural practices. Even the moon, once silver and white, would "go green."

At *Love Letter for Frogs*, Sara Rifqi tried hard not to let her nostalgia show through. Even so, more than a few of the paintings scattered throughout the exhibition hall were spattered with the telltale signs. In one corner, there was even a group of green frog statues piled on top of each other in the shape of a pyramid. Only this new generation of artists, with their incredibly severe guilt complex, could wish for the yellow pyramid itself to turn green. The phrase "if only" screws them from behind, every day, for the first time.

"If only" we had been more cautious . . . "If only" we had taken better care of the environment and the city's landscape . . . "If only" we had been less cruel to the environment . . . "If only" there had been more vegetarians in this city . . .

These cute little ducklings think the destruction of Cairo was an event as catastrophic as man's expulsion from paradise. They don't know that paradise is a garden of blind beasts.

For several years after the event, many made desperate attempts to save what they could. The Egyptian people were joined in the perpetuation of this farce by UNESCO and the people of the world. "Humanity faces a catastrophe." "Our heritage is threatened with extinction." To hell with all of it, really. As if Cairo's very existence were not a disaster in and of itself. As if abandoning it to such a sorry state long before the *naksa*, and the devolution of its human residents into soulless beasts, were not the real tragedy.

And still the rescue and recovery operations persisted. Search teams were sent to dig beneath the still volatile oceans of sand, only to be swallowed up and never heard from again. *So: Let us rebuild what was lost. Let us affirm that the spirit that built the pyramids, together with the legendary sweet-maker who designed our victorious Cairo, still dwells within us. Let us build Egypt anew, that it may rise from its grave under the sands. Let us sound forth the immortal words of our late great female contralto, Umm Kulthum, that "the whole world is watching."* Such was the new spirit that swept the country. Just as Paprika suspected, it would help propel Egypt and the entire region toward the future. But exactly what kind of future did she have in mind?

That future is now. And it stinks, I tell you.

It's the past with a different name. It's copies of the same, parading as a fresh start.

I pour some hot water into a glass, and stir the mint leaves until it turns yellow. Standing at my window, I can see the boats milling around in October's sand-port. Traffic's always light on Friday mornings. Here's to that.

I read a few pages of *The Brothers Karamazov*, then glance at my phone. I leave the book, and lie down on my sofa. I turn back to my phone. I'm waiting desperately for her to call, even though I know she won't. I scroll through my contacts list, looking for someone I might be able to spend the day with. There are dozens of names I don't know why I keep, and others I know are definitely busy. I start feeling what my mother would call regret, but shake off the shadows before they start to gather. Listen, my dear, now is not the time for self-reproach. I keep scrolling. I stop when I see her name, "Mona May." After only a brief pause, I shoot her a text: "meow meow :-)."

CHAPTER THREE

· · ·

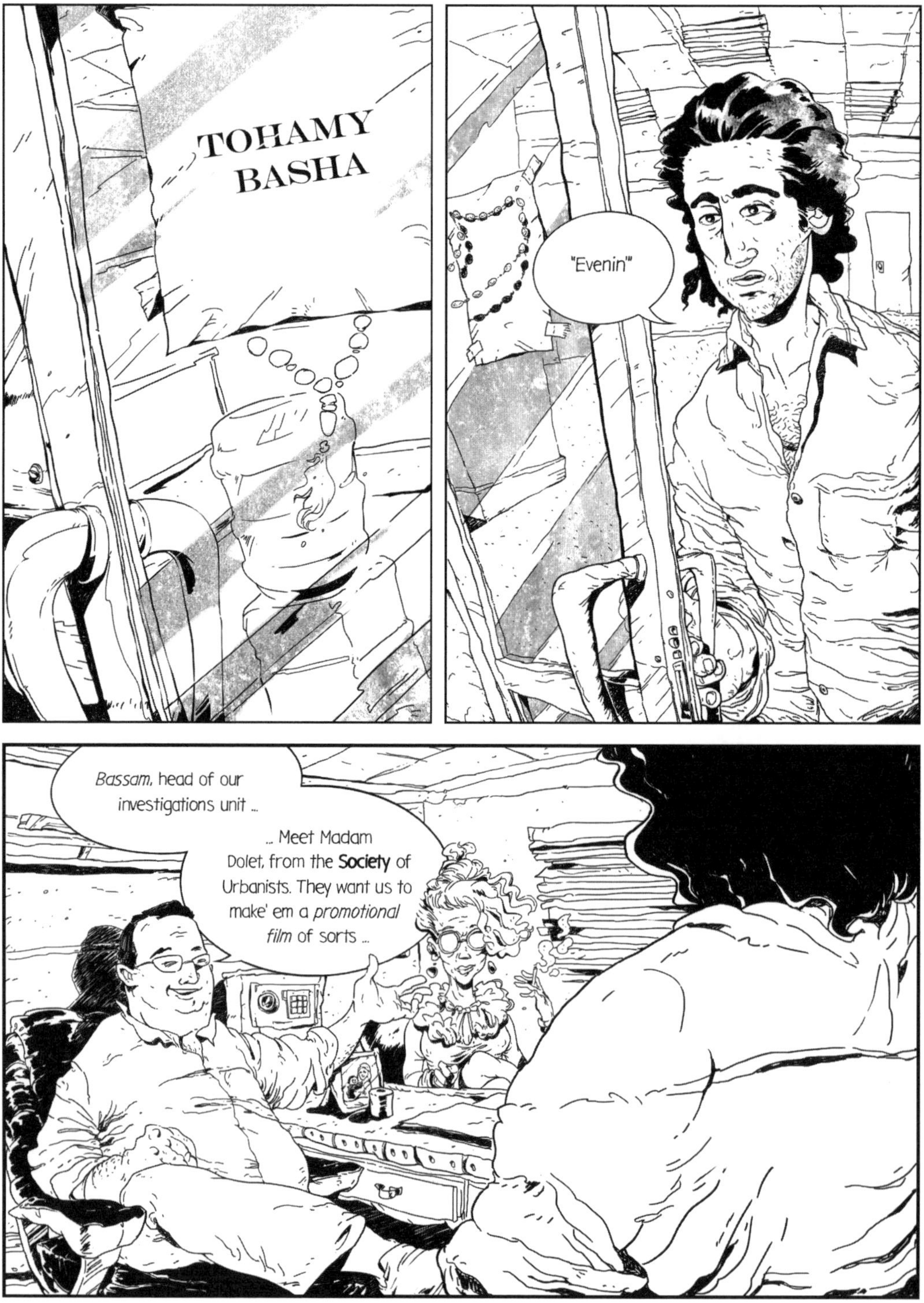
TOHAMY BASHA
"Evenin'"
Bassam, head of our investigations unit ...
... Meet Madam Dolet, from the **Society** of Urbanists. They want us to make' em a *promotional film* of sorts ...

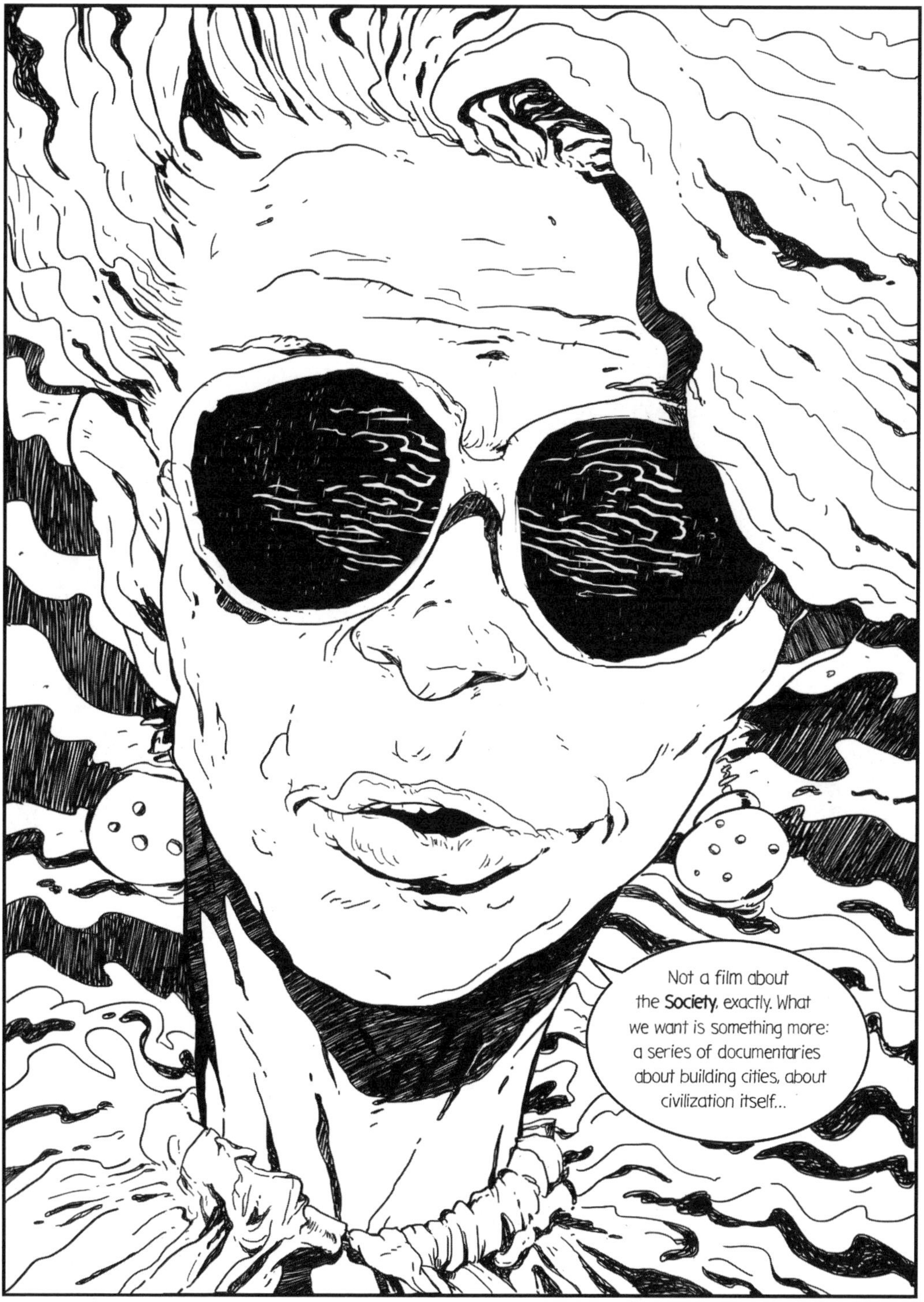
Not a film about the **Society**, exactly. What we want is something more: a series of documentaries about building cities, about civilization itself...

... about the Mother of all Cities, **Cairo**... her plots and planning, her grand design ...

. . .

A LETTER FROM REEM

Since you're pretending to ignore me, and not answering your phone, I had no choice but to send you this via email.

You know very well how difficult this is for me—writing, I mean. It burns me up inside. But I am all burned out anyway, and nobody cares.

My dear friend Bassam,

How are you?

I am well. I believe I've had a revelation. As I've already told you, I've quit my job. I can't stand all the noise any longer. I can't deal with sitting at my computer the entire day, doing nothing but responding to emails, all under the pretense of "saving the children." The only thing I've lost by quitting is that I'll no longer be able to travel, but at the same time, I no longer feel I need to go anywhere. I can stretch out on my bed and close my eyes, and have the whole world at my fingertips.

My dear Bisou. The whole thing was just an excuse. A petty pretext, a messy, misread text. And you, as per usual, were a complete fool. A total sucker.

But none of this should concern you. You weren't involved, and can't be blamed. Yesterday, as far as I'm concerned, is so far away. When I think about the past, I feel like it's the story of some other woman.

When I told you I was thinking of quitting, I found your whole reaction strange. I understand how you'd think that working from home for an international children's rights organization, with a monthly salary of four thousand Egyptian pounds, is all one could possibly hope for in this city. But I no longer have any hopes, not in this city. I don't care about comfort or working from home, I don't care about money, or love, or sex. Maybe a little hash now and then, as it's a respectable drug and comes from a good family.

Knowing you was indeed a delight. You are smart and have a good deal of charm. Our friendship shall continue.

But I still feel I owe you something, for something that might have nothing to do with you. Something of a coincidence, you might say, which opened up many doors inside me, and changed my relationship with the world.

It all began with a text message I received from your number, which read as follows: "Need 400 bucks, urgent. Resto called Magou's, Champollion St. Tomorrow 1pm." Don't think I had any intention of doing you a favor. "Fuck you," I thought to myself. "Go burn in hell." But I'm a good little girl, whose parents taught me the value of friendship. By sheer coincidence, I happened to have some errands to run downtown that very next day, and thought I'd go over to see what's up. It turned out the restaurant had closed a week ago, and the entire building had been bought up by some organization called "the Urbanists." By sheer coincidence, too, at the very moment I arrived, they'd been waiting to interview some girl who'd applied to be their administrative assistant. Mistaking me for her, they sat me down in a movie theater to acquaint me with the position's duties and responsibilities. At the Society, apparently, they do everything "sight before sound." Some of the other people in the audience, I later found out, were members of the Society's Cairo branch. The strange erotic film we watched wasn't so much about the Society as it was about their work philosophy. It was really something. What was even more something was the interview that followed with the Society's president, Ihab Hassan.[1] I tried to clarify that I hadn't come for the position, but he insisted I give it some thought. Afterward, we had lunch at Café Riche.

A really nice old man. It had been a while since I met someone as easy to talk to as Ihab. He helps you understand so much about the world you live in, as well as the world living inside you.

I think I understand now that the bullshit inside of us is noth-

---

1. Can I say for certain that this whole thing hadn't been planned from the start to rope me in? I sometimes think so, but then I'm reminded of something he once said: "Don't let paranoia get the better of you . . . More often than not, a subtle blip in the flow of things—a butterfly stalled in flight, a dog bark in the middle of the night—is merely nature getting back into sync, drawing you back into its regular rhythms."

ing but a reflection of the bullshit outside. Or maybe it's the other way round. In either case, the outside bullshit eventually seeps inside and settles into the depths of our souls. This explains why we've all lost the ability to communicate in a peaceful and civil manner.

I still don't know if it was you who sent me that text, or if you even know anything about the Society. I asked Mr. Ihab about you once, but all he said was, "Bassam Bahgat . . . I don't think I've had the pleasure."[2] The whole thing was probably just a mistake. Or maybe it was a sign from God that he was ready to welcome me back into his arms, and rescue me from the dense smog that permeated my soul.

Maybe it was "you" who sent me that message by mistake. In any case, I thank you for your name having led me, somehow, to this path.

Peace.

.   .   .

A PORTRAIT OF MONA MAY AT TWENTY

"It ain't just that, Tarantino. I mean, I sure is crazy 'nough to just give up and let my brain eat itself. But I's afraid my brain would still be hungry, see, and go on gobblin' up the resta me."

"Oh no, Bisou! No, no! We can't have that now, can we? If your brain started eating you, you'd have nothing left but your ass."

Nyahahahaha—bursts of laughter and, bam, there go the tequila shots lining up on the table. Her eyes rolled over my face as she licked her palm and sprinkled it with salt. She offered me the shaker too, but I was good enough with my slice of lemon.

---

2. Even when he tries to pretend, he does so in the mostly gentlemanly manner.

I licked the salt off her paws and we took our shots. I squeezed the lemon between my teeth and sucked its juices. She closed her eyes and opened her mouth. "Hhhhhhhhhhh," she hissed, her lips all smeared with salt. She pulled a cigarette from the yellow pack of Merits, and said in her usual unintelligible mumble, "Can I axe you a q'estion?"

"You can ask me two if it makes you happy."

"Tell me: What do you think is the most politest thing in the whole wide world?"

"I dunno . . . Like you asking permission to ask me a question?"

"No, you silly. It's when you're having anal sex, and the girl turns around and looks you in the face and says, 'Sorry, I've got my back to you.'"

Cracking dirty jokes was only one of Mona May's many special powers. She had countless others, including the ability to walk through the streets of Cairo dressed in a kimono, the fortitude to pour out a glass of beer like it didn't matter, and the confidence to trick Jack Daniels into paying for everyone's drinks at the end of the night. She could kill small children by jabbing them in the neck with the tip of her shoe, give you a blow job in a swimming pool, and swallow your semen in a single gulp. Then there was the way she would uproot small trees only to plant big ones with perky red flowers in their place. If she wanted, she could shoot rays of light from her fingertips while dancing, causing an immediate surge in hormone levels all around the room. She had expert knowledge of the finely intermixed layers of American cinematic history, and could manufacture biological weapons from simple household products. I was especially fond of her ability to turn the preppy kids at AUC into locusts, then sell them like slimy bundles of shrimp to sushi restaurants. She could be speaking five living languages one minute, and knock them dead the next. She could do the "hovering eagle punch," the "ferocious tiger grip," and of course her most important trick: the "five-fold palm slap," which would make her opponent disappear in the blink of an eye.

I fell in love with her. I fell in love with the tequila, the smudges of salt, the lemon and its sourness, too.

But I also knew better. In times such as ours, falling in love so simply is simply not allowed. If you stare too long into the blazing sun of romance, you won't be able to see the creaky microbus that's about to run you over in the middle of the street. In this city, expressing your true feelings—even if they happen to be mutual—will make you the immediate object of ridicule. They'll take you for a sorry little sucker who always cums too quick; they'll say you're a bit rash, and dangerous, too. For your own sake, it's better to act like just another one of the cold, dead creatures that surround you everywhere. Here, in this city, they tell you to "eat what you please, but express your feelings as pleases everyone else."

I acted like I had it all together. I gained control of my emotions, put my nerves on ice, and joined the hunt. Falling in love in Cairo, you have to prepare for the worst. You can't just walk over to her and confess, "Mona May, I've fallen in love with you."

Words like these could get a man hurt.

You wouldn't believe the amount of harassment, marriage proposals, or casual offers for "a quickie" that she gets exposed to on a daily basis. And if life for men in Cairo is a terrible nightmare, then for women it's a living hell with no escape. Their best option in dealing with members of the opposite sex is to imagine a nice and quiet friendship—the kind where you can sit and talk over drinks like respectable human beings—rather than to risk getting smothered by men whose emotions are all too sincere.

Things being thus, you have to pursue the hunt through deep underground tunnels, or across twisted roads and soaring bridges. And like it or not, you'll have to put on sheep's clothing, even if you're not a wolf.

And yet, who says love has to go anywhere?

With Mona May, I didn't expect for love to give me anything. I wasn't hoping for the next thing. In fact, I was hoping against it, whatever it might be.

I sat up naked in bed, watching her as she looked around for her clothes. It occurred to me that this might be the most we could hope for. I couldn't stand to lose her, and yet, I didn't have much to offer her.

This was many years ago, but the moment and all its little details stayed etched in my mind. Not just the colors. Not just her slender build and black hair. Also the smell of sweat mixed with smoke, shaken and dried together with the fluids of naked lust.

I could've been anything I wanted. And what I wanted, like any hot-blooded male with some twenty-three years and a pair of testicles under his belt, was to abide safely within the walls of an amusement park, sometimes allowing a few customers to enter, and sometimes peering out over at the world outside.

As the humidity gnawed at my flesh in a seedy cafe, I confessed, "Mona, I don't think this business can go on much longer."

"What business?" she asked, sucking up her grape juice through a long white straw.

"Our business."

She put down her drink, and after listening to the rest of my grumbling, took off without saying a word.

That look she gives when brushing away a lock of hair. The small quake she causes in a room when she crosses her legs. The way she lets her phone nest between her thighs; the way her chest bounces when she laughs: you couldn't pay for any of it. And you couldn't get rid of it either. She's a wildcat that knows where to point its claws.

She left me with a bite on the neck, and some vicious scratch marks just above my privates.

For a while she just disappeared. Then she magically reappeared. Or perhaps it's better to say I smoked her out. Every night before going to sleep, I'd close my eyes and emit invisible metaphysical forces to bend destiny's bow, forcing it to send "Mona" in my direction.

What we had between us wasn't like all those other stories. There was no flame of passion to be blown by the wind, no great drama to inspire fountains of tears. What we had was a common understanding, along with a certain degree of moisture whenever our libidos happened to align. Our friendship was, and remains still, powered by a force whose essence I could never grasp.

. . .

A FLOWER IN FULL BLOOM

I was surprised when he suggested his apartment on Adly Street for our first meeting. But Madam Dolet assured me, "Yes, you may see him at his private residence." When I got on the microbus from October to Tahrir Square, I gave him a call to confirm the appointment and get the exact address.

"Dr. Ihab Hassan?"

"This is he."

"Bassam Bahgat here. Madam Dolet told me I could see you today to discuss the details of the film."

"Yes, of course. I'm expecting you. Our appointment's in an hour, right?"

"That's right, sir. I'm already on my way."

"Splendid, splendid! Tell me, have you eaten yet?"

"No, sir. There's no need, really."

"Well, I've already starting cooking something, so I'll count you in. See you in an hour, then. Bye-bye!"

And with that, he hung up. *You kidding me, man?* I realized then that I hadn't asked him for the address, but decided I'd wait to call him back when I got to Adly Street.

I opened the window and got a hot slap in the face. Cairo in July. A few more days before July croaks and makes room for August, the month of real torture. The billboards crammed together along the highway, plastered with fresh, beaming faces. I took out my notebook, checked that I had a pen, and regretted I hadn't brought along anything to read. I took out my phone and started playing with it, and found I had an email from Reem. I began poring over it intensely, and became lost in a whirlpool of thoughts.

Once, when I was shooting a film up by Muqattam Mountain about the victims of the rockfall, I met an old woman. "May the Lord protect you from thinking too much," she said. I read Reem's email over again, thinking about the strange coincidence that had her go interview for a job she hadn't applied for, and meet the person that I was supposed to be on my way to see. And what was this text she got from me?

The clamor of car horns slapped me out of my thinking spell. Traffic had come to a near complete stop.

We've reached the outer rims of Lebanon Square. There's the nauseating stench of waste from dump trucks and pig farms; a tow-truck threading its needle into a stack of automobiles; a pileup of motorbikes and jaywalkers. I try not to stare at the three fat women in black abayas melting in the midday heat, trying to catch transportation of any kind. Out in this corner of the universe, a special sort of misery springs up from the earth and rains down from above. On the right, there's a great big church adorned with an image of the saint smiting the evil dragon. On the left, there's a mosque under construction; its builders have gone to great pains to make sure its minaret reaches higher than the church's steeple.

The microbus slowly nudges forward. I'm drenched in sweat, but like a good young man I remembered to use deodorant before heading out. I heave a sigh full of hot air and swallow my spit every few minutes. From the middle of this slow procession of cars, I'd estimate it stretches at least to Sphinx Square. And as a matter of fact, while it took only half an hour to get from October to Lebanon Square, it would take another full hour from Lebanon Square to Tahrir. Welcome to the hell that is Cairo, where life is one long wait, and the smell of trash and assorted animal dung hangs about all the time and everywhere.

I used to have a blog. But back in those days, I never really took any of it seriously. I didn't think the kind of writing I did deserved as much attention as, for example, politics, the mainstream media, or chasing after the real money. That was back then, mind you. In retrospect, I find it astonishing how clear cut life seemed to me.

Clear cut, but hopelessly miserable. I would wake up each morning incapable of smiling at myself in the mirror. I wasn't alone: no one else in this city knew how to smile either. Some had forgotten what a smile should look like. And if you ever happened to catch a smile from a waiter, parking lot attendant, or doorman, you could be sure that—according to the natural laws of this city—you were expected to reward this smile with a monetary equivalent. You could also be sure that, in spite of this reward, he'd curse you the second you turned around. Cairo was one big crucible of hatred; it was hatred in the raw.

My job working with Tohamy Basha was thrilling enough, especially since direct political action was out of the question as long as the General was in power. I could look forward to a career in media ("Raise your voice, raise it high! Freedom, freedom shall not die!"). I had many lofty goals. My job was all about ideas, about innovation, and about significantly revising these ideas to make films deemed acceptable to a wider Arab audience, and of course to the producer in Qatar. Part of our work was advertising and promotion. Actually, all of our work was advertising and promotion. As a child, I had a recurring dream about dogs breeding like rabbits along a dirty little canal that branched off from the Nile. Their howls were so terrifying that my heart almost died in the middle of the nightmare. What will Professor Ihab be expecting?

Rapid-fire interviews with the members of the Society. Wide-angle shots of Cairo's architecture. We might even get creative and have the Professor himself go for a walk in the city's streets, pointing out little details here and there. And then, let us shout in unison: *Pray for Cairo, Paris of the East! Our Great Cairo, the City Victorious, built by a one-time sweet-maker. Cairo, Cairo, Cairo! . . .*

. . .

Let Cairo go fuck herself, morning, afternoon, and evening; today and tomorrow and forever . . .

As I recollect memories for this report, I find it strange how I hadn't yet connected the Ihab that met Reem with my own Professor Ihab. Maybe that's because, as I read Reem's message, I was under the false impression that I was dealing with the Reem I knew. The Reem that would always hide the truth of things by constructing distorted labyrinths of detail. I just hadn't registered his name when I saw it.

It took me a while to put things together. Frankly, though, it wouldn't have made a lick of difference.

"So tell me . . . What did you study in college?"

I glanced around, trying to process the place's design. "My major was in political science," I responded mechanically.

In spite of his age, he seemed to hop about with extraordinary lightness. Lighter still was the décor of his relatively small apartment. Its total area could have been about 120 m^2, all designed without any walls dividing its various compartments. As you entered, you'd face the American-style kitchen at the opposite end. In front of the stove was a small table, where I took a seat. On my left, at the far end of the apartment, there was an enormous bed with purple sheets, arranged next to the door to the balcony, which looked out on Adly Street. On the other far end stood a black marble statue of a seminude woman, who held up a lamp casting a soft yellow glow. At the opposite end of the apartment there was a bathtub, and next to it I spotted a washbasin and latrine. This whole arrangement struck me as odd, and indeed rather flamboyant, for a person such as this—in particular the audacious purple that spilled out from the sheets and settled into various folds and flaps around the apartment.

No apartment in Cairo could have been designed like this originally, as one big open space. He must have done quite a number of renovations to mold it into its final shape.

"I know my cooking is a little unusual. I hope it doesn't bother you," he said as he began to set the table.

I smiled, already ready with my response. "It's really no problem, sir. There's no reason to go to such trouble."

It's true, I'm a professional kiss-ass. What else could you expect from an economics and political science major? A whole generation of young kiss-asses competing to out-kiss-ass each other. Politics has become basically an administrative science, with administration meaning the science of wielding power. In order to attain power, you must have a prerequisite in kiss-assing. And in this school of ours, dear colleagues of our collective four-year struggle, we shall learn the goddamn ABCs of kiss-assery, or else . . . Or else we'll learn them in the school of life, which is capable of impressing upon even the stupidest among us the rigor and discipline needed to achieve true ass-kissing.

As my bladder was about to burst, I politely requested to use the bathroom. Professor Ihab was presently extracting a full chicken from a pot of soup. He turned his head and shot me a crafty sort of smile, looking like he'd just auditioned for a part in some Nadia Guindy spy thriller.

"Of course. The bathroom's right over there." He nodded in the direction of the latrine.

With my back to him, I unzipped my jeans and started taking a piss. This proved irksome, given that there was no wall or door that might prevent the splattering of my urine from echoing all around the room. The room was the apartment and the apartment was the room: the outside was all inside, and the inside dissolved into the outside, and it was surely easy enough for the sound to carry. It just didn't seem right that he should hear me as he took his first sip of that chicken soup. Perhaps I was embarrassed. My nose turned red. I wiped my pecker with a tissue, washed my hands, and returned to the table.

My dish was a chicken thigh drowned in water. That and a lot of onion. Next to this was a bowl of boiled vegetables, also drowned in water. I smiled and pretended to smell the food.

"Was it you, sir, who designed the apartment, or did it come like this?"

I noticed that my knife was unusually long and sharp for such a meal, and was set alongside a blue leather glove. *You're hardcore, my friend.*

"That is correct. It was I who designed it. Still needs a few more tweaks before it's done." Pointing toward the bed, he added, "I think a nice oval-shaped mirror would go well over there . . ."

Then, without finishing the thought, he slipped on his glove, lifted his chicken thigh over his head, and squeezed out a drizzle of pink juices into his mouth. He put it down again and started cutting it into slices. The chicken appeared to be still raw. I poked mine with my knife and found it, too, to be raw. How awkward. Should I tell him, or just excuse myself? He glanced at me, seeming to notice my confusion, when the doorbell rang. He took off his glove and went to answer.

"Thanks," he said, and came back to the table carrying a bag with the McDonald's slogan printed on it: "I'm lovin' it."

We used to have a lot of fun pronouncing the slogan as "I'm a dirty whore," a pun that only works in Arabic. One might find it strange that in Cairo, any random McDonald's you go to will be better than its average American counterpart, according to the sworn testimonies of actual Americans. Business for the Golden Arches was good here, and it wasn't hard to see why: for a restaurant to succeed in this city, all it needed to do was combo up things that didn't belong together, and hand out burgers and fries boiled a dozen times over in battery acid.

"Really, sir, you shouldn't have."

"I told you I'd have you for lunch, but I knew my cooking wouldn't really appeal to you."

"Actually, I—"

"By the way," he said, interrupting me, "I ordered you a Sprite, not a Pepsi."

He grinned; I didn't get the joke. I went along with it and opened the bag.

"But why is it," I began, "that you eat your chicken like this?"

He had almost finished gobbling down the poor animal, its white skin muddied together with its pink flesh.

"I don't just eat my chicken this way. I eat everything this way. Just water with a dash of spices, and lots of meat. It's the only way you can be sure you're getting the best juices out of your food. The flavor is pure and unrefined. Its nutritional value is truly amazing."

He reached into his dish with two fingers and plucked out a small morsel of flesh. Then he wiped it in a dish of salt and pepper, and tossed it in his mouth. "And the taste," he continued, "is a flower in full bloom!"

I somehow sensed the piece of meat as it slid along his tongue and pressed against his molars. He chewed with the calm of a young and wealthy dowager sniffing the perfume of a rare yellow bush. I slowly lost consciousness, mesmerized by the slow movement of his lips: two finely crafted strips of flesh, not too thin and not too full, circled by some light wrinkles that branched out across his face. They stayed pressed together, yet I could feel the mincing and mashing of raw chicken between his teeth. All this had a truly hypnotic effect, and I had no sense of time passing until he went in for another bite.

"Tell me," he said, snapping me back awake, "why did you leave political science and economics and go into filmmaking?"

"Huh . . . Wha . . . What?" I said, as if jolted from a dream where I had been drowning in sand.

Lunch was followed by a full three hours of yakety-yak. Boiled coffee. L&M cigarettes. Then another cigarette whose brand and country of origin I couldn't make out. More yakety, followed by yak. Then more yak, followed by yakety.

His manner of preparing food accurately reflects the essence of the Society's own architectural philosophy. Architecture, for them, is not the search for beauty or efficiency. Rather, it is conceived of as the exploitation of all of Earth's natural resources, of squeezing them to the very last drop for the best taste. History, style, beauty, cultural specificity: all these things are mere trivia, a kind of superficial growth upon the base structure that is architecture. The cultures and arts that constitute civilization would not exist were it not for this base; it would thus be illogical to subjugate design to such random peculiarities. Architecture is a leader, not a follower. Flaws in design arise only when this arrangement is reversed. When architectural evolution comes to a halt in a particular city, its spirit becomes riddled with cracks and fissures, and time itself freezes over. Everything, from the fruit on the trees to the meat on the table, becomes rotten to the core.

I'm in the middle of listening to Professor Ihab when I get a text from Mona May.

"Whatya up 2 city kitty?"

I turn off the phone, with a mind to deal with this later.

"Way back when, certain cities like Cairo had reached a point beyond repair. In fact, Cairo had deteriorated to little more than thousands of mounds of rubble, which had been hastily patched together here or there without any imagination, foresight, or ambition. The only question that faced the city's few remaining architects was how to mold this rubble into a form that might somehow benefit—or at least not harm—its human inhabitants. In order to change all of this, we have to start by changing our perspective on the city and how we relate to its architecture. We didn't come to Cairo just to repaint a few old houses or redesign a few streets—beauty is relative, it's not our main concern at the present. We hope only to make life in Cairo less miserable and more joyful, to open a few windows so that light may pour into this vast wasteland."

"So then, Prof . . . We're talking here about a film on the architecture of Cairo?"

"Oh no, not necessarily Cairo. And no, it doesn't need to be just one film." He poured himself a glass of mineral water. "Let us be more precise. What we want is a series of films. It doesn't matter how many there are, and we're ready to pay you any price you ask. All that matters is that we're pleased with the final product." He looked at me with blue eyes so clear I could see my reflection in them. They held me in a grip as soft and gentle as a silk sash. "And that you're pleased, too."

My phone rang again, and it was Mona May. This time I felt the need to pull away from Professor Ihab's rather unnerving field of attraction.

"If you will excuse me, please. I've gotta answer this."

"Please."

I took a few steps away, then realized it didn't really matter where I stood in an apartment without any rooms.

"Hello?"

"Where you at, kitty cat?"

"What's up?"

"Come over to Zamalek tonight, there's gonna be an amazing party on Hasan Sabry Street."

"Whose party?"

"Youssef Bazzi."

"What did you call me? . . . Oh . . . No, I don't know him."

"Neither do I. Just come over, I'll get you a ticket."

"How much are we talking about?"

"My treat, kitty cat."

When I got back to the table, he'd just finished wiping the cig-arette ashes off the surface with a big white handkerchief. It dan-gled from his pocket as he sat down, looking like a decapitated pi-geon spilling blue blood.

"I'll make it easy for you," he said, taking notice of my con-fusion. "We can get started by working on the Ring Road." He took his hand out of his pocket and laid it open on the table, then continued. "This area's quite something. Aesthetically, it's the ugliest place on the face of the earth, you won't find anywhere uglier. At the same time, the kind of popular, grassroots archi-tecture that's sprung up around it is truly astonishing. You won't find a comparable highway anywhere else in the world that's been reclaimed and repurposed like this. Regular people invaded what would normally be considered a no-go zone, and created excit-ing new possibilities and opportunities. This is a very promising model for what can be done given Cairo's current geographic and demographic reality. All it needs is a sort of rehabilitation—or, to be more precise, the place needs an identity. The basic problem with the slums, just like the Ring Road, is that they lack any clear identity. So the question that we want to explore in the first film will be, What sort of architectural identity suits a place like the slums around the Ring Road?"

As I left the apartment, my brain felt like a ship sinking in its own cranial fluids. Throughout our conversation, it seemed as though every sentence he spoke had been crafted with the utmost refine-ment and precision to deliver a particular effect. This was due less to any great wisdom he may have uttered than to his unique pres-ence and manner of articulation. His was a rare and powerful at-traction, untainted by the brutality of force.

The moment I closed his door behind me, I knew I'd be back.

I had the sense that I'd left something behind and would return for it as soon as I knew what it was. As for Ihab Hassan himself, I was certain this was only the beginning. Going down in the elevator, I dialed up Tohamy without knowing how I might possibly explain to him the nature of this project, let alone the nature of our new client. "All right, got it, we'll talk it over tomorrow," was all I could manage. Out in the street, everyone was busy talking on the phone. As soon as I hung up my own call, a small child pressed up against me and whined, "Uncle, uncle! A pound for food!" He repeated his pitch like a broken record, however much I ignored him. Feeling my phone ring in my pocket, I opened it with one hand as I tossed the child a pound with the other.

"What's up, Moud?"

"Sweetheart, how are you?"

"Great. Everything's great."

"Coming to Zamalek tonight?"

"Probably, yeah."

"Holy cow, man. It looks like tonight's gonna be a real party."

"You bet. What time you thinking of heading over?"

. . .

SHAFIQA OF ALEXANDRIA

Cairo's not what you'd expect from a city of its size. In spite of its teeming millions, this is a city that is hopelessly repressed.

A coalition of social, political, and religious taboos conspires to keep everything that ferments in the city's underbelly from rising to the surface. The rare puff of light or glimmer of rot that happens to simmer up from below will be snuffed out in a snap, either by the swarms of flies that patrol the city's hangouts, or the seasonal Black Cloud that seals its atmosphere, or the thick layer of dust that blankets its crumbling streets and alleyways, or the shrieks of pain from circumcised women whose husbands force them into a quickie before the metro closes at eleven.

On the surface, Cairo's residents appear as a wretched assortment of women wrapped in layers of cloth, and pitiful men whose ravenous sexual appetites go forever unfulfilled. A more penetrating view, however, reveals this city of twenty-odd million to be buzzing with shadowy gatherings of all sorts, each with its own secret rituals and languages. The casual visitor will be unable to crack their codes, unless, by happy coincidence, he stumbles upon someone who holds the keys. Cracking the codes by yourself, or acquiring your own personal key, requires a long and toilsome journey in which you abandon yourself to the city in all its filthiness, until it becomes part of you and you become part of it.

The secret societies of the Cairenes include religious fanatics who move about in cohorts of brothers and sisters; homosexuals who organize cocktail parties and meet-and-greets in homes out in Dokki and Mohandeseen; young artists drowning in rivers of beer stretching from Zamalek to downtown; wife-swapping groups in Imbaba; street children overdosing on soda in the shadows of slums and abandoned railroad yards; hashish dealers making the rounds in the brothels of Dar al-Salam; a Church that's maintained its control and influence over its flock for centuries; bodybuilding fanatics; boxers obsessed with their fists; mendicant musicians and worn-out belly dancers in the backstreets of Faisal and the Pyramids District; gluttonous businessmen organizing hunting trips to begin after midnight; junkyard dogs; foreigners who ride motorcycles in Maadi; youth committed to charity and public service in Agouza; folk singers in Shobra; S&M fans in apartments that overlook the Nile in Maadi; families begot of incest with a biological map stretching from the corniche at Rod El Farag over to Ahmed Helmi Street; fornicators with donkeys in Ezbat Antar; the men in black, defenders of security and stability; dog catchers and dog dealers roaming about in bands in the desert; private security firms in the Fifth Settlement; killers-for-hire hiding out in al-Ataba . . . All these secret societies grow up and mature in close geographic proximity to each other. They greet

one another by sniffing each other with the tips of their noses, or
by licking each other's necks, or by looking each other in the eye:
each one's secret is safe with the other.

In the decade preceding the Tsunami of the Desert, the tele-
communications revolution contributed to the rapid propagation
of these groups, portions of some of which actually succeeded in
rising to the surface. The police made a game of hunting them
down and tormenting them. They would randomly expose some
of their members and throw their meat to the media, which would
happily take the bait, add some spices, and throw it in turn to an
audience always hungry to devour the flesh of someone the police
told them was sharing his wife with other men, or smoking hash
at Sufi festivals. Simply lifting up the lid would leave a member of
one of these groups exposed. He'd be wrenched out of the city's
long intestine and left starving out in the street, easy prey for the
junkyard dogs. With a mixture of sorrow and longing, I still remember the one time I met Sally, and my disgraceful disappear-
ance afterward.

To be more precise, what I remember is the partially torn poster
of Shafiqa of Alexandria, which I noticed in the building's entrance as I waited for the elevator. I found it strange that someone
would put up a poster of Shafiqa in an upper-middle-class apartment building in Nasr City. It was touching to still be able to make
out Shafiqa's special glow behind the layers of dust, sweat, and
filth left by the many hands that had tried to tear the poster down.

It startled me to find Sally opening the door in a chiffon robe
with dappled filigree, worn over a blue silken nightgown. She
had just stepped out of, and I into, a hardboiled film noir. The
first words out of my mouth were about Shafiqa of Alexandria—
her violently passionate songs, her smoked-out voice, her dra-
matic end amidst rings of powder and white narcotics. At one
point I found myself telling her about a friend of mine who'd met
Shafiqa's manager and former husband, and learned about the absolutely tragic state she was in just before she died. I went on and
on, trying to distract the both of us from getting to the point of

my visit. I could barely control the sorrow in my voice each time I mentioned Shafiqa's name.

Sally stretched out her hand and patted me on the back. I almost gasped at the sight of her red nail polish, but was quickly distracted by the joints of her fingers, which struck me—or was it just my imagination?—as those of a fully grown man.

Trying not to pull away, I looked her in the eyes and reminded her about the promise we'd made to each other online. "Today's just to get to know each other, right?" For a moment, I hovered between the excitement of adventure and the strange pleasure of acting like a coy little girl. I wondered how big her penis would get when erect. I was now the prey chased by the hunter; our roles were reversed.

"Of course," she said in English as she rose to her feet. "What would you like to drink?"

"Beer if you have any."

"Sure."

"Unless you've got anything else?"

"I have wine."

"No, I prefer beer."

As I recall, the conversation began with her talking about her job as a manager of one of Cairo's international hotels. It gave her the opportunity to come back to Egypt, where she was born and raised, after living in Canada since her college days. Back then, her name was Samir. He was the only child of two college professors, who sent her to study in Canada before emigrating there too. After his mother's death, he suffered a terrible depression; he pulled himself out of it by traveling to Thailand. Later he returned to Canada to begin his career in hotel management, before heading back again to work in Thailand, where his interest in changing genders began to take shape. He didn't transform into Sally completely. She had an excellent pair of breasts, a well-shaped behind, and silky smooth skin that she knew how to take care of. But she still kept her shy little penis tucked away between her thighs.

I remember Sally telling me about her suffering at the hands of strangers and friends alike. Back in Cairo, even among her gay friends, she was treated as a sort of oddity. As soon as she would make a new friend he would disappear, revealing himself to be no friend at all.

She gestured profusely as she spoke, mixing Arabic together with English. After a few drinks, I imagined it'd be nice to have her fingers on my back and her breasts bouncing against me each time she laughed. But each time my mind wandered in that direction, I'd pull back with the feeling that the hurdle to be overcome was too great.

"But I feel you're different," she said to me, while all I could think of was the soiled picture of Shafiqa of Alexandria hung up in the entrance of an upper-middle-class building in Nasr City.

. . .

A COCKSUCKER'S REPRIMAND TO HIS FELLOW COCKSUCKERS

All we used to think about was sex, sex, and more sex. But for a bunch of teenagers in a city like Cairo, all that was available were the images of sex, not sex itself. One had to be satisfied with its mere scents, its colors, some appetizers and soap.

In an apartment out in the Sarayat District, there were four of us sharing two rooms and a common fantasy about a hot chick who'd knock on our door sometime after midnight and come make all our dicks wet. It was only a fantasy, though. Any chick that might try to get to our apartment would have to pass through an endless series of hurdles, from the doorman all the way to the neighbors, who'd be carefully monitoring the habits and behaviors of a group of young men from the provinces. Our only refuge for our first few years in Cairo was the university and the surrounding cafes. I formed a number of close friendships with my female classmates, who greatly outnumbered the males in my graduating class, without really trying to commit to one of them.

Quick-witted, a regular joker, full of enthusiasm, and optimistic about the future. A bright little flame of passion, you might say. By the time I turned eighteen, all I'd had was a high school crush, a few kisses, and a girl whose chest I once fondled.

I came home one day to find all of my belongings tossed out into the street. Our roommate Yacoub Qannawi, from al-Minya, had taken advantage of our absence during the morning period and invited over a girlfriend from the law college. The doorman wasn't there when they went up. But if the doorman himself didn't catch them, he had a thousand other eyes on the lookout who might alert him with a wink or a whisper. Thus, after fetching the landlord and another neighbor, he went up to the apartment and banged loudly on our door. And boom! We were out on the street, reeling from our first taste of Cairo's generous hospitality.

I found myself unable to fully absorb the situation, and it festered like a black mark of shame deep inside my soul. Every time I passed by the neighborhood, I had to stop myself from boiling over with rage. I thought of breaking into the doorman's house, or calling the landlord and insulting his religion, or just taking it out on the entire building by blowing up a gas cylinder in the staircase. I didn't get any further than lighting a cigarette. Revenge is a dish best served cold. Come to think of it, it would be best to take revenge against this rotten mess of a society as a whole. That's it, my friend: take one good shot right at this damn society, straight in the balls, and watch it burst open like a steamy sack of sperm.

I called a relative of mine who studied at a private university out in 6th of October City and asked if I could stay with him for the time being. This would be my first encounter with the enchanting suburb. Even though October was impossibly far from my university, at least I'd be comfortable there. It would become the city of my dreams, and I stayed for my entire junior year. I later moved out to the Pyramids District. After graduation, I set sail across Cairo's boroughs and bridges until finally dropping anchor, once again, in October. In the entire city, I found no place else where my nerves could relax and my mind could settle, free from memory's heavy sorrows.

Quite simply, being in Cairo means being violated. *God has destined for you some heavy bullshit.* Summon all the powers in the world, and you'll be unable to change this simple fact. If it's not a goosing from the left, it's a goosing from the right.

My first complete sexual encounter, from penetration to pulling out, took place in an apartment in Falaky Square. Whenever I entered or left the building, I'd speak with the doorman in English to give the impression that I was an American colleague of the American girl who lived upstairs, thus foiling his attempts at prying.

In Giza Square, my heart almost stopped when I heard violent knocks on the door in the middle of having oral sex.

In Zamalek, a single joint of hash would be enough to make "Lady Spoon" paranoid. She'd spend the entire night having nightmares about the Morality Police storming the apartment and dragging us naked from our bed—driven by the same motives as those who make Egyptian movies, focusing more on the scandal of sex than its pleasure. If not the police, she would dread a sudden visit from her father, who was living abroad.

In Manyal, I would always be careful to make sure the staircase was empty before going up, and wait for the "all clear" signal before going out.

Every romantic relationship in Cairo is an anxious one. As a rule, romantic relationships are always anxious everywhere. But the sheer amount of pressure this city and its residents exert on you amplifies the anxiety beyond belief. A man could lose his honor at any moment because of a prying doorman or shrewish neighbor. What comes to mind is that verse by Amal Dunqul, "How can you look in the eyes of a woman you cannot protect?" More to the point, How can you protect yourself? In Dunqul's poem, one had to protect oneself from enemy attacks from Mount Zion, or from the oppressive power of a military regime. To all of this, you can now add any random son of a bitch you might come across in the street. Everyone wields power. Everyone feels afraid and violated. Everyone is ready to pounce, and everyone is ready to goose everyone else.

Some of the worst moments I've endured in this city have been while taking a simple stroll in the streets with a girl, especially if she's finely dressed. In such circumstances, the fear that regularly possesses Cairo's female residents[3] now passes on to her male companion as well. He'll turn into a human radar, monitoring for all possible sources of danger. You might think you're ready for anything, your adrenaline is pumping, you're alert. A gang of sporty young fellows might come your way, and you'll have to choose between defending your female companion or pretending that you didn't notice their lewd looks and gestures, even though she certainly did. You feel like a tiny little seed wrapped up in a tiny little shell. But just as you've mustered all your might, you suddenly realize nothing really matters. It was all just your own fear.

Why trouble yourself?

Give yourself a break. You aren't in control of yourself, you aren't in control of anything in this city. It's she who controls you. You're nothing but a cocksucker among cocksuckers. Quit the drama, little one, and enough blaming yourself. In the end, it's not so bad to be a cocksucker in Cairo. Just relax and take it all in. You might even find that cocksuckery guarantees a certain amount of protection, a certain amount of security, a good deal of prowess, and an incredible lightness of being.

---

3. It is scientifically proven that a large percentage of females in Cairo walk in the street at a rapid pace. With their gaze cast down or focused ahead, they avoid all eye contact, don't smile, and are careful to not even twitch. They exert great pains to turn into shadows. They are possessed by a deep-seated fear of words uttered by random men in the street, or of any accidental slip that might cause them to fall down or draw people's attention to their face.

(8-11)

Optimum Tech __MUST__

(1) Fix Modem -
       Internet ↙ -
       phone — dial Tone.

(2) Fix Cable Box in
        Bed Room.

when he is done - Before
he leaves -
TURN ON ALARM -
open sliding door - Activate
                         alarm

Shut off alarm -
Give code to Central Station
alarm will now be __reset__

Returns & exchanges

I gladly accept returns and exchanges

Contact me within: 14 days of delivery

Ship items back within: 21 days of delivery

I don't accept cancellations

But please contact me if you have any problems with your order.

+ More

Shipping policies

We aim to dispatch all orders as quickly as possible and always within 5 days after payment has been received.

Please note that as a seller we cannot be held responsible for problems experienced by carriers during busy periods.

Our shipping costs are fixed and we offer consolidated shipping, so you extra regardless of how many items you add to your basket. Shipping cos calculated when you add items to your basket and may vary according to currency exchange rate at the time of purchase.

Orders containing print sizes up to 8 x 10 inches will be packaged in a cle sleeve and shipped inside a board backed envelope for their protection.

Orders containing prints larger than 8 x 10 inches will be gently rolled into

CHAPTER FOUR

• • •

I first thought about writing all this down about a year ago. I was with Mona May at a swimming pool in the New Ville Hotel, out on the western edge of October. I jumped in first, diving down to touch the bottom with my fingertips. Back on the surface, the sun glowed just behind her head, forming a saintly halo of photons.

She took off her clothes. Underneath, she had on a bikini in sky blue. She jumped in, and settled against the edge of the pool with her head above the water. I swam two full laps before going back to lean up next to her.

We talked about a novel I can't really remember. She expressed her desire to start writing again. Sometimes she'd write in Arabic, but by virtue of her education and reading choices, she felt more comfortable in English. As she rose to get out of the pool, her fair, silky skin and beautiful legs left me, as always, with a warm rumbling in my stomach.

She stretched out in the sun.

I followed her, and grabbed a beer from the barman. I put it down next to me and glanced around, realizing there was only me, three girls stretched out in the sun, and an old man reading a newspaper in English.

"Mona May, lemme lay down next to you here in the shade."

I spread out on a chaise lounge, lit a cigarette, and finished almost half the beer, before dozing off. I dreamed of a visit from Ihab Hassan after an absence of many years.

Sometimes, after smoking too much hash,
I get a little washed-out.

You like me with rose, or with henna?

I might start remembering all the lovers I've lost ...

... or the friends that gave pleasure and pain ...

Their lies and deceit have cast me away

... or I might just forget them all, together with the past.

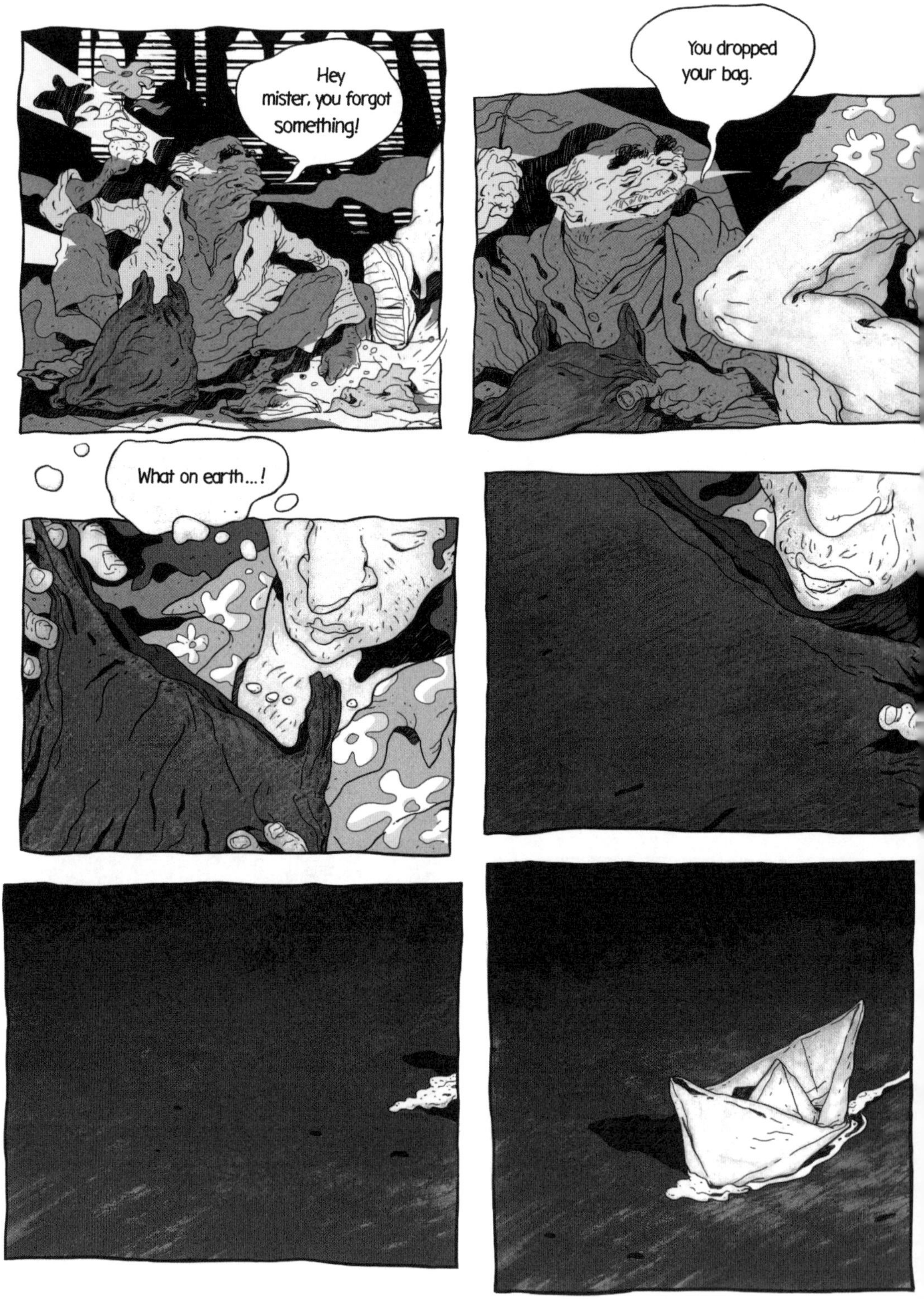
Hey mister, you forgot something!
You dropped your bag.
What on earth...!

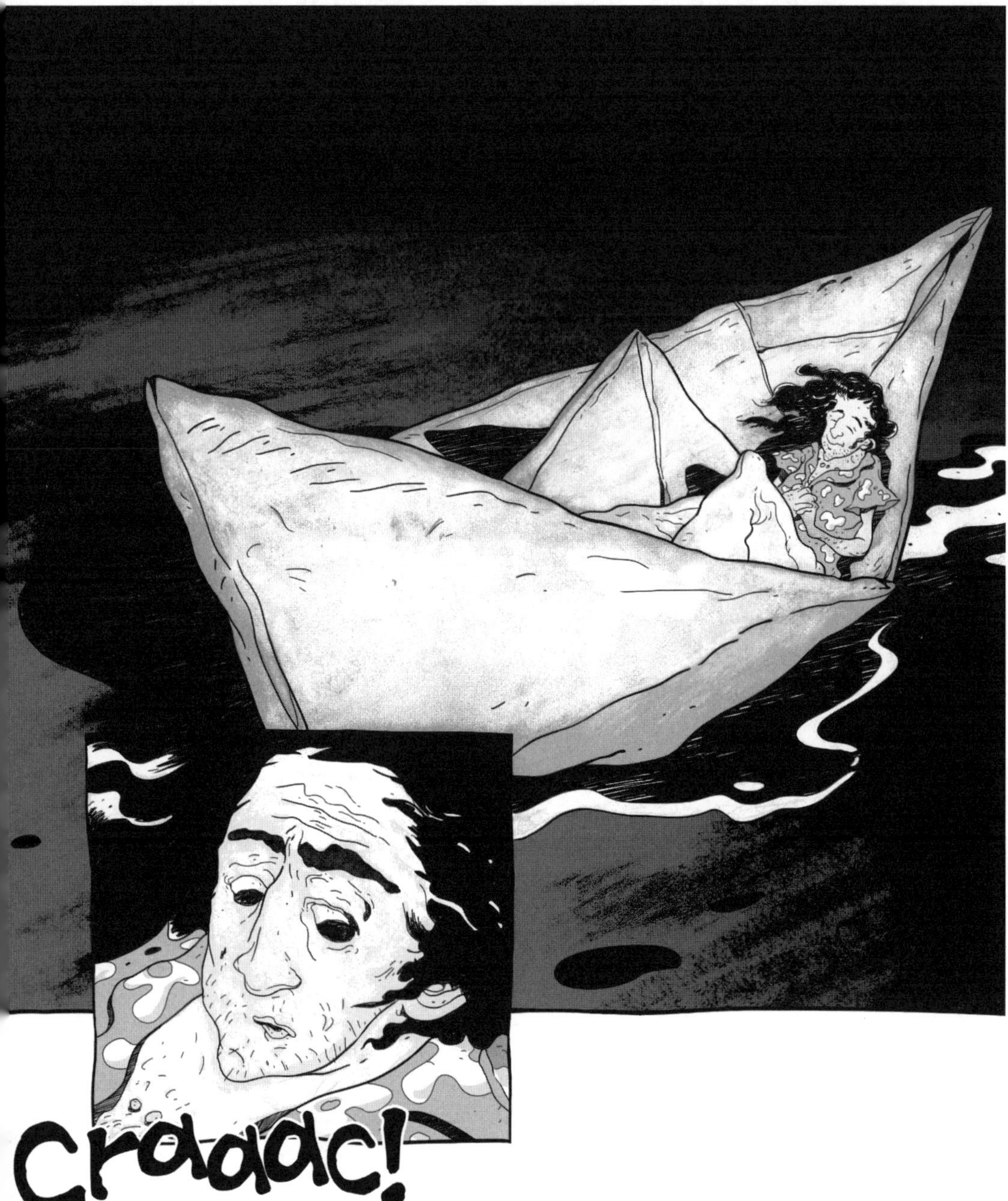
Craaac!

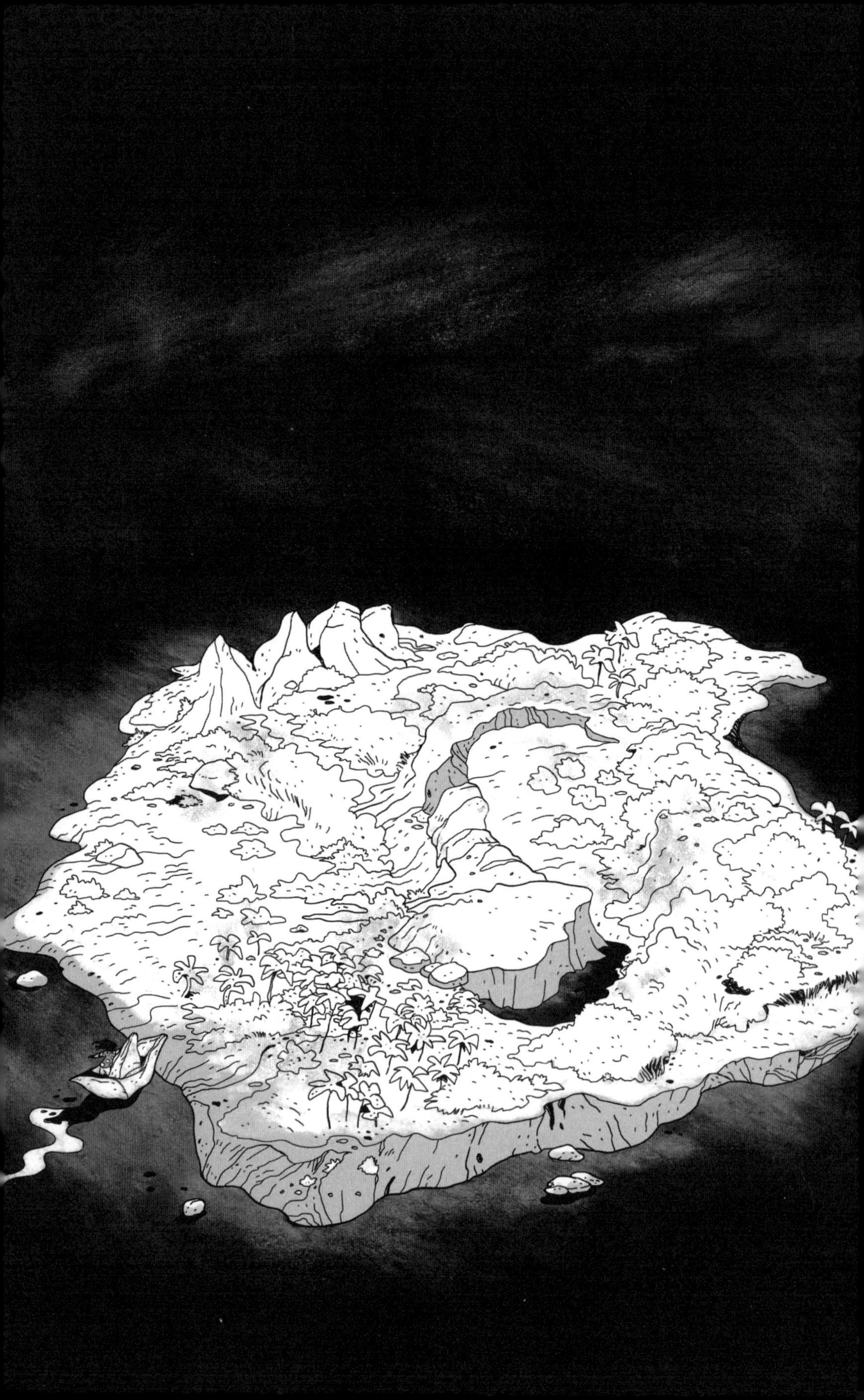

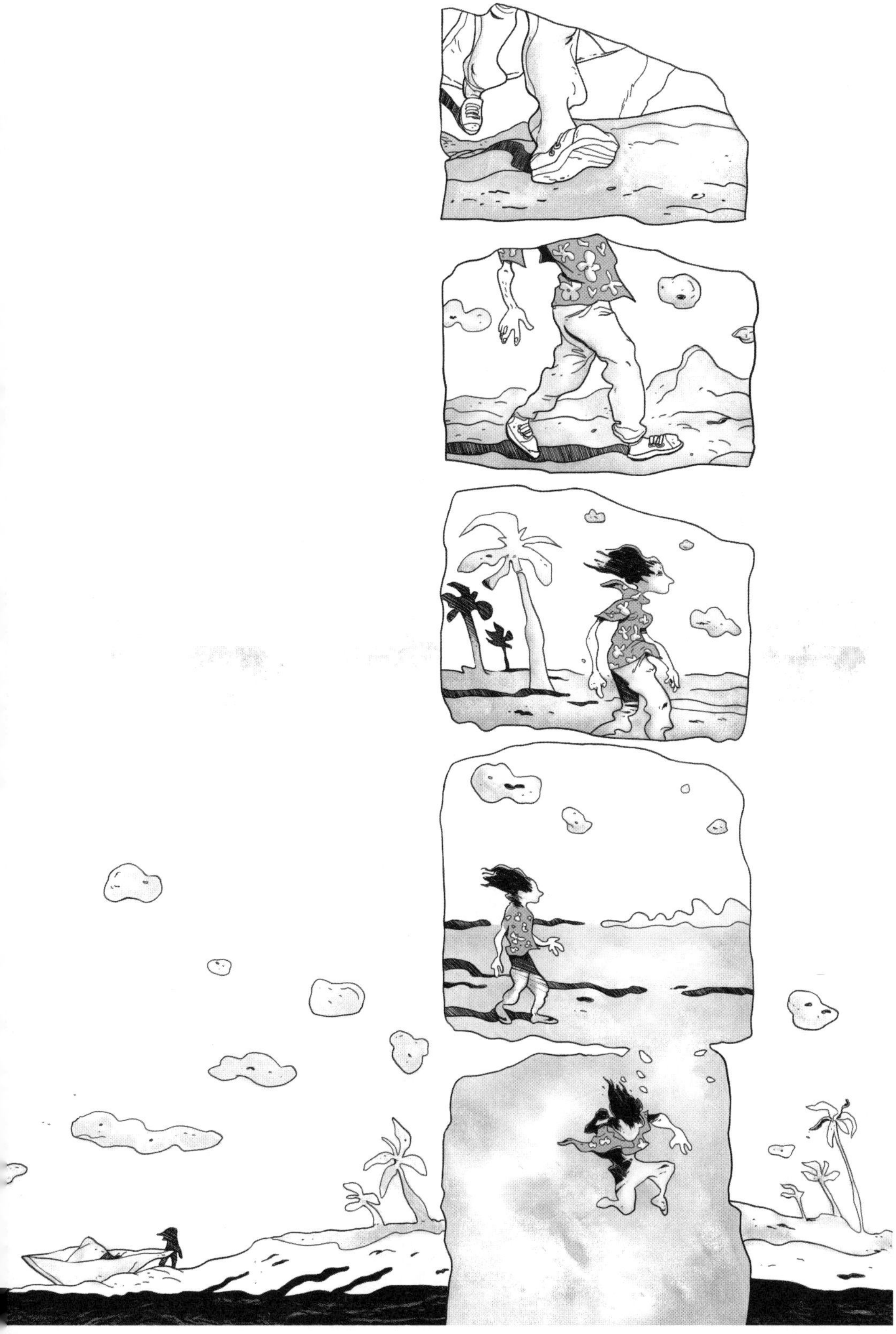

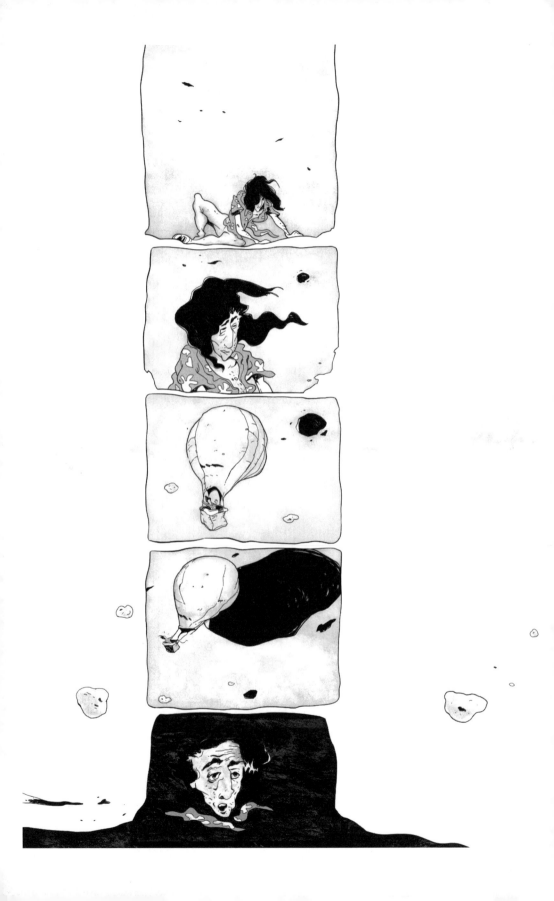

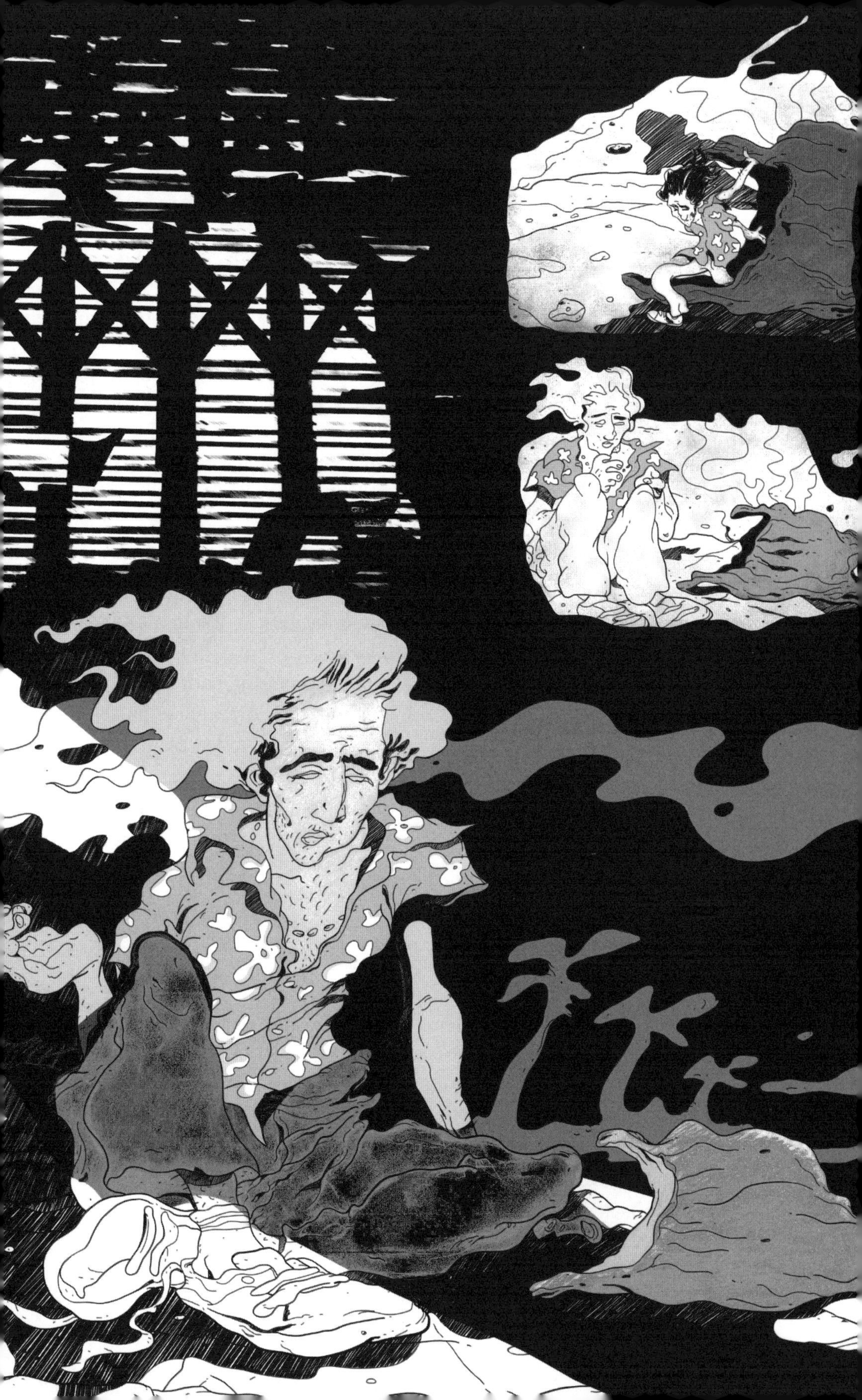

.   .   .

THE ROAD OF PASSION

The last day of shooting started at dawn, and we were finished by the early afternoon. A sweeping view of the al-Warraq area on the edges of the Ring Road. Heat and humidity, and the dust of microscopic little creatures, unknown to modern biology, sticking to our skin and sucking up our energy. In a place like this, the sand and soot are both inside you and all around you. Your clothes dampen with sweat until your jeans stick to your thighs. The whole crew smells absolutely disgusting. Everyone wishes he'd put on more deodorant.

Out shooting, we saw hog farms subsisting on trash dumpsters. Big black hogs with scraggly-looking puffs of hair and myriad skin diseases grazing among playgrounds of refuse, living alongside a community of humans. The children would play in the trash along with the hogs, giggling and pissing and mating with one another, prancing and dancing and smelling each other's behinds. We saw entire neighborhoods living off electricity stolen from the lampposts along the highway. We saw tremendous pyramids of mixed organic and artificial refuse, engineered in such a way as to keep out the wind year round. Any breeze that might seep through would inevitably pass along the particles of odor-causing chemical compounds and specks of mold that dance about in Cairo's atmosphere.

We found ourselves in al-Warraq again. The director was Tohamy Basha. He moved about laboriously, wiping his forehead and neck with his handkerchief, and now and then stuffing it through the front of his shirt to wipe his armpits. The production team brought chicken pané sandwiches from Cook Door. The day was full of running about, as we repeated the same shot over and over from the same angle but at different times, in order to record the scene as it appeared under different degrees of sunlight.

I went back home to 6th of October City, letting them take the footage back to the company. I took a cold shower and grabbed a bottle of water out of the freezer. I spread out on the bed naked, with the fan spinning at top speed.

Dear customer: The chicken you eat comes frozen, packaged, and wrapped, fresh from the factory. A single chicken takes about twenty-one days to produce according to company standards. At the end of the process, it comes out in a form that is suitable for human consumption. The age of the genuinely organic chicken has come to an end. The government, with the generous support of chicken manufacturing companies, has made great efforts to exterminate the poultry that people used to raise in poorly ventilated nests on the roofs of buildings. These measures were taken in the interest of combating bird flu and protecting public health. The new industrially produced chickens are uniquely free of the flu virus and other illnesses. They're also 100% halal. Some like the breasts, and some like the thighs. Others prefer the wings. Our chickens come fried, grilled, or spiced. We've also got chickens that are half cooked, so you and your family can enjoy a delicious meal in a matter of minutes. We all love our chicken, especially with that magic Kentucky mix.

I woke up dripping with sweat. I reached for the bottle of water, which was covered with a thin layer of condensation. I took a good gulp and laid back down, and started fondling my weary little organ. I tried imagining something to help me get off, but stuck between the specters of Reem and Mona May, all I could gather was "some like the breasts, and some like the thighs."

The phone buzzed. A text from Moud:

"Estoril, 9:30, vodka and tequila."

It was eight o'clock.

I felt like throwing up. The microbus was jammed in traffic in front of the Egyptian Radio and Television Building. I opened and closed the window, and as I caught whiffs of the pure rottenness that hangs in the air around Lebanon Square, my mind was taken back to the scenes we had shot over the last few days.

Outside the microbus, the air was hot off the grill, and burned to the touch. Inside was a shut furnace of human perspiration. I opened the door and leaped out.

I couldn't handle an emotional relationship with Mona May. I knew all too well that her love would consume me and push me to the very edge. There was a moment in the midst of it when everything seemed good enough to be real. But separation was like wearing a coat made of nails. I could only take it off by painfully extracting each little iron spike from a sensitive part on my body.

It took weeks before we started to lighten up with each other, either through a "hi" on Messenger or a "poke" on Facebook. There was really no way to avoid it. Since we shared seventy "mutual friends," we were bound to meet again, sunrise or sunset.

It was another one of Cairo's curses. In this city, there's no such thing as a relationship that ends after having begun. Even if two people slammed the door in each other's faces, they'd inevitably run into each other again, whether at a concert, a traffic light, a shawarma restaurant, a cafe in al-Ghawriya, or a bar on the Nile. What's more, even if coincidence conspired with their decision to stay apart, then surely their large and closely intertwined networks of friends would bring them back together at some point. They'd be forced to find other ways of thinking about their relationship. For me and Mona May, our best option seemed to be a close friendship sealed in period blood and dried-out sperm.

A white tiger struts along Cairo's corniche. The realm of dreams and romance. The legacy of roses and fresh juice. Arms in tight embrace. Passionate males trying desperately to hide their erections. The wondrous things on display along the Nile corniche.

I wanted to be Mona's friend, and I would never forgive myself for losing her.

Hey sweetheart, won't ya tell me how to love you . . .

And yet, I didn't want our relationship to have a label. Nor to be a poem, or a spare piece of paper. I didn't want our relationship to be a chicken thigh or a chicken wing, or even a whole chicken itself. A way of sliding down together to some unknown depth of depravity.

Moud leaned over to whisper something in my ear. I sat at the head of the table, and besides us two there was some nice and charming company. Most of them were companions from life's journey, and had escaped from Cairo after successfully establishing themselves abroad. They had been set free from Egypt, but like addicts, they'd always return to sniff the rotten horse shit they had grown up on. Coming back for periodic visits, they'd bring along bottles of liquor you couldn't find here. What a lovely reunion. A laugh at the end of the evening. The latest developments of the latest stories. There was always a new story, and it always had new developments. Even though we hadn't gone anywhere, these developments happened. Whatever the story, it always ended in rounds of laughter at the end of the night.

I went to the bathroom, then came back and started on a cigarette. Moud was telling me about the last girl he'd met. He'd pause every few seconds, expecting me to offer an analysis or opinion. I calmly smoked along and said nothing. Eventually, he threw the ball directly in my court, saying, "So I dunno, what do you think?"

"Moud," I said, turning to face him, "what is it you really want from women?"

I quickly realized that I'd asked the question at precisely the right moment. A look of yellow frustration came over his face. He blurted out a bunch of confused and contradictory nothings, at the end of which he concluded, "I want to surrender to a woman, for her to make me believe in her, or believe in the value of a relationship, any relationship, with any woman."

In spite of Moud's awkwardness, it was this romantic face, resting atop that enormous trunk of his, that always attracted me to him. He had an idealistic take on things, relationships included. It was a source of deep frustration and sorrow for him that Cairo would never reward this idealism. In reaction, any form of idealism he might happen across would be the target of his immediate ridicule. His image on the outside, as with many people, was different from his image on the inside. In fact, to exaggerate somewhat, you could say his external image was a directly inverse projection of his interior image. Pessimistic on the outside, idealistic on the inside. Tortured by the inverse dualism of Cairo's residents. The city of striking contradictions.

I went into the office. Good morning, peace be upon you, how's it going . . .

Morning small talk and idiotic smiles. A black cloud gathered around my eyes. A hangover. Last night, the bumpy road and creaky microbus on the way back to 6th of October City was more than I could handle, and I vomited out the window.

But the morning light was like a gentle feather on my behind. I took out my computer, which I have with me at all times: a stone on my back in the searing desert heat. Gulping down several mouthfuls of water, I hoped to replenish the fluids that had been drained out of my head. Why couldn't the brain be a nice little pool of liquids, instead of this disgusting spaghetti ball shape it has? How marvelous it would be if your brain cells floated about freely in some sort of cranial liquid, so that if you shook your head to the right, you'd shake up new ideas and repressed memories, and if you shook your head to the left, you'd shake up other ideas and other memories.

In my inbox, I had an email from the "Society of Urbanists." Before opening it, I thought I'd scroll a bit through Facebook. That's when Tohamy Bey walked into the office.

He lingered for a second in the doorway, a billowy cloud puffed up like a dinosaur.

"Bassam, good morning."

"Good morning," I said, slowly lifting my gaze and trying to seem more beat than I really was.

"What's wrong?" he asked, coming closer. "You sick or something?"

"Not at all," I replied, reaching for my pack of cigarettes. "Just had a bit too much to drink last night."

"Okay, all right then," he said mechanically. "You see the email?" What exactly is okay, and what exactly is all right? I never knew. But that's what he always said. "Okay, all right then."

"No," I said, also mechanically. "Not yet." I fished around for my lighter.

"Okay, all right then." He took a step backward. "You'll wanna check it out. Your friends at the Society wanna make a film about the Nile this time, or something like that."

"The Nile?"

"Yeah, no kidding. And what's more, they wanna have a meeting in an hour."

"Okay, all right then," I said, imitating his voice perfectly.

"Oh, and one more thing," he said, stopping at the door. "Have they got Reem Abd al-Rahman working for them now?"

Somehow, I wasn't surprised. Maybe I'd just been waiting for the news to reach me, like a serpent slithering toward its nest of eggs.

"How come?" I asked in a flat tone, pretending not to care. I opened my drawer, trying to seem distracted by looking around for my lighter. I only found matches.

"Well, 'cuz it'll be her that's sent the email."

"You're kidding?"

"You can quote me on it. You'll find her name there at the end: 'Reem Abd al-Rahman, Administrative Coordinator.'"

"My oh my."

"You can say that again."

He paused for a moment, before coughing up another "Okay, all right then." As he was about to leave, he turned back again and asked, "But how'd she get mixed up with that crowd? A guy's gotta wonder."

I shot him a look that said, "Red line, don't cross." But I knew he wouldn't leave without an answer, so I threw him a bone. "It's a small world, my friend."

I whistled the old tune. *The Nile and the palms. The waters so calm. The breeze through the trees.* "The buffalo carcass covered in fleas." I went back to my inbox. The email's subject line read, simply, "The Road of Passion."

. . .

THE ANIMALS OF CAIRO

THE SLIMEBALL

He could be a sad song or lonesome tune.
His love will just melt your heart, and make
it open, honest, and green. He's not ashamed
to be weak, his indecisiveness doesn't bother him.
He believes in manliness and sometimes suffers from
    contradictory values,
but his fragility always makes you feel sorry
for him. To keep him out of your heart,
you'd have to build a wall of earth and stone between you.

THE GIRL IN THE VEIL

The garden, once upon a time. I went in, smelling flowers.
"My angel," he whispered to her. From the cup of intercourse
we drank. Off she flew, leaving him alone in his misery.
What a poor little soul! His sweetheart fell for the next guy.

JUNKYARD DOGS

The first specimens appeared in old black-and-white films, but the breed really started to propagate in the seventies. They generally live close to the Nile corniche, and prefer dimly lit spaces. They communicate in more than one language. The males breed outside of the pack, and the females are forbidden to commit to a single mate.

THE EGYPTIAN WOMAN OF TODAY

The youngest generation of Amazonians, warriors of the Nile Delta. They are known for their skills at making poisons, jousting with spears, performing abortions and fertility operations, street fighting, tracking the movements of stars, predicting the paths of comets, and employing entomology in the service of anthropology.

They are also known for being tough on the outside and soft on the inside, and for their disgust of parasitic house pests and dark-colored rodents.

In addition to the aforementioned traits, the Egyptian woman of today is known to be beautiful, despite having only a single breast. She dislikes sharing personal information, but enjoys gossip. Power gives her a sexual jolt that bursts forth from her pussy and turns everyone around her into junkyard dogs submissive to her will.

COCKROACHES

A species of winged insects that moves about by means of sprints and jumps. The cockroach has brown, translucent wings, and feelers in the form of two long hairs sprouting from its head.

Male cockroaches emit a disturbing sound known in Arabic as *sarsara*, which is derived from the name of the insect itself (*sarsur*). This sound attracts the females of the species as a preliminary to the act of copulation, and is produced from a mechanism particular to the cockroach. The mechanism originates in the wings: the pointed tip of one is located opposite the protruding edge of the other, with a taut layer of skin stretched between the two of them. The so-called *sarsara* is produced when the ends of the two wings touch.

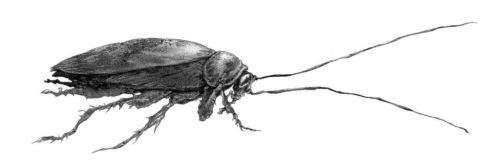

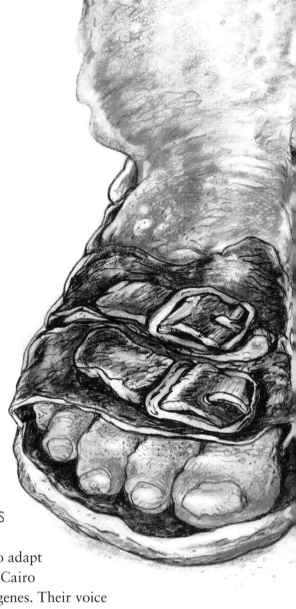

THE WILD RHINOCEROS

Certain creatures are able to adapt
to the pollution and filth of Cairo
through mutations in their genes. Their voice
acquires a particular coarseness. The voice box is replaced with a
live frog that subsists on carbons monoxide and dioxide, sucking
up cigarette smoke and the exhaust of automobiles.

During childhood, the skin of the wild rhinoceros undergoes a
process of shedding and regeneration. The flesh becomes covered
in a thick, inorganic mix of dust particles and noise pollution.
This unnatural coating serves to protect the animal's internal organs, but at the same time seals him off from any communication
with the outside world. *Lo: upon their hearts has been placed a
stone*. Or the heart itself is the stone.

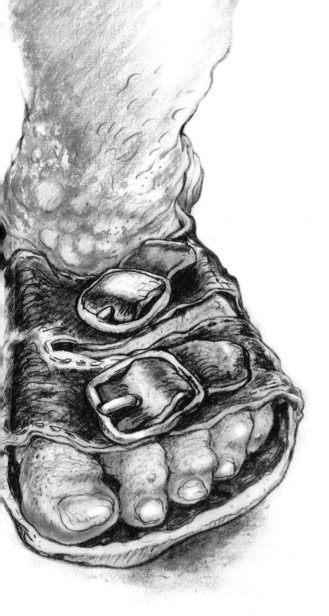

THE DERVISHES

Time has ravaged me. Fate has bitten me in the back and bent me over. Outside, no one recognizes me; I don't recognize myself. My only food is the filth of her streets. My clothes are the pitch of her asphalt.

A fugitive, a stray. His exterior is coated with oil. Every time you try to grab hold of him, he slips through your hands. He is equipped with whiskers and sensory antennae.

They fixed him up with a studio on the roof. His girlfriend got pregnant. After the abortion, she said, "I want to sleep in your arms." But his exterior is coated with oil. His mother didn't feel any pain when giving birth to him; he slid out of her vagina like a drop of blood during menstruation. You can't see him, but you can see the traces he's left. Following these traces makes you feel dizzy, like trying to read for a long time by candlelight.

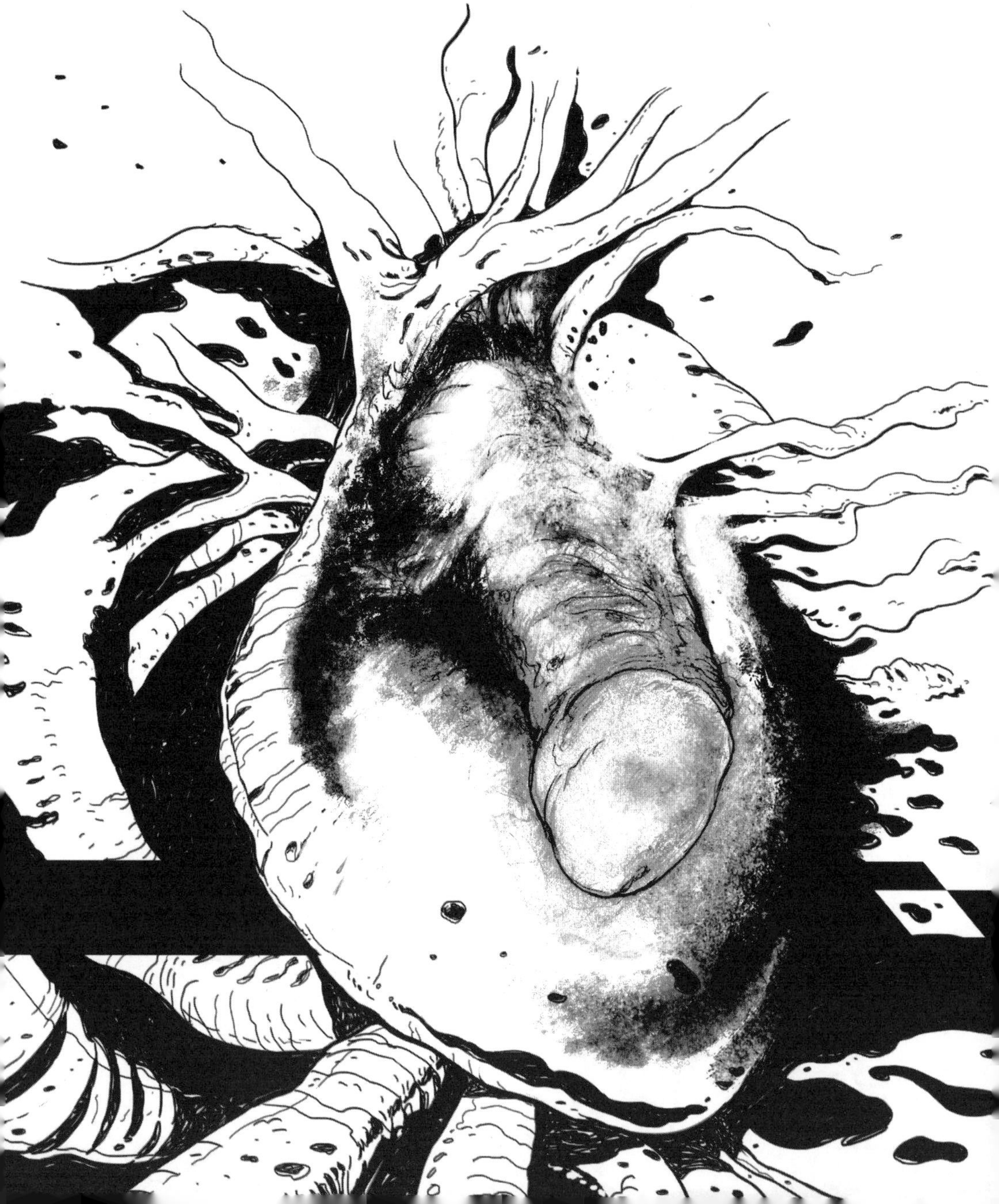

THE BIOLOGICAL TAXI

Let's tell a story, a joke, an anecdote. Let us laugh, let us make merry. I'll suck your blood at the next street corner, and spit you out as a housewife might take out the trash, wrapping it in a black plastic bag and leaving it out as a naked lunch for the cats in the stairwell.

We'll ride only to the end of the street, but I'll deceive you into thinking that your whole future is with me alone. When I leave you battered and broken, there won't be anyone after me to gather up your pieces and put you back together.

أجرة ٤٦٠٥

Here let us take a short reprieve.

Out in front of a cigarette kiosk, there stood a group of kids consuming foodstuffs manufactured according to the highest nutritional standards. They drank carbonated beverages that filled them with a good deal of self-confidence. There was no sun or moon in the sky. The clock pointed to nine.

Nearby was parked a police car in the shape of a kiosk—the kind of vehicle that in Egypt they call a "box." A group of soldiers spilled out of its rear and rushed over to the actual kiosk. Out of the front came the black rat, wearing sunglasses even though there was no sun. They approached the kiosk and began tearing it down and scattering its contents out into the street. The kids-consuming-foodstuffs-manufactured-according-to-the-highest-nutritional-standards got out of the way. The soldiers went on demolishing the place for a few more seconds, then went back to their highly stimulating conversations. The kiosk's owner came out and headed straight for the black rat.

"What are you doing! What are you doing! Stop them, sir! Stop them, you bastard!" Thus shouted the old man, who had been a tiger in a past life.

The rat swung its tail and smacked the old man on his head. Another smack, and the old man was sent flying through the air with a broken back.

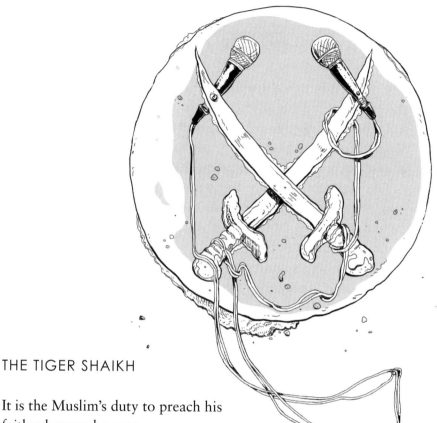

THE TIGER SHAIKH

It is the Muslim's duty to preach his
faith wherever he goes.

"What about settling the land and spreading civilization, O Shaikh?"

Look around you, and observe your Muslim brothers: Is
this not the "best nation produced for mankind"?

"What is love, O Shaikh?"

We have no time. If, when the Hour arrives, you have a
seedling, go plant it in the earth.

"What is the rule concerning nudity in front of one's wife,
O Shaikh?"

Let us build the ideal Muslim man, then let us build the
ideal Muslim family, then let us build the luminous society.

"What comes after all this?"

Paradise, my son, paradise. There you will find that which
no eye has seen and no ear has heard.

. . .

THE NILE MEETS PAPRIKA

You heard it from me first: if there's one reason Reem got in with the Society, it's Ihab Hassan. That's where things got started, at least, before other reasons happened to present themselves. (Personal reasons mingled with professional ones, together with the assorted aches and ailments of the soul.)

The dog's sitting at her feet with its eyes fixated on the television, while she massages its neck. Sure, she looks like she's watching too, but she doesn't hear or see anything that's on the screen. Her mind is elsewhere.

She sees a jeep spinning around in circles out in the desert.

A machine somewhere, whizzing and whirring, sputtering out of control.

A sandstorm.

A desert storm.

She takes a sip of her Nescafé. She stands up and unplugs her phone from its charger. She looks at her watch: six thirty in the morning. She puts her phone in her bag and checks to make sure she has everything she needs. Then she steps out like a white cat with fizzled hair. No make-up, as usual. Just a t-shirt, and a pair of jeans hung around her slim waist.

"Taxi."

The white taxi, driven by an elderly man, comes to a stop.

"We're going for a pretty long trip."

He smiles. "It's in God's hands," he says, pointing to the meter.

The taxi leaves El Manial heading south toward Maadi, then Helwan, then Tibbin. The address mentioned in the email is on the corniche in Tibbin, across from the iron and steel factory. She checks the meter before handing the driver the fare and getting out.

She looks up and down the corniche until she spots the black limousine. Cars zoom past in both directions. The sky is blue; Cairo's summer sun hasn't yet arrived. There's a certain degree of humidity in the air, but the wind blows gently around these parts.

As she heads toward the car fitting the description given to her, she thinks of whistling a little tune.

The car door opens, and out steps a rather fetching young woman. She's a full-spectrum blond, with shades ranging from light brown to pure yellow. She's got a red t-shirt pulled tight over her figure, with a neckline low enough to show some cleavage. Below this she's got on a pair of jeans, and oh, by the way, let me tell you about jeans.

I like jeans. You like jeans. We all like jeans. Jeans come in all sizes for all ages. Jeans are always there, just waiting for you. Just like this blond's smile was waiting for Reem.

Why kill yourself all alone? Why don't you consider martyrdom over suicide? Why not sacrifice yourself for some loftier ideal—for love!—to lift your spirit up toward a higher level of existence?

Tohamy always liked to ask me if I had any "good books" to suggest. He'd ask me the same question over and over again, then change topics and ask me if I knew about any "good movies." And on again.

Tohamy, slouched over in his chair like a dead bull, would strike most people as an insensitive brute. In truth, Tohamy was a victim of his own prurient desire, the rotten fruit of thoroughly disgusting times.

He'd made a decision before I ever met him. "The content of your work doesn't matter one bit. What matters is that the final product looks sexy—and, if at all worldly possible, *novel.*" He had long ago decided to sell himself to the bright lights. "Ideas come and go." And then, as if suddenly remembering my own hard work, he flashed me a smile. "But at the end of the day, fortune favors the wise."

Tohamy's philosophy seemed interesting at first—but this distinction he was making between form and content struck me as contrived and deceitful. There's no such thing as content without form or form without content. And at the end of the day, what does he mean by sexy? And what does he mean by bright lights? Strike a match and watch it burn.

I felt disgusted listening to him tell me about his romantic escapades, blabbering on with all the airs of a fearless conqueror. At a certain point in each of his stories, my disgust would turn into genuine pity. It became evident that these romantic escapades were actually a source of disappointment for him. In the middle of each story, he'd say, "She just totally turned me off. Didn't know what she thought she was doing." What made me feel sorry for him even more was the way he belittled all these women. "A bunch of bimbos. Totally shallow." The whole world, according to Tohamy, was a bunch of shallow bimbos. Thus my disgust would give way to pity, which was so overwhelming I wouldn't know how to put it into words.

He was a little kid who liked lighting matches and watching them burn. But one day, there would be no more matches, or he'd discover that each match wasn't very different from the rest.

I was never able to explain to Tohamy the reason for his misery. Back then, I didn't know myself what that reason might be. But I now realize how Cairo was able to endlessly reproduce certain kinds of people from a single mold of misery. Since his childhood, Tohamy, like any kid, had wanted to be popular and successful. He wanted to be in the limelight. So he soon found himself in the School of Media and Communications, from which he was led, by a series of coincidences—or, more accurately, by the capricious fate of Cairo—to his present occupation. He became a director of documentary films, then started his own company. Funding for this venture was provided by a group of idle investors who'd come back after working in the Arab Gulf countries. They let their veiled wives play with their children all day at the sporting club, and sat around not knowing what to with all their accumulated wealth. A young man with a film company seemed like a good enough investment, and the young man himself had little other choice. He would have to get married soon—seeing his friends had already started having children, he felt out of step. He wasn't like the rest of them, but it was imperative that he try to be. Every bad decision he made tore at him on the inside, but he insisted on going through with it anyway.

In his youth, Tohamy spent a lot of time at the mosque with

other young men, who gave him a sense of moral direction. And even though he was no longer young, nor particularly religious, these old perceptions of right and wrong had stuck with him. Thus he still felt a certain pain inside when he did something wrong, without quite being able to explain to himself why it wasn't right. Nearly everything made him feel this way. Thoroughly disgusted with himself, he saw his life as one big sin. The only way he could go on was to dive even deeper into sin—or what he considered to be sin—in search of anything that might be "new" and "sexy." But all he found was misery, and the blue-tinted dullness of spent desire.

"Ihab's told me quite a lot about you," she said in English. "And I always trust his taste."

Reem responded with that sideways smile she makes whenever she's tempted by the devil of sarcasm and mischief. "I trust his taste too. That's why I came to meet you."

Paprika approached the edge of the corniche and looked out over the Nile. Back in the black limousine, the driver had the day's *Al-Jumhuriya* spread out in front of him and was busy reading. Reem came over and leaned on the railing next to Paprika. A minute passed, then two. She rested her eyes on the gentle flow of the water. Three minutes, then four, then five. A full six minutes passed. An unspoken game of roulette to see who would speak first. Paprika had her hands in her pockets and a true poker face. Eight minutes, ten minutes. Reem shifted her weight from one leg to the other. A quarter of an hour. Seventeen, eighteen. Paprika took in a deep breath, then let it out in one big puff. "How pretty."

Reem nodded. "Yeah."

Paprika turned to her with a big smile, as green as the open fields. Gesturing toward the river, she said, "So . . ."

Reem didn't respond, so Paprika went on. "So, Reem. What do you think? How can this Nile of ours be more beautiful?"

Reem gave a shrug like someone casting away a cigarette. "I don't know."

"Why's that?"

Reem fell silent for a moment, then turned back toward her companion. She appeared to be shocked to find Paprika staring right back at her. But there was no escape: her eyes fell into the line of Paprika's gaze. The matter had been decided. Reem felt as though a gentle hand had wrested her heart away from the depths of despondency. In that moment, she realized she'd fallen in love with Paprika—exactly as in the movies, when the magic turns against the magician. Paprika drew closer, and repeated her question in a whisper: "Why. Is. *That?*"

"Because I don't know."

"You don't know what?"

"I don't know how the Nile might be more beautiful." The words dropped out of her like a silken scarf tossed in the air.

"What about beauty?" Paprika persisted, still in a near whisper. "What do you know about beauty?"

Pressed under the weight of this woman's sheer presence, Reem tried to collect her thoughts. "It seems pretty," she gestured, trying to dodge the question. "But the problem is . . ." She paused to gesticulate, as if gathering the words up out of the air. "The problem is all this *sorrow.*"

There, on the banks of the Nile opposite the Helwan iron and steel factory, the idea was born. In a moment of acute emotional catharsis, it came out as a gasp for air, a sigh of relief from a sickness of the soul.

"It's simple," Reem continued. "All this river needs is to avoid this city altogether. The Nile gets depressed when it flows by Cairo."

I never thought of it like that, given the great estimation I had for Reem's intuition and strength of character. Now I have my doubts, and find myself thinking *maybe* as I give the dice a roll.

Fear of solitude, maybe, was a good enough reason for her to get that dog. Dogs, after all, are loyal companions, and have that damn cute look that makes you feel sorry for them. They're little babies, full of adorable innocence. And their fur has got such a fresh and cozy scent after a bath.

"Documentary hyperrealism." That's the expression Reem used to describe what the second film was supposed to be. As she explained in her email, this meant that rather than capturing scenes from current reality, the film was supposed to document an imaginary event, an event that could best be described as "hyperreal." What she had in mind wasn't removing the Nile altogether. All that had to be done was change its course, such that instead of flowing next to Cairo, it made its way along the border separating the adjacent provinces of October and Giza. From there it would continue its path toward the Delta, which would naturally have to change as well—but this was another topic altogether.

As was stipulated at the beginning of this film project, each installment was to be concerned only with "*Cairo, Cairo*, and nothing but *Cairo*"—thus spoke Tohamy as he jabbed the air with his middle finger. "If they want a documentary film about the sex lives of ants on Faisal Street, then *that's* what we're givin' 'em!" He was fond of this expression, which he repeated to me more than once.

Also in her email, Reem indicated that the next meeting would be attended by the head of the Society's branch in Austria, one Miss Paprika. I found this rather disappointing, as I suspected I'd never see Dr. Ihab Hassan again. We hadn't seen each other since our first meeting nearly two months ago. The first film was picked up by Madam Dolet, who came back later with an envelope containing the handwritten remarks of Dr. Hassan on a single sheet of paper. Also inside was a check for twenty-five thousand dollars, all as compensation for a film whose production costs I was sure could not have exceeded ten thousand Egyptian pounds. And all Tohamy had to say was, "If they want a film about the architecture of my goddamn ass, then *that's* what we're givin' 'em!"

The meeting was to take place at the Four Seasons Hotel in Garden City. "Just some casual brainstorming about the project. Lunch will be served." I prepared myself for the worst.

The Nile in October.

I played around with Google Earth, imagining some possible scenarios. It could come up from Helwan, then bend eastward past Giza with its worthless Great Pyramids, in order to cut off 6th of October City decisively from all the trash on the other side. The Nile had always been changing its course. I looked at old pictures showing it passing through Ramses Square. Once, long ago, it had seven good branches cutting through the Delta. It took seven thousand years of civilization for *Homo aegyptiacus* to exert control over the Nile. And when he was finished, it was little more than a slim canal, slow as a turtle on the verge of suicide.

And if this was the way things were—and indeed this way they were—then there's nothing to prevent them from being this way tomorrow, and the next day, and the day after that. Nothing too much to ask of "documentary hyperrealism." What cocksucking Frenchman came up with such a lame expression?

Documentary hyperrealism.

As I expected, Reem greeted me with a smile and a kiss on the cheeks. "What's up? How you been?" No need for formalities between the two of us. We took our seats at a table at the end of the hall.

"Paprika . . . she'll be ready to head out in about ten minutes."

"Okay, all right. No problem, no problem." I went on muttering some routine nothings and nodding my head.

It seemed we'd be sitting alone here for a while before the honorable Lady Paprika would make an entrance. There was no use looking away at the pale-looking family seated next to us, or pretending to stare at the tablecloth. Reem wouldn't be the one to start the conversation, of course. She liked to sit and enjoy the awkwardness while you fished around for something to start with. Her mood for the rest of the conversation would depend on where, exactly, you decided to cast your first line. I decided to aim somewhere safe.

"So how you like working with these people?"

"How do *you* like working with them?"

Great shot, my friend! Right on the mark. Reem plays a good game.

"I work *for* them, making movies, but I don't work *with* them. But anyway, it's been all right. All these characters and their ideas are pretty weird, but it's been all right. You could say it's been interesting, really. Maybe a little frustrating too. That's how it is, starting from nothing."

"Hmmm." She nodded, and grabbed a pack of cigarettes from her bag.

I crossed my legs and leaned back in my chair. "But seriously. I wanna know where these people get all this money."

Was Reem thinking of revenge? And for what, exactly? For her failure at life, maybe. For the mountains of anguish and despair that stood between her and her goals. For lost love, for the early advance of old age. For being stuck. For not knowing who or what she was taking revenge on in the first place. All she needed to explain herself was to say with a deep sigh, "Just take a look outside . . . Take a look at this filthy city, this goddamn wasteland."

It wasn't just a matter of garbage piling up everywhere, of hideous architecture or jaundiced faces. It wasn't just about the constant swirl of traffic, dust, and pollution.

"The air itself is rotten here, Bisou. The very air we breathe has given us cancer. There's no cure for what we've got. We'll carry this disease with us wherever we go, until we die of sheer hideousness." And so I ask myself, Why wouldn't she want revenge?

The idea behind the film was simpler than I'd thought. Just a series of interviews with architectural experts, some of them foreigners, whose expenses would all be covered by the Society. They'd be flown into Cairo and asked to explain what might happen if the city lost the Nile. It had been suggested that such a scenario was one way to save the city from its nightmarish present. Cairo would wither and empty out as a result, with a massive population shift to the suburbs. As every crisis is an opportunity, the heart of the city would be much more easily redeveloped, and possibly turned into an open-air museum of sorts. It's equally likely that the new suburbanites wouldn't care about what happened to their old city, so it would just be abandoned and life could start anew elsewhere. Millions would be saved from their misery. The western provinces of the country would certainly benefit, and it might even be possible to revive Alexandria as the capital of Egypt. Alex is a dump, too, but by no means beyond repair.

In our discussions, I suggested that we might want to interview ordinary people on the street and ask them what the Nile meant to them. Especially those whose immediate livelihood depended on it. Paprika, however, just shook her head.

"This is a promotional film," she said, pointing directly at me. "Its purpose is to represent the Society and its ideas. Ordinary people's opinions don't concern me: they're relative, and vary from one place to another."

I nodded as though I agreed, even though it was clear she didn't care whether I agreed or not. She looked at Reem and then back at me. "I mean," she said, "if we did the same thing along the banks of the Yangtze, people would tell you the same thing. Nothing new under the sun."

Paprika's ideas seemed confused. More worrying, they seemed to contradict most of what I'd been told by Dr. Ihab during the first film. For him, people came before urban planning. They came before history, before everything else. Everything about this new film seemed to contradict the first one we'd made about the Ring Road. Then, the focus had been on trying to recover signs of life, energy, and innovation hidden beneath all the apparent ugliness and waste. Now Reem and Paprika seemed to want to uproot the only beautiful thing the city had left, and watch from a distance as the ugliness devoured itself.

In the middle of our discussions, I noticed that Paprika's hand had been resting for nearly the entire time on Reem's thigh. I pretended not to notice, while they went on eating and I continued to sip my beer.

Paprika did like some of what I had to suggest. She seemed particularly interested in the historical dimension of things: how the Nile played a role in the very shape of the city, and how the city, in turn, forced changes on the Nile.

At the end of our session, I presented a series of questions about this scenario we were supposed to imagine. The first was about Cairo's lakes. Where had they all gone?

For centuries, the lakes and pools left over from the seasonal floods had been a defining feature of the city's geography. Then they all disappeared. What happened? Had little green spacemen come down and abducted them?

Paprika smiled. "What a nice idea," she said, in English as always.

The river used to crisscross the city at different angles. But at the beginning of Muhammad Ali's reign in the early nineteenth century, operations were undertaken to control the river's flow through the city. As a result, these lakes—or "pools and swamps," as they began to be called—were gradually hedged in and depleted.

"So as you can see," I said, switching to English, "things were not always thus. All this was the end result of a series of unfortunate mistakes, which can be rectified. All we want to do is *fix what went wrong*." And with a final flourish, I flashed a cheesy television grin.

"You really believe what you're saying, Bisou?" Reem said in Arabic, firing a bullet right in my face.

"Sure, why not?" I replied. "Something to think about, anyway. It's only hyperrealism, after all."

More importantly, Reem's hand was on top of Paprika's.

CHAPTER FIVE

• • •

I rang the doorbell twice before turning the key and walking inside. The drapes were flapping about wildly in the wind. She wasn't in her room.

"Mona May?" I called out.

"Hallooo . . . ," her voice rang out from the bathroom. The door was open. I found her relaxing naked in the bathtub with a comic book. "You got a light?"

I gave her one, then went over to sit on the toilet. My eyes rolled over to her breasts bobbing up from under the water. I watched as she tried to keep the cigarette high and dry.

I remember telling Mona May about Ihab Hassan on the same day as Youssef Bazzi's party. The name sticks in my mind because it sounds funny. "Youssef Bazzi." (That's another one that only makes sense in Arabic. Call me for lessons some time.) But for the life of me, I can't put a face to the name. Don't remember anything about him. Probably some kid who got educated abroad. Had a duplex in Zamalek, where he used to host parties just for his close friends. That was until he discovered that a city the size of Cairo suffered from a shortage of *cool* places, and decided to open his place up to all sorts of people: artists, pseudo-artists, wannabe artists, foreigners of mostly European or Anglo-Saxon origins, fluent speakers of English, experts in Third World development, private school graduates, anyone with some spare change.

In the middle of the living room was an enormous Jacuzzi, where a guy and two girls were playing in their bathing suits.

Outside of the only bathroom, there stretched a long line of drunk boys and girls with bladders about to explode. Music so loud you couldn't quite make it out. I stood next to the balcony with Mona and Moud, sipping a can of beer and telling them about an old man who prefers his chicken raw.

Moud wasn't paying attention. Mona, however, seemed impressed.

"That's amazing, dude. You've gotta introduce us." I couldn't tell if she really liked my story, or was just a bit beyond tipsy.

I left the office and hailed a taxi to downtown. The heat coming off the passenger seat nearly burned my ass.

"What the hell, man?"

"Sorry, my friend, can't do nothing about this weather."

I put on my headphones and checked out. When we got to Talaat Harb Square, I decided to walk the rest of the way to Adly Street. As I was crossing the street, another taxi flew by and clipped me in the elbow. "Goddamn son of a bitch!" I shouted.

Quite unexpectedly, the taxi came to a stop right in the middle of traffic. I was ready for a fight, if that was how it was gonna be. The driver was a thirtysomething, heavyset bull of a man with a thick black mustache and even thicker lips. He sported an old pair of plastic flip-flops, a yellow polo shirt, and a beer belly with matching double chin.

"Why ya gotta swear, huh?!"

"You blind or something?"

"What did I do wrong?" He took another step toward me.

"Whaddya want? You gonna hit me or something?"

I waved my hand in his face, but he grabbed me by the fingers and twisted them back. My fingers felt like they were going to break. I gave him a good slap in the face with my other hand—like I was too much of a sissy to throw a proper punch or something. He was about to return the favor when I managed to push him off me, and that's when the crowd intervened.

"Take it easy, you two!" someone shouted. I stumbled away, holding my fingers tight against my chest. They hurt so bad I couldn't even feel them.

The driver retreated to his car as dozens of bystanders came along to pat me on the back. I was in too much of a daze to write down his license plate number. I could feel that last slap he didn't manage to get in. I could feel the insult together with the injury. So that's how it is, then. In a split second, in the blink of an eye, this city just snaps and takes it out on you. Whether it decides to hurl you up into the clouds or push you face first over a cliff, it'll come at you from behind like a twenty-foot pole.

My phone was playing Shawqi Qinawi—or was it Ibn Arus?— humming something from the beginning of the Banu Hilal epic. Quatrains plagiarized from an imaginary artist.

Cairo. The heat. The scowls, the sliminess, the sweat. The *pain*. The scream muffled inside. The streets that don't let you laugh or smile, or even cry or shout out in pain. My relationship with this city was no longer quite the same. Something had changed inside me. Perhaps that something had been there all along without me noticing. Perhaps it had only decided to emerge when I started this whole business with the films, then finally burst forth in full form after my defeat at the hands of the taxi driver with the thick moustache and even thicker lips.

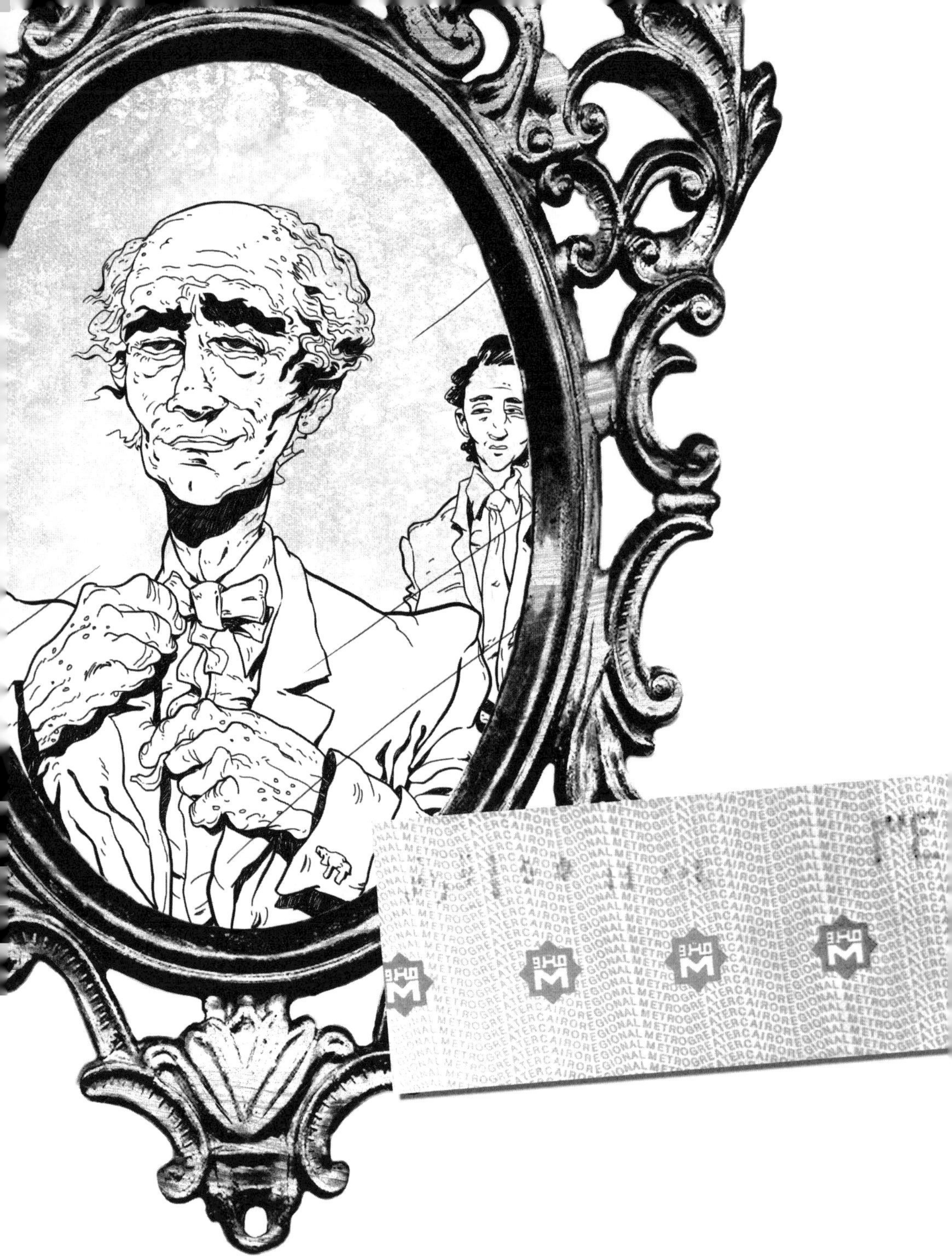
REGIONAL METROGREATERCAIRO

Ihab Hassan: I'm quite certain you'll like where we're going
tonight.
Bassam: How can you be so sure?
Ihab Hassan: The same way I knew you wouldn't like my
cooking the last time we met.

A limousine drove us from Adly Steet to the corniche along Garden City. We were quiet for most of the way. Each time our eyes happened to meet I'd flash him a smile, but he seemed not to notice. Perhaps something was on his mind.

I suspected he'd be taking me to a restaurant, but was surprised to see us turn into a garage underneath a highrise. We were waved in by a guard who looked like he worked for a security agency of some sort, but which one I couldn't be sure. He flipped a switch, and a wall in the back opened up, revealing a hidden passage descending yet further below ground. Could it be another garage?

After another 500 meters or so, we found ourselves in another concrete chamber. Ihab gave me a smile, and I followed him out of the car. He took off for an elevator in the back, but I managed to keep up with him. Inside there were only two buttons, one for up and one for down. Down it was. Ihab stood with his face to the door, and I behind him, utterly perplexed. Without looking at me, he said, "I know a man who went around the world in twenty years, and spent the next forty years remembering what he saw."

On the level below was a short passageway leading to a wooden door. Ihab took out a key and turned back to glance at me as he turned it in the lock. I'm sure he could read the confusion plastered all over my face, but he just smiled and went into the room.

A small office with a desk and some shelves. I was just a little disappointed, you'll understand. A few books and papers scattered here and there. Where's all the hidden treasure? Where's the long-lost tomb? Where's the damn pot of gold, you filthy little leprechaun?

The place had clearly been neglected. Only a faint neon bulb dangling from the ceiling. Ihab reached over and turned on a lamp on the desk. He took a seat behind the desk and beckoned me to join him.

"You know where we are, exactly?" He sounded like he was about to propose.

I could guess. "Underground, maybe?"

"Let me ask you something, Bassam. Where did Cain go after murdering Abel?"

"Beats me."

"But you know the gist of the story. And you know that right now, we're underground."

"There's a lot I don't know, too. But I don't exactly have a crystal ball."

"You want some answers, then, eh?"

Instead of answers, however, what I got was a story that whistled like wind through the woods. Out in the field, Cain had heard a wind something like this. The first murderer, brother to the first farmer. While Abel continued to herd goats, Cain was destined for the city. He represented the desire to control nature, not to submit to it. The desire to plunder its wealth, to harvest its fruits, and to excavate its treasures. And the Lord said, "What hast thou done? The voice of thy brother's blood crieth unto me from the ground. And now art thou cursed from the earth, which hath opened her mouth to receive thy brother's blood from thy hand; when thou tillest the ground, it shall not henceforth yield unto thee her strength."

Cain defied the curse. With patience, he sought to acquire knowledge. And thus, though deprived of progeny, he built a legacy for his future disciples to honor.

Forty years later, the cult of Cain went out from the family of Adam. Lead by Naqraous the Mighty, son of Misraim, son of Markabil, son of Douabil, son of Ariab, son of Adam, the caravan traveled until it reached the Nile. Impressed by its seasonal floods, they decided to abide therein. They called this place "Misraim," after their first disciple—whence "Misr," the Arabic name for Egypt.[1]

---

1. I found echoes of what Ihab Hassan told me in al-Maqrizi's *Al-Khitat*, as well as in the first part of Jalal al-Din al-Suyuti's *An Agreeable Discussion of the History of Egypt and Cairo*. In addition, a fuller description of this "Naqraous the Mighty" can be found in Evliya Çelebi's *Book of Travels*. There it is stated that he was the first of a dynasty of men who rejected Adam's account of paradise lost, promising instead to create paradise here on Earth. His brothers branded him a heretic who had forsaken the covenant made with God.

Ihab suddenly grew animated as he concluded his story. "These people built the very first *City*, Bassam! *City* with a capital C! Say it after me, Bassam: Amsous! *Am . . . Sous*! Am . . . Sous, Bassam!"[2]

I popped a cigarette in my mouth. "Can I smoke in here?" I said.

He shrugged as if he couldn't care less about the place. "Why not?"

I took a good puff, gathered my thoughts, and said, "But I've always been told that Egypt, or 'Misr,' was so named after Misraim, son of Noah. I've never heard of this Misraim descended directly from Adam."

"That's a whole 'nother story. The two sometimes get mixed up, or one is taken to contradict the other. What we have, in fact, are two separate stories, one coming before the other. In the great river of knowledge, each drop in the stream flows together with the next one. Sometimes one drop will force another toward the bottom, and its echoes are lost to us.

"It's quite heartwarming to hear that a young man like you knows the story of Misraim, son of Noah. But have you heard of Philemon? This was the name of the priest who refused the call of Noah to build his arc. But when it was clear that the end was

---

To prevent bloodshed, Naqraous and his followers departed from the tribe, thus forming the first society of utopians to set out in search of heaven here on Earth.

2. The general fogginess of perception in those days made it difficult to identify, with any great precision, the members that constituted the Society. Thus it was all the more remarkable that al-Maqrizi was able to speak specifically of Amsous and the disciples of Naqraous who had originally founded Egypt. He describes in extraordinary detail how, through their own inventiveness, they fixed the course of the River Nile and irrigated the land. Before them, the Nile had not been the river we know today. It was little more than a series of tributaries and fractured pockets of water flowing in a mostly southerly direction. Yet the mighty disciples of Naqraous, in al-Maqrizi's words, "managed to engineer the Nile, such that it flowed where they had built their cities, and passed alongside their capital, Amsous."

nigh, he went to Noah and asked for forgiveness, and was thus allowed to board the arc with his family.

"Philemon had one request for Noah: 'O Prophet,' he said, 'I wish that you might bestow upon me nobility and prestige, that I may be remembered by generations yet to come.' And thus Philemon's daughter was married to Misraim, son of Ham, son of Noah, and bore a child who was named Philemon in honor of his grandfather.

"Philemon the Priest took his small family—his daughter and her husband—to Egypt. There he took pains to instruct his grandson in the sacred sciences and divine measurements, and revealed to him the forbidden knowledge preserved by the disciples of Cain and Naqraous. He invested his son-in-law with political dominion, backing him with the power of his priesthood and a finely engineered social order.[3] In return, Philemon the Elder demanded special custody of Philemon the Younger, that he might initiate him into the special rites of the Society of Urbanists. The brotherhood was to be founded anew, and thenceforth adopted secrecy as its modus operandi."

At this point, Ihab took out a small slip of paper and said, "Allow me to read to you an excerpt from *Philemon's Counsel to Philemon*:

> Knowledge is the Flower of the Flame. It is the Sun that kindles the Stars. Thus the Flower of Flame needs not the Sun,[4] nor must it

---

3. The following eloquent passage occurs in the anonymous *Kitab al-Istibsar fi ʿAjaʾib al-Amsar* (ed. Saʿd Zaghlul Abd al-Hamid, 1958): "And Philemon did reveal to his son-in-law, Misr, son of Yinsir, the occult knowledge and sacred mysteries of Egypt. He instructed him in hieroglyphs, and brought out of the earth its gold, silver, gems, and turquoise. He showed to him the quarries in the eastern mountain, which was thence named 'al-Muqattam,' or 'that which is broken off.'"

4. The reference here to "the Sun" represents a singular challenge to the divine in its most potent manifestations. It is as if Philemon were predicting the rise of all subsequent religious and social orders in ancient Egypt over the next

be left without Cover, lest unto Ruin all be doomed. In the Name of my Ancestry, From Philemon to Philemon, we hereby give ourselves to the God above all Gods: to Knowledge that created God Himself and was revealed to All."[5]

I tapped at my cigarette, and watched my scorched little thoughts scatter over the floor.

. . .

NIGHT

Ihab Hassan was a small fry compared to his grandfather, Hassan Shaarawi.[6]

Toward the end of the nineteenth century, it so happened that this Hassan should travel to Europe to study engineering. It was the will of God, the will of the Khedive, the will of the wind, the

---

three millennia. We may read here as well a coded allusion to the deification of knowledge itself, as the quest for enlightenment would eventually turn toward ritual worship and devotional practice. Through obsessive preservation and archiving, knowledge would become the new god: the sublime source of light, the selfsame Sun, transcendent to all of creation.

5. Here I reproduce this text straight from memory. Ihab also gave me his own translation, which I still carry with me and peruse from time to time.

6. Although I haven't discovered any solid proof, there's a lot of circumstantial evidence to suggest a connection between Hassan Shaarawi and Muhammad Mazhar Pasha. The latter was one of the first Egyptian students of Monsieur Goumard, a loyal follower of the Saint-Simonians and Barthélemy Prosper Enfantin. He was also one of the first Egyptians to join the Society of Urbanists during its second reawakening. But he's perhaps best known today as the first Egyptian head of the Artillery School, and the builder of the modern lighthouse of Alexandria on the Ras al-Tin peninsula. Having been charged by the Society with hemming in the Nile, he constructed the Delta Barrages north of Cairo, as well as the barrages at Rosetta, according to his own designs.

water, and the moon. By pure coincidence—or perhaps, by the sort of manufactured coincidence that tended to intervene on behalf of the Society's most important members[7]—Hassan became acquainted with the Belgian engineer.[8]

It is not enough to suggest the two were "acquainted": let us say that Hassan and the Belgian became *familiar* with one another. That is, they developed a special bond, like that which ties together the members of a family. There was nothing unusual about this. The Society insisted that its members eschew hierarchy in all its shapes and forms. It implored them to always search out new, more lasting forms of familiarity, new kinds of knowing, new ways to wisdom. This was the essence of the Society's being, the secret source of its survival.

This Belgian was among a group of engineers who laid the foundations of Cairo's modern infrastructure. Together with "the Frenchman" and "the Englishman," he assisted in the development of the city's first sewage system. The Belgian felt disgusted.

---

7. Whether or not he was aware of it, Muhammad Ali was a pawn in the hands of the neo-Masons, who used his iron fist to purge those members of the Society who rejected its move from Gnosticism to politics in the early nineteenth century. Many had seen this move as a betrayal of the covenant of Philemon. In his unpublished work, al-Jabarti documented the crimes committed by Muhammad Ali and his followers against Egyptian and Sudanese members of the Society. Indeed, al-Jabarti himself was a target of Muhammad Ali's brutal regime, but he managed to avoid the terrible fate suffered by the Mameluke princes, some of whom were in fact members of the Society. One reason for this was the high regard al-Jabarti enjoyed in the Society as the result of his vast, encyclopedic knowledge and his renown well beyond Egypt. Moreover, when the schism erupted between the Masons and the Gnostics, he refused to take sides. His great aspiration was to craft a third way that might reconcile the two groups: on the one hand, those members who, through direct and often violent intervention in the affairs of mankind, hoped to deliver it from its miserable existence, and on the other, those who remained committed to pursuits of a purely occult or academic nature. With few exceptions, then, the Khedive sent Egyptian pupils to schools run by the Masons, or to teachers associated with the Saint-Simonians.

8. Ihab told me the name of this engineer, but it gradually slipped my mind.

Hassan—who was his adviser, or assistant, or something of that nature—became fed up with the whole idea of making the city any better. Eventually, the Belgian decided not to tire himself with the details, and was satisfied enough that his company had been awarded the construction contract. He would often say to Hassan that the Khedive was a mad fool. All he wanted, the Belgian complained, was to consolidate power in his own hands, and prevent the possibility of any kind of competition. He ruled with the mindset of a provincial strongman, and this was not appropriate to the governing of a modern city. What was required was real competition. Without competition, there would be no city.

Cairo, in the opinion of the Belgian, could not handle any further "development." His French and other European partners, on the other hand, had an easy counterargument. The city had a horrendous smell, and its pools and swamps were breeding grounds for microbial infestations and diseases of all sorts.

But who really cared about all these diseases, anyway? Did the Khedive? Did the Egyptian people? Most Egyptians, the Belgian reminded his foreign friends, were not originally from Cairo. They lived in small villages and hamlets, and the towns and cities of the countryside. It would be an incredible waste trying to rebuild a city that's rotten to its very core. Why not have a fresh new start? Why not look around for someplace more hospitable, and there build a city capable of sustaining new life?

But the Belgian's friends simply didn't understand. In those days, the idea of building whole new cities seemed to be something beyond imagining. Urban planning as we know it today was still in its infancy. The Belgian, together with Hassan, had thought it possible to exploit the Khedive's megalomaniac ambitions in order to build a new, fully functioning urban center down to the last detail. The new city, it was hoped, would take some of the demographic stress off Cairo, and allow those who remained to dream a little bigger.

Hassan belonged to that small cadre of educated elites who would be responsible for introducing the general public to a whole host of new expressions—"patriotism," "the Egyptian nation," "rights," "despotism," "freedom," "bread," and so on—that would acquire profound emotional resonance. But when he returned to Cairo, he found that he didn't quite fit in, either with the good old bourgeoisie or with the rising ranks of nationalists. He seemed forever destined to remain alone, yet with a sense of belonging that extended here and there. Both one with the people, and one with himself.

No city was meant to be like this. Cairo was supposed to be more intelligently designed, more precise, more efficient. Not just a bunch of buildings that seem pretty on the outside to a rarefied class of Egyptians and foreigners. These people don't know what they're looking for anyway. A genuine lack of imagination has befallen architecture and urban design. Ideas have dried up. What we need is a revolution, or something.

Back in Cairo, Hassan fell into a depression. Foreign construction companies were in control of the city. The Khedive and all his men—including even those scoundrels who bragged of being "patriots"—wanted nothing but the kind of architecture they saw in the West. Hassan often felt the need to express to those around him his great dissatisfaction with everything that was going on. From the general outline of the streets to the finer details of the sewage system, nothing met his approval.

Eventually he took off to China. And what did he do there? What did he see, and whom did he meet? How did he spend his time for two whole years? Perhaps he learned Chinese. Perhaps he learned some other language. The truth is, we don't know. Perhaps Ihab, if anyone, knows what he was up to.

At the age of forty, after returning from China, Hassan received an invitation from the Belgian to come to Paris and be initiated as a member of the Society's inner circle of administrators. Here, one story ends, and another begins.

I remember Ihab's face in the pale yellow light of our bunker underneath Garden City. We were there for the second time. Now Madam Dolet was with us, complete with her tiny spectacles and eyes like Safia El Emari (think Joan Rivers). Her look was only half the mystery. Meanwhile, Ihab was on the verge of a nervous breakdown. Somewhere between the erratic tenor of his voice and the Madam's hypnotic gaze, I forgot exactly where I was.

Up above ground, Cairo was being inundated by a tsunami of sand and dust. We were waiting things out here until Paprika decided how it should all end.

I remember asking Ihab if I could smoke.

Dolet cracked a grin and lit a cigarette. I snatched her lighter and lit up too.

"But don't you think," I said, turning back to Ihab, "that you were sometimes looked upon as having betrayed the spirit of so venerable an ancestor?"

"Well, things aren't so simple. At the end of the day, I see Hassan as a product of his own times, as someone whose actions made sense in that particular historical and geographical context. I consider it unfortunate that he passed away before he could see his architectural philosophy adopted on such a grand scale. You can see his influence everywhere. Without him, I find it difficult to imagine such things as those affordable housing projects that sprouted up everywhere after the Second World War, providing shelter to all those who had lost their homes. Even such modern notions as imitating nature and the surrounding landscape in the design of buildings: here, too, we might give credit to Hassan. Back in the thirties, he was already talking about the necessity of urban green spaces, of using the rooftops of buildings to grow crops. His idea was to take some of the burden off the countryside, and integrate agriculture into the regular life of the city. It took decades for these ideas to be implemented in any organized fashion, and then only on a rather small scale. Chicago City Hall is one example. The man was a genius, pure and simple."

Just as he finished talking, his phone beeped, alerting him to an incoming text. He donned his reading spectacles. From the blank stare on his face, I couldn't tell whether the news was good or bad.

"By the way," he said, "you know he was a friend of Walter Gropius. You've heard of Gropius, no?" It was obvious he was trying to hide something from me.

"The name sounds familiar," I said.

"Gropius was a young man when he met Hassan. The two became close friends. But Gropius soon developed his own independent method of design, which we know as the Bauhaus School. That's not to say that the two no longer had anything in common. But Bauhaus took a decidedly romantic turn toward harmony and fluidity of design. Where exactly had the two departed? The Nazis had decided that Bauhaus was against the German zeitgeist, so Gropius fled to America, where his work received an enthusiastic reception. Hassan, meanwhile, spent the remainder of his days busy with administrative tasks. Seldom venturing out of his house on Pyramids Street, he committed himself to widening the Society's ranks and spreading his ideas among its new talent. To the end, he was an armchair architect, really more of a theorist than a practitioner."

"And what about Paprika?"

"I don't have much of a problem with her. She's something of an extremist, to be sure. Really committed to my grandfather's ideas. If anything, she fails to grasp that my grandfather wasn't a saint."

"Wait a second—you *don't* have a problem with Paprika? Now my understanding was that we're all trapped down here on account of her . . ."

"Believe me, I've got nothing against her as a person. This isn't about individuals. It's a war of *ideas*."

"By the way, speaking of ideas. There's one thing I don't get about Paprika's Great Plan. I agree, of course, that Cairo's a miserable, hideous, filthy, rotten, dark, oppressive, besieged, lifeless, enervating, polluted, overcrowded, impoverished, angry, smoke-filled, simmering, humid, trashy, shitty, choleric, anemic mess of a city. But isn't it the architect's job to work within this mess?"

"Sure, my friend. But at a certain point, one will find it simply impossible to work with the way things are. The only way out then is just to demolish everything and build again from scratch."

Sure, it all sounded ludicrous, but then here we were cowering in a bunker under Garden City. Still, to watch him and Madam Dolet talk it over like they were reviewing some sort of science fiction movie—well, it just seemed rude. As if they didn't realize that they themselves were two very involved parties and that, moreover, they had involved me in this mess with them. Perhaps they felt that in the face of so tremendous a loss, nothing of any use could be done. Perhaps that's why they had chosen me, a young man of no particular use, to begin with.

I'm not exactly sure how to explain what happened next. Ihab seemed to accidentally let out a small sort of snicker and then awkwardly try to cover it up. But it was too late. The man was suddenly cackling at the top of his lungs. Whatever it was, Madam Dolet caught it too, and soon the three of us were convulsing with laughter. Madam Dolet's eyes filled with tears, and Ihab doubled over the top of his desk. I laughed till my stomach hurt. We laughed louder. We laughed like it was the last thing we'd do before being buried alive.

Despite making a good living working for some multinational corporation, Moud soon found himself a victim of that endearing, uniquely Cairene brand of misery. Perhaps that is why we became such good friends.

He watched the best of American television, and closely followed the electoral skirmishes between the Democrats and the Republicans. He became disenchanted with everything, and felt his life had no purpose. I once suggested that he try his hand at writing.

He would write in English. Every page he wrote, he would send to me or another close friend. More than the writing itself, what he enjoyed was the look on our faces as we read. That's all he seemed to aim for. But as long as he was in Cairo, he felt everything added up to absolute zero. Even if, most of the time, he had everything anyone could ever ask for.

Behold the turkey. He sings for no one.

Behold the peacock. Any peacock. Does anything he does make a difference?

"I want outta here," says Moud, taking a shot of Bacardi.

If you do manage to escape, my friend, throw down the rope for me too.

Five years after the destruction of Cairo, I met with Paprika in 6th of October City. She was one of the principal architects behind the Dalí Desert. More precisely, she was *the* architect behind the Dalí Desert. Now, at the height of her power, she controlled the most important not-so-secret society in the world, as well as the largest conglomeration of construction companies.

Behold the peacock. What does he do?

He pecks at the emptiness. He ruffles his plumage in the winds of despondency.

She ordered a plate of boiled vegetables. "I don't want vegetable soup," she warned the waiter. "Just want you to boil some water and throw some raw vegetables in it. Capiche?"

As she waited for her order, she started stabbing the tablecloth with the tip of her knife. Back then, I had gotten into rolling my own cigarettes. I took out some paper and started filling it with tobacco. The restaurant was called The General. It was nighttime, and the moon was half full. From the window you could see the boats gathered at the docks.

"I'm sure Reem would be happy," Paprika said, breaking the silence, "seeing the way things turned out."

I shot her a quick glance before returning to my cigarette. She called the waiter and asked him to open the window. The wind blew in as clean and fresh as ever. After the storm, it had taken four whole years to purify the air of Cairo, or what was left of it. During the night, the massive pumps along the border with 6th of October City would begin sucking up the air. After purification, small quantities of fresheners would be added to the air, and mixed together with some innocuous bacteria to break down the carbon monoxide and other pollutants. This made the air perfectly fresh each and every night, as though it were a kiss from the gods, a kiss from Reem.

I finished rolling my cigarette and popped it in my mouth.

"I never asked Reem to sacrifice herself," Paprika said. "You know that, don't you?"

"You want me to help you clear your conscience, is that it?" I lit my cigarette.

"Bassam. I have no conscience."

"Then why'd you bring up Reem? And if you didn't take Reem's life, what about Ihab, and Madam Dolet, and the millions of others who lost their lives for no purpose whatsoever?"

And what does the peacock do?

From the tips of his feathers hang the ropes of execution.

I poured myself some mineral water. A scene from the old Egyptian movie *Ibrahim the White* flashed through my mind. I looked up at her and said, "Miss Paprika. I'm not interested in digging up the past. I couldn't care less about you or what you're planning for the Society. I've only come here because you said you could offer me a job. So please: I'm all ears."

She stopped smiling.

The peacock will befriend anyone, follow anything, as long as little stones keep falling out of his feathers. Because they're shiny, he thinks they're jewels.

The waiter brought my coffee, along with the boiled vegetables and broth for her. I drank my coffee, and she her broth. In silence. That song by Mahmoud Abd al-Aziz, "Lion and he's got a kingdom," started buzzing in my head.

She finished her broth.

And what does the peacock do? He goes after the little stones. Each one differs from the next in terms of color, size, taste, and brilliance. They're really just stones, but he thinks they're jewels. He tries to chew on them. He picks one up with his beak and shakes it from side to side. He can't quite grind it down, and he's unable to swallow it whole. He might croak like the chicken that tried to swallow a pecan.

"So. How would you like to be *Guardian of the City*?"

"Guardian of what city, exactly?"

"This one here. 6th of October."

. . .

REVENGE HAS NO PLACE
IN MODERN LIFE (1)

The Society had no official headquarters in Cairo. There were, however, several affiliated organizations, such as the Rotary Club, the Lions Club, and the Green Youth Movement, who were able to lend them office space. They could also reserve entire restaurants, like Taboula, for their meetings, or even hold emergency gatherings at the base of the pyramids. If need be, they would all sit naked together in a Jacuzzi, or have a plane fly them in circles over the city. They could, if they wanted, meet in any one of these places. But, whether because of the sensitive nature of the matters to be discussed, or the potential gravity of events to come, or even disagreements among the twenty-one members of the High Administrative Council, it had been decided that their meeting should be held in Ihab Hassan's little apartment on Adly Street.

They arrived in small groups, and were put up in accommodations that differed according to their tastes. Architect Uzami Murakama (Japan) and nutritional expert Samara Khan (Indonesia) chose the Marriott Hotel in Zamalek. Professor of urban planning Dr. Hanna Isa (Lebanon; the United States) and Jean Rashid, the agricultural expert, along with his partner, Vivian, professor of interior design (France), all chose the Grand Hyatt in the middle of the Nile. Mr. Kim Young, lecturer in military affairs (South Korea; the United States), traveling with Mr. Gonzo Smith, restaurateur and professor of ancient magic (the United States), chose the Ramses Hilton, as did Lars Jacob, professor of graphic design (Denmark), Mrs. Teresa Pepa, the renowned architect (Italy), and Nicolai Brasso, professor of ancient languages (Italy).

Meanwhile, the Hotel Amin in Bab al-Louq was to host Mr. Xia Chin Lin, expert in security systems and nuclear reactor management (China), the famed writer Su Tung (China), and writer and literary critic Pankaj Mishra (India). The historian Gilberto Freyre (Brazil) chose the Conrad Hotel on the Nile. Salif Kali (Mali), specialist in rural medicine, as well as violinist Karin Boye (Sweden), the visual artist and professor of psychology Herbert Grönemeyer (Germany), and businessman and professional magician Ahmad Faheem (Egypt) all chose the Semiramis Hotel. Arms dealer Yuri Shevchuk (Serbia; England) and the specialist in Arab magic Jameela Aal Saud (Saudi Arabia, of course) both chose the Sheraton in Dokki. Finally, Paprika, architect and specialist in modern magic (Austria; Japan; the Philippines), had a private apartment in Zamalek, and Ihab Hassan, professor of literature and current president of the Administrative Council, had his little place on Adly Street. Also attending the meeting would be Madam Dolet, and Reem, who was Paprika's assistant.

As per the Society's normal operating procedures, the meeting's participants did not arrive at any binding decision. Rather than voting on a particular policy, each member would cast a secret ballot to express personal support for that member who had first suggested the policy, and then conduct sideline negotiations with said member to determine exactly what kind of support might be needed. Those who refused to offer support would simply take it upon themselves to do everything in their power to stop the policy from being implemented. This was not democracy, exactly. It was survival of the fittest. The wheel of evolution spun by having everyone pitted against each other, and the process also adhered to "Rule Zero" of the Society's constitution. The particulars of "Rule Zero" were not known to all, but the spirit of the law as generally understood was a pledge to preserve the secrecy surrounding the Society's overall structure.

Dolet explained it all to me later. This latest meeting had been nothing more than a ruse by Paprika to strengthen her authority and promote her ideas for the future of Cairo. And it was just the first step in her scheme to wholly upend the prevailing understandings of architecture and the environment around the world.

What Paprika had in mind went well beyond Cairo. It struck at the very core of the Society's mission, aiming to change the direction of humanity as a whole. No one knew exactly who this woman was, or where she originated. She had collected dozens of different stories about herself, each one contradicting the other. A puzzle in a box tossed into the depths of the ocean millions of years ago. It was said she held exclusive knowledge about the design of the world's first strand of DNA, from which all subsequent life was to flow.

She rose quickly through the Society's ranks, after first joining at the recommendation of a low-level priest in Tibet. She had presented herself as an expert in "green" architecture and professor of sleep studies.

Her ideas fit well with those of some of the Society's members, though these were by no means a majority. Her argument, to put it simply, was that "the Society should exploit its vast archive of knowledge, accumulated since the beginning of time, for the sake of humanity's deliverance from its present misery. If the only point in keeping this invaluable treasure locked away was to protect the laity from hurting themselves, the Society could maintain guardianship of its sublime mysteries but still intervene forcefully enough to change the world politically, economically, and scientifically."

Ihab, however, considered that such an argument greatly exaggerated the Society's potential influence and capabilities. "Even if the Society were able to open its archive," he protested, "deciphering and analyzing all the information it had accumulated over the centuries, in languages both living and extinct, would be no small task." Instead, Ihab had been actively engaged in pushing the Society to invest in the world's best research universities, as part of a gradual process of liberalization or "opening up" of the archive. Moreover, the Society's great storehouse of knowledge was not located in a single building or facility, but was spread out among many locations around the world. Even if all the current members were to come together in one place and delve into its sublime mysteries, they wouldn't be able to finish reading everything in their lifetimes—let alone attempt to properly fathom all that they had gathered. For these reasons, Ihab much favored a gradual process of liberalization.

But after the fiasco in Iraq, it appeared to many—especially Nicolai Brasso, professor of ancient languages—that any step toward liberalization would be a grave error. Secrecy must be preserved. Thus the stage was set for Paprika to unveil her own plan. It was time, she insisted, to change course. The battle had to be taken to a whole new level.

Cairo was just the beginning.

I'm not sure if what happened was good or bad. People in general, especially today's youth, seem to be happier than we were at their age. While it's true that some of these happy folks are taking drugs, and that others get depressed and commit suicide, such things seem to be a basic part of the human condition. At the end of the day, the Great Wheel spins on, human productivity continues apace, and the natural laws of action and reaction are enforced with fresh resolve. Pundits in the press compared Cairo favorably with Japan's rapid economic growth after the Second World War. "The rabbit's jumped out of the hole," they were fond of saying. Perhaps they didn't realize that the whole world was now more or less the same: no room for rebellion, no space for screaming. The forests had been masterfully redesigned, and temperatures kept carefully under control. Machines dug deeper below the planet's surface in order to harvest her secrets. Peacocks were placed under strict surveillance, as the number of endangered species increased with every passing hour. Chaos itself was reined in and confined to predetermined areas, or incorporated into the Great Wheel itself, helping to keep things moving along calmly in the interest of a global, well-maintained equilibrium.

Art, too, was made to submit to the rules of the global market, to the extent that any act of artistic transgression would itself become commodified and sold to the highest bidder. The few lunatics who decided to self-consciously embrace commodification, in a pitiful effort to bend the rules of the market and the media to their own purposes, formed merely a small and easily contained blemish on the ever robust, resplendent edifice of the Law.

CHAPTER SIX

• • •

That's not to say life in Cairo was completely miserable. There were good times to be had year round: some during our long summers, and quite a few during our short winters. Such times were, invariably, either days off work or days without it. They say the city never sleeps, they say it bursts at the seams. The city rotates and revolves. The city branches out. The city beats, the city bleeds.

In their places of work and worship, the people of this city swarm. They shop and scurry and go for a piss, so the Wheel of Production might go on spinning despite the traffic. That's how it all looks, if you're an eagle soaring up above. But if you're just a little mouse of a man spinning inside that Great Wheel, you never get to see the big picture. You go to work and do your job, and might even earn a reasonable salary. If, by some great fortune, you manage to see the fruit of your labors, it still won't move you an inch. Whether you work or not, the Wheel of Production keeps on spinning, and the current carries you along.

Which brings me to the time Mona May and I went with a group of friends over to Moud's apartment in Garden City. This was after a party at Youssef Bazzi's place. We stayed up until the morning smoking hash and competing to finish a whole bottle of vodka. I remember seeing the music dissolve into monkeys that clung to the ceiling. There was a blond German tapping her leg to the beat. Erections popping around the room. A young Palestinian-American, with poor Arabic, talking a lot about racism. Smoke, cigarettes, hashish. And more smoke.

"Bassam," says Kiko, turning to me with a totally bloodshot look. "I've got smoke in my eyes."

"Go easy on 'em, baby."

I pull a tissue over her eyes and blow gently. The German girl watches with a confused look. As I pull the tissue away, my palm drips with the dark freshness of Kiko's face. I plant a light kiss on her lips.

"Did you know there's a kind of sexual fetish called 'licking the pupil'?" says the German girl in English.

"How exactly do you mean?"

"Yeah, I read about that once," interjects Moud.

"That's disgusting," objects Kiko, wrapping her arms around me.

What are your typical twentysomethings to do in Cairo? Might they go for pupil licking? Are they into eating pussy? Do they like to suck cock, or lick dirt, or snort hash mixed with sleeping pills? Or one might ask how long it would take for any of these fetishes to lose its thrill. Are they good for life?

Everyone here has done lots of drugs, both during and after college. Yet here we all are, little islands unto ourselves, with no greater aspiration than to hang out together. We manage to stay alive by sucking our joy out of one another.

Mona May is standing next to the speakers. Her eyes are glazed over as though her soul's been sucked up by the music monkeys on the ceiling, and her body sways to the beat.

After a while, taking drugs clearly gets old. Or they are just not enough. And if one of us ever gives in to total addiction, his life would be over in a few months: this we know by trial and experience. Those of us left in this room are too chicken to end our lives in this or any other way, maybe because we still cling to some sort of hope, some sort of love or friendship.

For all that Cairo takes from its residents, it gives nothing in return—except, perhaps, a number of lifelong friendships that are determined more by fate than any real choice. As the saying goes, "He who goes to Cairo will find there his equal." There's no such thing as smoking by yourself. And the food's only got taste if you have someone to chow it down with, happily, carcinogens and all.

In this city, you'll be lucky if you can get over your sexual tension, and appreciate sex as just one of the many facets of a friendship. Otherwise, your horniness will make you a testy bitch. Kiko rubs my back, and I feel a heat between my legs.

As dawn came up, Moud went to his room, and everyone else went home. Too lazy to head back to 6th of October City, I lay down and fell asleep on the couch. I woke up early with a slight headache, an army of ants marching in the space between my brain and my skull. I went to the bathroom and took one of the pills Moud had brought from overseas to fight hangovers. After taking a warm shower, I called Lady Spoon and agreed to breakfast at Maison Thomas in Zamalek.

On the way, the streets were clean and empty of traffic. It's a holiday: perhaps the Islamic New Year, or Victory Day, or Revolution Day, or Saltwater Catfish Day. Whatever it was, the city looked drowsy and everyone was checked out. At moments like this, I barely recognize the place. When I'm able to get from Qasr El Eyni to Zamalek in under twenty minutes, I almost feel like she's decided to warm up to me. But I know that wicked smile on her face. She's telling me, "At any moment, I can have you stuck in traffic for over an hour, with nothing to do but sit back and feel sorry for yourself as the noise of the streets slowly sucks the life out of you." Open veins spewing blood all over the bathroom.

I met Lady Spoon outside the restaurant. She had on a long white dress showing her arms and a bit of cleavage.

"You smell really nice," she said, kissing me on both cheeks.

"It's Moud's cologne."

It was her neck that made me fall for her. She's nine years older than me, but she knows how to stay youthful, exercising regularly and always eating healthy. She's pretty, cheerful, and has a successful career in advertising. Unfortunately for her, she's a Protestant and happens to love Egypt, and her chances of meeting someone with both these qualities in Cairo are slim at best. She studied overseas before spending quite a long time being terrified of getting married or settling down. Sometime, she'd like to have children. She had been used to dating men who were older than her, but suddenly, they had stopped showing an interest. Those that did show interest didn't interest her. This was the first time that she would be dating someone younger than her, which made her embarrassed to tell her friends.

The name "Lady Spoon" was given to her by Mona May. She saw her at a concert once wearing a pair of spoon-shaped earrings.

These were the same earrings she had on now. They swayed with the movement of her hand as she sliced a loaf of bread. In spite of the dryness in my throat, I'd been smoking since I woke up this morning. Cigarettes have a different sort of taste with the morning breeze in Zamalek: something resembling bliss, desire, a softness in violet and orange.

Our breakfast was eggs, along with slices of the finest quality pork, imported from abroad. After honey, jam, and a glass of orange juice, I'm back to life. As the poet says, "You ain't you when you're hungry." At Maison Thomas, her smile nudges me awake under a white bed.

We walked around the streets of Zamalek in the direction of her apartment. She had a thin silver bracelet around her ankle, and toenails painted red. Sometimes we would walk hand in hand, and sometimes with my arm around her waist. Under the shade of the trees, we laughed. We shot smiles at the officers standing guard outside different embassies, but their solemn demeanor didn't change.

I thought . . . Do I love her?

Of course I love her. I can't touch a woman I don't love. But then, what is love exactly? It's a relaxing of the heart, a tranquility in your soul, a warmth in your stomach. It's like any love in Cairo, always ready to disappear. A lover of companionship.

In her apartment, we smoked a joint of hash. I rubbed her knee as she played around on her computer looking for an old Madonna song. I lifted her dress above her knees and slid to the floor. Nestling between her legs, I lifted up her foot and started licking her big toe. I walked my tongue in gentle taps along her leg until I reached her knee, which I pummeled with kisses.

"It tickles," she giggled in English.

I gave her knee a parting kiss, and continued my tongue's journey up her thigh. I planted a kiss, soft as a butterfly, on her thinly lined underwear and pulled it away with my hands. I plunged my tongue into her pussy. I drank a lot that night. I drank until I felt thirsty. I gave her a full ride with my tongue before she took me into her room, where we had slow and leisurely sex. She turned over, and I put my fingers in her mouth. Wet with her saliva, I stuck them in her pussy. Slipping and sliding. I stuck them in from behind. I grabbed her short hair and pulled it toward me. I humped her violently and then lay on top of her for a few seconds. I got out of bed and threw the condom into the trash. As I gave her a smile, the phone rang.

"Hey dude, where you at?"

"Mona . . . What's up? I'm in Zamalek."

"So, you still up for a beer tonight?"

"Maybe . . ."

"I'm with Samira. We're going up to Muqattam Mountain."

"So you've got a car?"

"Yeah."

"Okay then. Why don't you come pick me up in Zamalek?"

"When?"

She climbed out of bed with a gentle smile. Sex was over now. We've still got some friendship and goodwill on our faces. People are eating each other alive out there, so why can't we keep things civil?

"How about in an hour or so?"

"Let's make it an hour and a half. Outside Diwan Bookstore."

"Okay."

"Bye."

"See you later."

After a quick shower, I gave her a kiss and a pat on the ass, which was my way of showing gratitude, or something like that. My hair was still wet as I went out. On the way to Diwan, I whistled to myself these words: "Okay . . . Bye . . . See you later." I had a smoke in front of Diwan's display window, which was full of those trashy English books that sell best in airports and supermarkets—the kind that soak your mind in grease and fry your heart in oil. It won't be long before they start selling them with Kentucky Fried Chicken. I tried calling Mona, but she didn't respond. Then I caught her sticking out her head and waving at me from Samira's car. Her hair blew in the breeze, or maybe it was just the loud music spilling out of the radio. Flags fluttered along the street, the car stopped, and I hopped in.

In order to get to Muqattam Mountain, we had to pass through the decaying remnants of Old Cairo. Oddly enough, it took us only seven minutes to get from Zamalek to Abd al-Khaliq Tharwat Street. On a typical day, it might take us a full hour and a half to get to the Azhar Bridge at the end of Abd al-Khaliq Tharwat, but on an atypical day, like this one, Cairo seemed to be liberally bestowing her gifts on all those traversing her streets.

All this emptiness was due to a lack of spare change on holidays like today. The streets, especially downtown, take on a completely different appearance. Mona's wearing a long skirt of some light fabric. I stick my head between the seats and see she's bunched up her skirt in her lap and is rolling a joint. I'm distracted by the glow of her knees, and Samira's turning up the music. Jimi Hendrix's guitar shrieks like a hen laying its first egg. I open the window as we pass over the Azhar Bridge, and imagine I catch a whiff of cumin, pepper, and spices. As we exit the bridge and enter the Husayn District, I smell some burnt coffee beans that, without being an expert, I can tell are of poor quality. The scent fills my nostrils. Among the tombs in the City of the Dead, the smell of liver fried in battery acid lingers like a rain cloud. We finally emerge from the torrent of odors that fills Cairo all the way to the edge of Muqattam Mountain. We go to Bar Virginia and order some beers.

We only talk about things that will lighten the mood: films we've seen recently, some interesting new music, tales of the wonders and oddities recited by taxi drivers, the jesters of the city.

The sun is about to set, and Cairo's laid out before us like a grid, a two-dimensional image from Google Earth. In the middle of this mess of satellite dishes, horrendous-looking houses, and high buildings, there appears one of the city's old ponds. It's a small spot of water, the last that remains of the many pools left over from the Nile after it was circumcised by the Aswan High Dam. In the background there echoes the voice of Muhammad Muhyi, singing a song by Hefny Ahmed Hassan.

A gentle breeze blows. Condensation collects on the green bottles of beer. A moist handshake of appreciation between the beer and its connoisseur.

Samira's fooling around with her phone. Mona takes her beer and clinks it with mine. Her smile, a lock of her hair blown by the wind, and Cairo at sunset in the background. For a few moments, I feel something resembling happiness.

. . .

REVENGE HAS NO PLACE IN MODERN LIFE (2)

I made only two visits to the secret bunker underneath Garden City. The first time, it was just me and Ihab Hassan. The second time, Madam Dolet joined us too, as the three of us took shelter from the evil spirits that prowled the streets above. It was the beginning of the Storm.

The location of our bunker was a secret even to many in the Society of Urbanists. The Society—or should I call it the Organization? I don't really know the difference—kept a well-maintained archive of the mysteries and truths it had discovered over the millennia. Yet its contents remained scattered and dispersed, beyond the control of any single member: were it all to be assembled, no mortal could withstand its blinding light.

Ihab only found out about this place by chance. He had been investigating the construction of Cairo's sewer system when he learned of an obscure faction within the Society that, long ago, had obsessively set about constructing complicated networks of tunnels under major cities. These tunnels led only to empty rooms. With time, many of them disappeared. Some became rivers, or filled up with ground water. A few, however, remained intact. In the 1950s, this information was brought to the attention of one of the Organization's leading members, who went on to form a secret subcommittee dedicated to the maintenance of the tunnel networks in several locations around the world: Cairo; the suburbs of London; Washington, D.C.; Rio de Janeiro; several boroughs of New York City, with the exception of Manhattan; Port Said; Santiago; and so on. Ihab became privy to these networks as well, but the other members of the Administrative Council—including Paprika herself—remained totally unaware of their existence, save for the more famous ones such as the catacombs of Paris.

It was during my first visit to the Garden City bunker that Ihab unloaded on me his whole family history, beginning with the story of his grandfather Hassan and the "idealistic crazies"—his words—of Egypt's nineteenth-century Renaissance. He wound it all up by lamenting his current plight as the Organization's chief administrator. He was at war, and defeat for his side meant nothing less than global catastrophe.

I didn't get why he was telling me all this. When I asked him, he replied with the simplicity of a man peeling a peanut: "Because you're an intelligent young man, someone I can trust. Besides, you're not one of them."

He paused, before confessing, "I want you to make me a website." After repeated attempts to explain himself, he suggested we create something similar to WikiLeaks.[1] Being an intelligent young man, I didn't find it difficult to guess what he was after.

"So we're talking about exposing the Organization?" I asked.

"You want to play this game with me?" he countered. "I mean, like most kids your age, you're not easy to impress. I get it. But don't you want to make something of yourself, to have your own story to tell to future generations?"

---

1. A website that came out not long before the Storm, dedicated to publishing leaked documents about American military operations in Iraq.

I accepted the offer, perhaps because I really was worried about turning twenty-five without having a good story to tell. My life might pass by in a single shade of misery. This "game" opened a new window and gave me the energy to jump through.

Mona had recently been telling me about how disgusted she was with her job at some local programming company, so I shared the offer with her as a possible way out. Ihab had promised to pay cash, out of his own pocket. She was unimpressed at first.

"Dude, I don't do websites. I'm in IT. You know what IT is?"

"But you've done websites before, no?"

"Way back, when I was in college."

"All right, why don't you come over and meet this guy. Just to make his acquaintance."

I can say without a doubt that the look on Mona's face when she first met Ihab was unlike any I'd ever seen. She was actually impressed. This guy was legit. It was love at first sight, and when Ihab brought out a bottle of aged wine, it was like he'd tickled her clitoris with his tongue.

"I'm screaming with excitement," she says with a voice as soft as honey.

I want some excitement too, and getting my cock sucked won't quite do the trick. I need to discover a whole different erotic zone. I need someone to dig a well in my side and accidentally hit upon a site of pleasure long buried under layers of skin, spleen, and bullshit. I need, not so simply, Mona May. I don't totally buy everything Ihab's telling me, but I wouldn't totally reject any of it either. What he has to say blows like a gentle breeze on my face, and I can sense something new on the horizon.

"Let's follow the light," Mona says, "and catch fire like a bunch of moths."

And so she returned to her old hobby of web design. Of course, this meant she would meet Ihab often, alone, without me. Of course, they developed something of a relationship. Was I jealous?

Of course not. The whole thing was so cute it was enchanting, and I was content to see the joy on their faces each time they were together. To see her finally regain her appetite for life was enough to make me feel optimistic. "Someday I'll get what I want," I started telling myself. "Someday I'll succeed."

I only wished, sometimes, that I could be part of their relationship, something of a third rib.

I wished the same thing with Reem and Paprika. I wanted only to exist in their presence. I realized for the first time that this was the kind of love I needed: to be that sort of "third party," suspended somewhere between reality and delusion.

When I met with Reem to be briefed on the topic of the third film, I felt for the first time that the Society had swallowed me up. It was as if my whole life were a puzzle, a network of mazes designed by one of the Society's architects, sprawling underneath the city of Cairo.

This time we met at Cilantro in Dokki. The first surprise she had for me was that she arrived all alone, without Paprika. The second surprise was a red scarf wrapped around her head, which I would later realize was a hijab. And the third and final surprise: this was to be a forty-five-minute film about her, the one and only Reem Abd al-Rahman.

"I've been trying to quit," she said, asking me if I could spare a cigarette. I gave her a light. She puffed out a thin cloud of smoke as the waiter took away our coffee.

. . .

HEFNY AHMED HASSAN[2]

The better part of the Organization's archive of mysteries is shared orally, not among all members, but in a chain of transmission that binds together "teachers" with "companions." The Society, eschewing hierarchies, does not have masters and students. Indeed age itself is not a factor, as a particular "teacher" may be only twenty-one, while his "companion" has long passed sixty.

Arthur Rimbaud, the French poet, was still a young man when he moved to Ethiopia. Yet he happened to have given birth to an idea that would be valued as one of the Society's most important mysteries. It was not made known to all, of course. Ihab wasn't among those so initiated, while Paprika and others were. Madam Dolet claimed that it had something to do with the chemical infrastructure of rainforests, which allowed certain individuals to modify their ecological parameters while under the influence of a plant-based drug compound.

A secondary part of the Organization's archive consists of two subsections. The first subsection contains ancient manuscripts composed in languages both living and dead. Some of these are to be found scattered among the museums of the world, and while publicly accessible, the languages in which they were written remain indecipherable. Most, however, are stored in libraries buried underground or in the depths of the ocean, where they are watched over by appointed custodians.

The archive's second subsection is made up of published works, some of them written by the Organization's own members. They include mostly poets, novelists, sociologists, architects, artists,

---

2. An Egyptian folk singer known for the popular epic *Shafiqa and Metwelli*. Set in the late nineteenth century, the epic tells the story of a man who murdered his sister in order to avenge the family's honor. Let us remember that this took place in the past, since, as we have already seen, *revenge has no place in modern life.*

and intellectuals whose membership in the Society is kept a closely guarded secret. Some of their works are written under pseudonyms, or are attributed to other authors. The *Epistles of the Brethren of Purity*, the poems of Abul 'Ala al-Ma'arri, the fairytales of the Brothers Grimm, the *Epic of Dhu al-Qarnayn* in its Malaysian recension, James Joyce's *Ulysses*: these works and others that remain shrouded in history.

For the Society's members, secrecy is not a luxury. It's a fundamental aspect of their existence, a strategy necessary to achieve their goals.

Another fundamental aspect of their existence, as already stated, is their rejection of any manner of hierarchy. But this applies only within the Society itself. With regard to the rest of the world's population, members have long believed themselves to be distinguished by a superior intellect. As such, they are qualified to lead, and are alone capable of providing true happiness and prosperity for all. The only problem, as members see it, is that humankind happens to be governed by those beholden to fear of the strange and unknown. Such ignorant men are not only an obstacle to the general progress of humankind—they are a threat to the very existence of those who are not so ignorant.

One of the Society's members was a British surgeon credited with devising ingenious methods of organ transplantation, as well as with performing the world's first successful open-heart surgery. (Naturally, these innovations were kept secret for decades before being shared with the medical community at large.) In addition, the surgeon—who spent his last years hidden somewhere in the south of India—was known as the originator of a powerful legend that is told by Society members to this day.

"Naturally, it's all a bunch of bloody nonsense," the surgeon would say of the legend. "None of us believes a word of it. Still, it gives a lot of symbolic weight to our existence, and explains in a metaphorical way how we, as members of the Society, came to be. In any case, the story concerns the first man to lead his tribe to reside in a cave. Let us observe how radically life would change for this group. Let us feel the warmth they felt, having retreated from the winds outside to bask in the sun-soaked rocks of the earth. This warmth would have been a totally new experience for the species. Subsequent generations of humankind would come to know this warmth as 'safety.'

"This first man—and by the way, he might have been a woman—wasn't the strongest one in the group. He was no fierce warrior. With his weak and emaciated figure, he was the one most sensitive to the cold, and the one most fearful of being attacked by wild beasts. However, he was different from the other weaklings in the group. Perhaps it was something in his nerves. Perhaps he had a different sort of memory, or an odd mutation in his genes. Perhaps it was a preplanned coincidence that led him to find sanctuary in the cave, and thus teach humankind what it meant to feel safe.

"This man's tribe would not consider him a hero or a ruler. The power he wielded was not political in the primitive sense, but psychological, and he would subsequently be known by many different names: the magician, the priest, the wise man, the poet, the playwright, the thinker, the mathematician, the physician.

"But the most significant change the tribe witnessed after inhabiting the cave was that their number soon doubled. So it was after the first year, and again with the passing of the next. The population grew until the cave was no longer big enough for all of them. The first person to attempt to expand the cave from within, or to build an extension outside, was the world's very first architect. It is from him that, according to the legend, all members of the Society are descended."

To return to the Organization's notion of secrecy. This was first discussed in the streets of Thebes not long after it was founded. After centuries of conflict and unrest, it was finally put into practice in the months preceding the burning of the Library of Alexandria.

Transmitted like phantom genetic material between its members, the Society's occult knowledge grew and mutated year after year. Some of it spilled out into the open, but most remained jealously guarded. Occasionally, something unexpected would happen. The Internet, for example, emerged completely independently of the Society. The same thing happened with television.

Sometimes, certain members even forgot that they were part of the Society. At other times, it was the Society that forgot about them. But eventually, there would be a knock at your door, or a text on your phone. A delegate might even tap you on the shoulder while riding the subway, pull closer, and whisper in your ear a few precious words, his eyes glowing with the warmth of brotherly love.

The most precious secrets maintained by the Society concerned the spreading of a sense of safety. You'll feel it when you shake hands with one of them. The heaviness will be lifted from your shoulders and you'll become almost sleepy. You'll feel like an infant returning to its mother's womb.

You'll be running around from place to place, running across time, when you realize it's totally unnecessary. The idea will take hold in your mind. It will travel from companion to companion, carried along with the humors, and settle into the great archive of knowledge.

.   .   .

CONCERNING THE INFLUENCE
OF THE PAST ON THE FUTURE

I entered the College of Economics and Political Science under the influence of my father, who passed away when I was in high school. He left behind a fantastical sort of library consisting of the complete works of Mohamed Hassanein Heikal and the writings of Abdel-Halim Mahmoud, former Grand Imam of Al Azhar. In college, I received an eclectic mix of continental philosophy, centering mostly on the works of Foucault and Arendt. (Unfortunately, neither were members of the Society.) Perhaps my wit was stronger than my foresight, but the lesson I learned from the two of them was that there was no longer any hope.

With the turn of the millennium it seemed that ideology had been replaced by culture, and that politics had become a form of business management. There was no longer any vision, nor any missions to achieve the impossible. It was as clear to me as it was to many others that there was no longer any hope, and that the fate of humankind was pain and misery. Nothing could be done to stop what was now inevitable. We might throw up dams to try to halt the flow, but no sooner would our work be finished than the torrent would burst through.

I could therefore easily understand why the Society would want to preserve their secrecy. Until we're able to find some way to put an end to the pain once and for all, we best remain hidden. Only then can we reveal ourselves and bring our full plan to light.

In October, it's night outside. The only sound you hear is the music blasting out of a car whose teenage driver thinks that going faster and louder will make things better and better.

The other day, I stopped at the grocery store to pick up a bottle of hot sauce, some bread, and cigarettes. A news report on the television suddenly caught my eye . . .

A recent incident in the **Media Zone** has raised the concerns of biotech experts, and placed the laws of **demographic** stability under renewed scrutiny.

Kareem Abdel Rahman, a simple employee who lived with his wife in the Earthquake Housing projects.

We've been married for 5 years. Kareem always hoped for a child to carry his name.

He worked at the **printers**, right here in **October**.

To raise a **family**, everyone **said** we'd need to find someplace bigger than 53m². Kareem worked day and night so we could afford a new place.

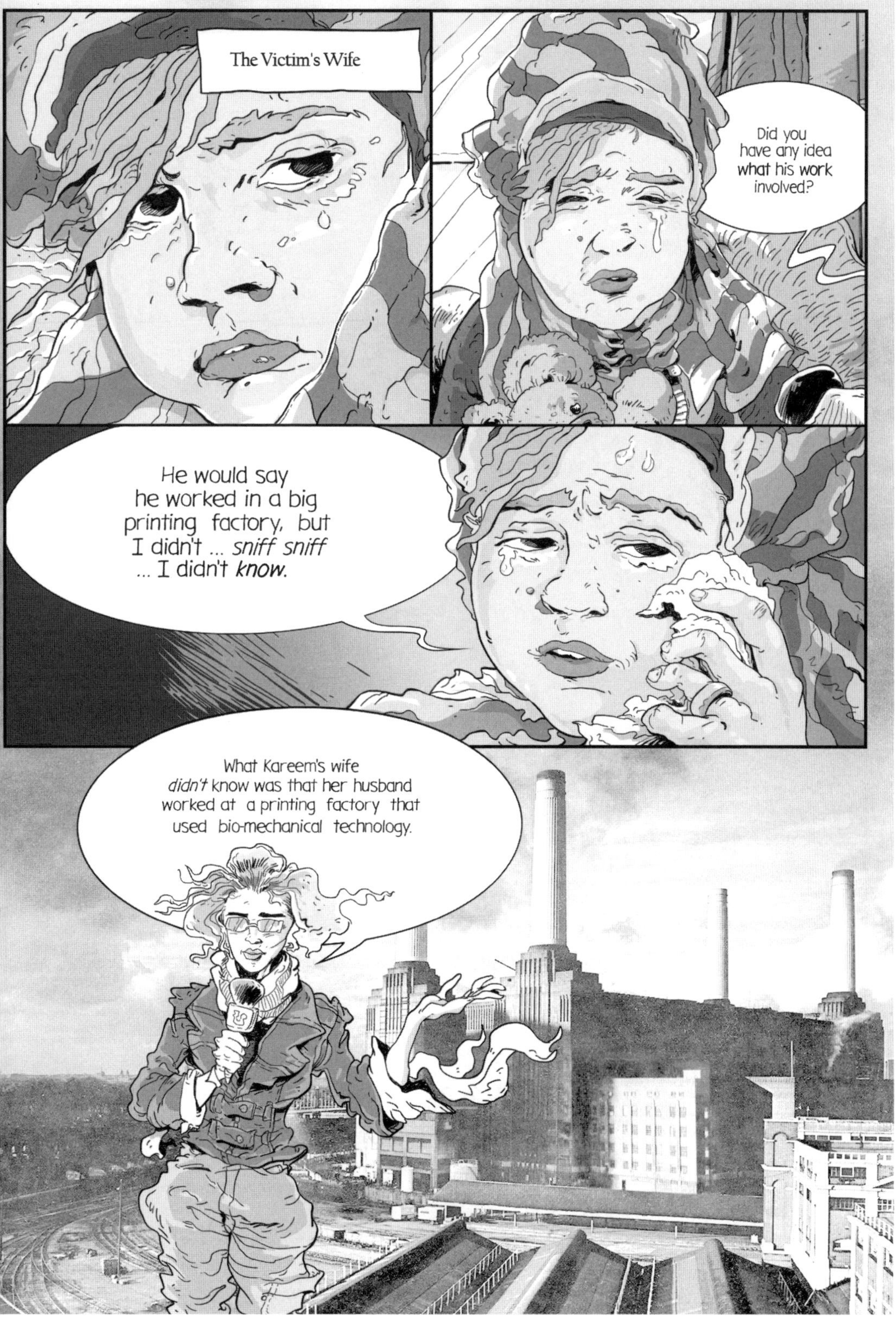
The Victim's Wife
Did you have any idea what his work involved?
He would say he worked in a big printing factory, but I didn't ... *sniff sniff* ... I didn't *know*.
What Kareem's wife *didn't* know was that her husband worked at a printing factory that used bio-mechanical technology.

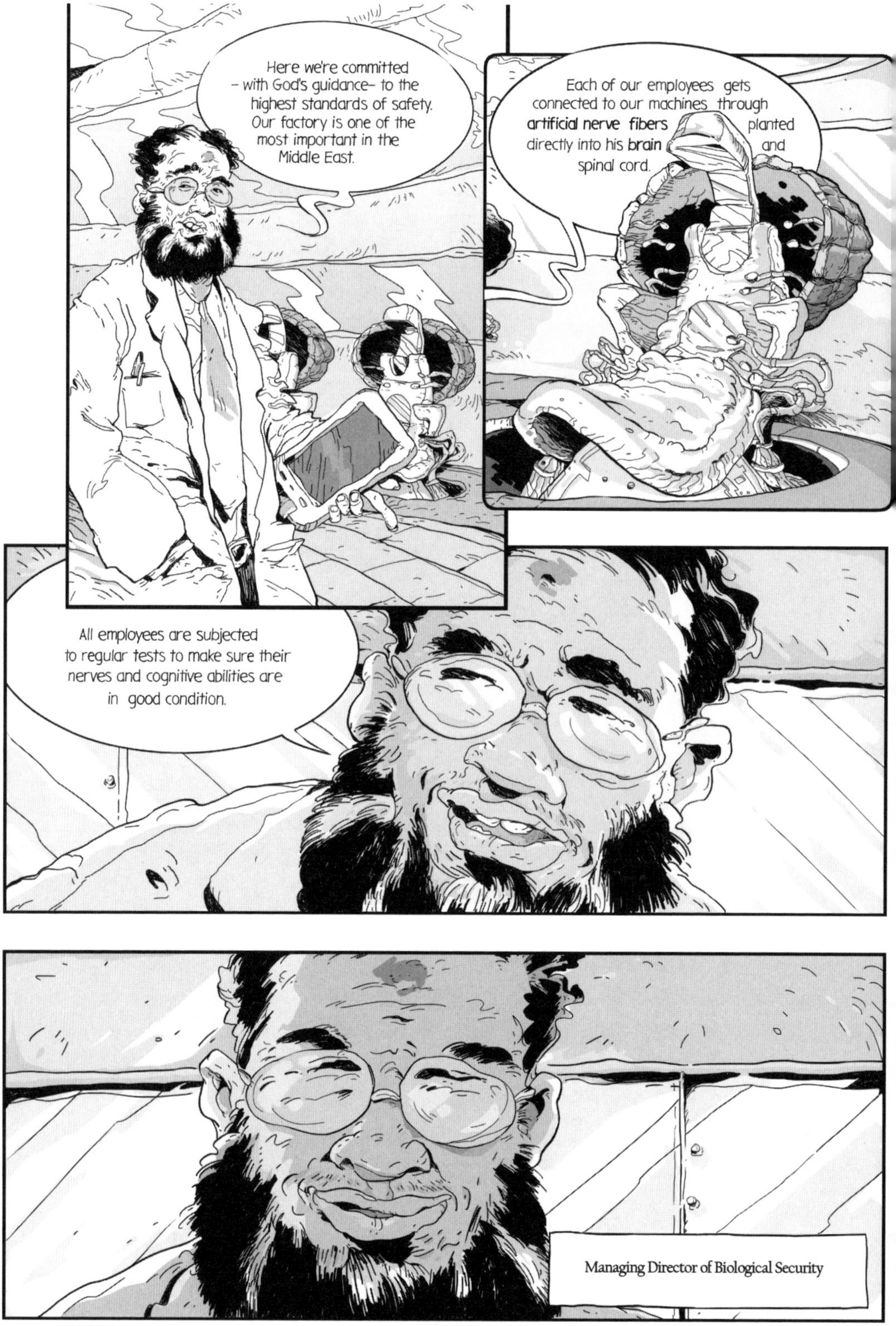
Here we're committed – with God's guidance– to the highest standards of safety. Our factory is one of the most important in the Middle East.
Each of our employees gets connected to our machines through **artificial nerve fibers** planted directly into his **brain** and spinal cord.
All employees are subjected to regular tests to make sure their nerves and cognitive abilities are in good condition.
Managing Director of Biological Security

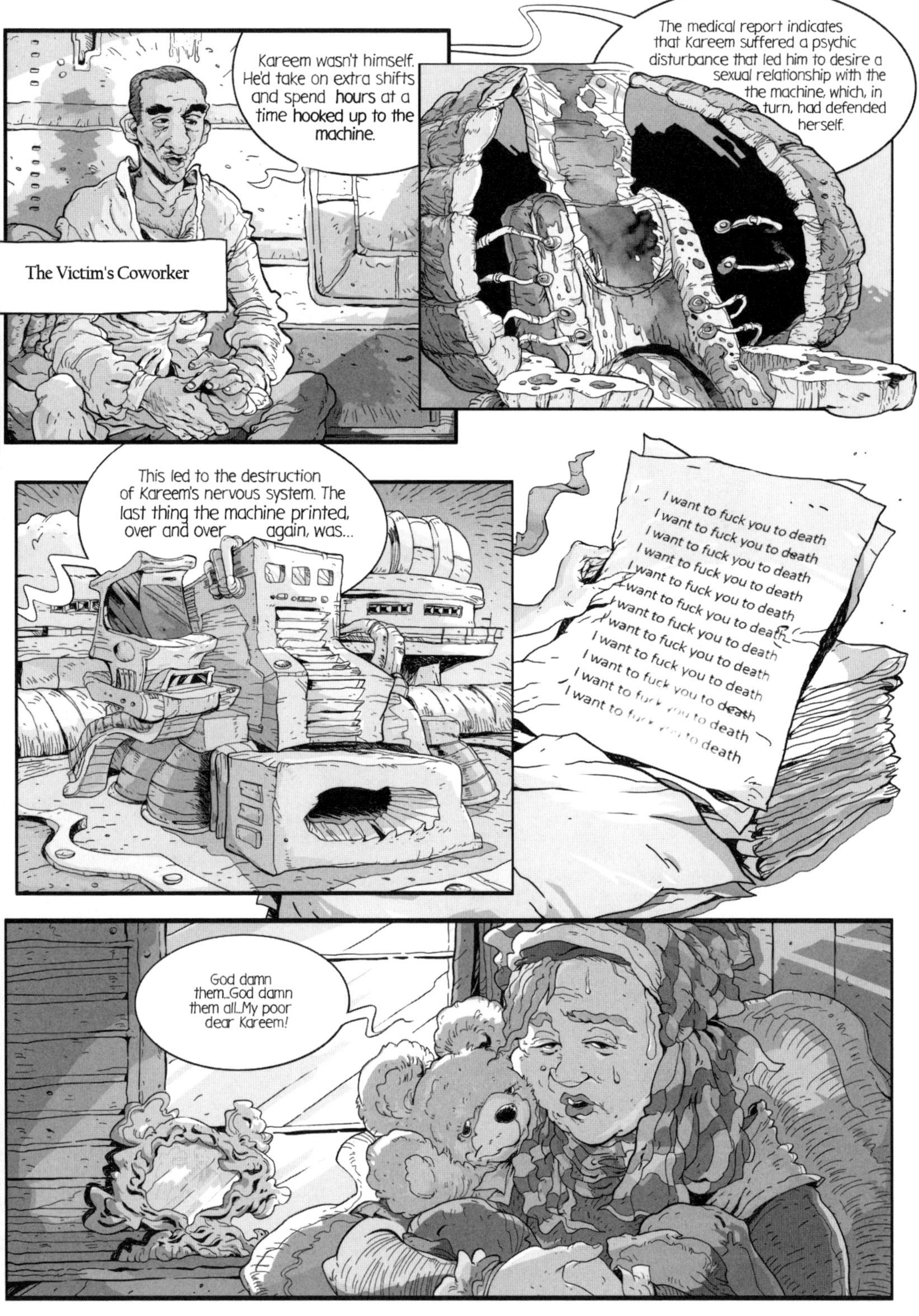

The Victim's Coworker
Kareem wasn't himself. He'd take on extra shifts and spend hours at a time hooked up to the machine.
The medical report indicates that Kareem suffered a psychic disturbance that led him to desire a sexual relationship with the the machine, which, in turn, had defended herself.
This led to the destruction of Kareem's nervous system. The last thing the machine printed, over and over again, was...
I want to fuck you to death
I want to fuck you to death
I want to fuck you to death
I want to fuck you to death
I want to fuck you to death
I want to fuck you to death
I want to fuck you to death
I want to fuck you to death
I want to fuck you to death
I want to fuck you to death
I want to fuck you to death
I want to fuck you to death
God damn them...God damn them all...My poor dear Kareem!

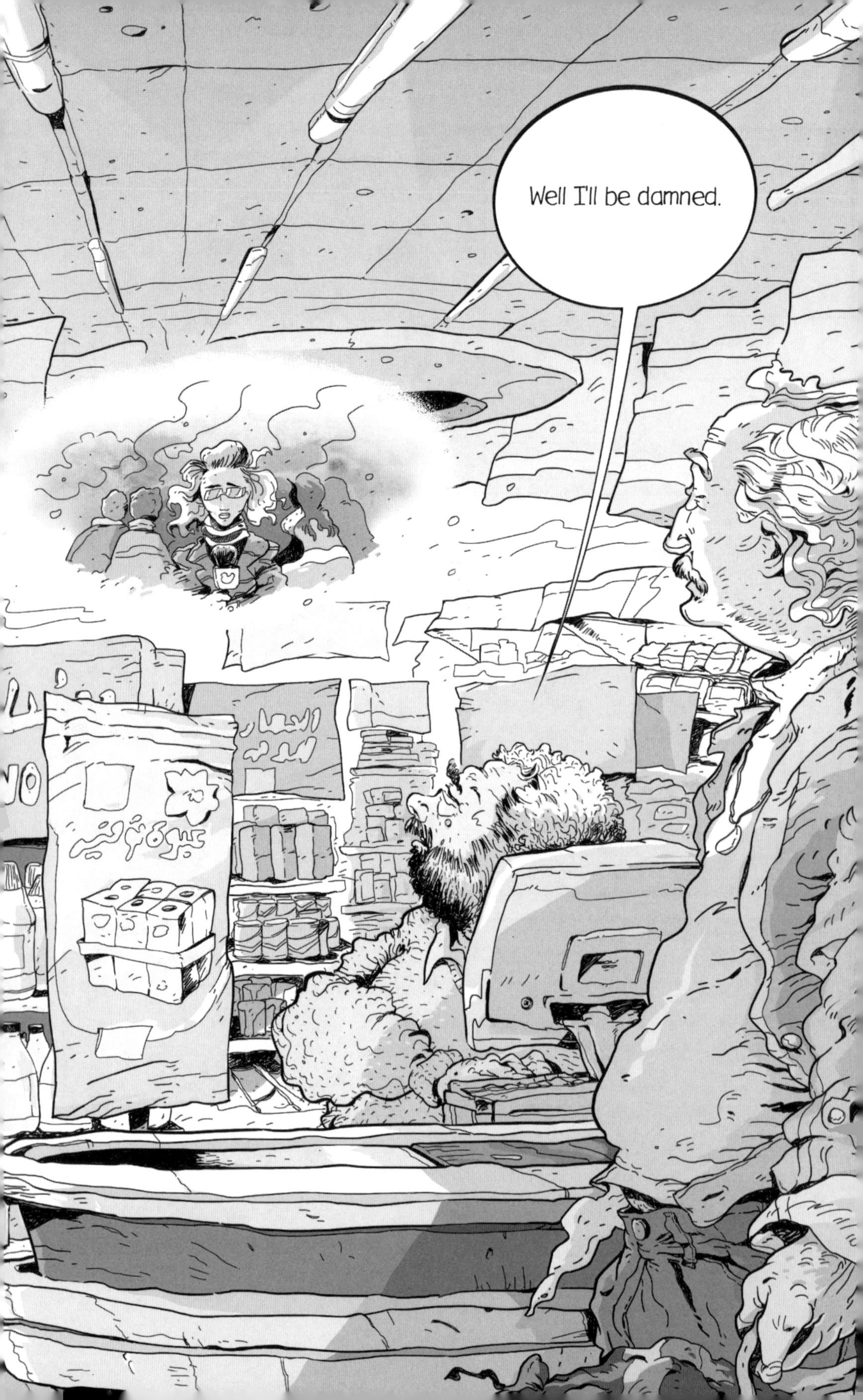
Well I'll be damned.

CHAPTER SEVEN

• • •

Cairo had such a vibrant nightlife. There were house parties, there was sitting around on cheap plastic chairs at the cafe and smoking shisha mixed with glycerin. You could choose between walking the streets to the point of exhaustion, sleeping in front of the television, masturbating in front of the computer screen, work, seedy cabarets, or sucking up some of the noise that spilled out of bars and music clubs.

Beer, beer, and more beer.

A friend of Moud's had just returned from abroad, and was thus permitted by law to purchase four bottles of alcohol on one passport. He donated one for our party that night. After some warm-up beers at Cairo Jazz Club, we were ready for him. He'd brought tequila. We began to commence our rituals, but Mona wasn't in her best mood. The light was dim. The band was getting ready. Moud was complaining about work.

"Believe me, this country's a mess. You'll never be able to understand how it all works."

Imad, the friend who'd brought the tequila, was an Egyptian-Canadian who had a job at a bank overseas. Mona May was playing with her phone. Kiko moved her head to the music—tonight's performers specialized in classic Western hits. Some girl from the German University in Cairo (GUC) seemed shocked at everything going on around her.

"What is it you are all drinking? Why do I have to put salt on my hand?"

"It's cactus juice, darling," responded Imad, the tequila man. "The salt gives us the patience to endure."

"Hey, beautiful," I asked the girl with the black fingernails, "what do you do in life?"

"I study graphic design at GUC."

"She's the one who designed the poster with 'No' written on it," Moud butted in. "You'll remember it from the demonstration."

Which demonstration? "No" to what, exactly? It didn't really matter. The important thing was she'd made a poster. In those days, demonstrations were all about posters. Political activism was headline news. Headstrong youth raging against the system got precious screen time on all the satellite channels.

She lit a cigarette and started talking politics. Kiko stood next to me, the boredom visibly gnawing at her soul. The poster girl seemed outraged at something the tequila man had said. Her voice raised as she said something about poverty and hunger.

"I went to this village called Ezbat Antar. You wouldn't image the suffering of the children there."

Like many youth in those days—youth in any days, really—she seemed so concerned with poverty and hunger that she forgot how hungry she was herself.

The place started to get crowded. There were high-class prostitutes, and women in their late twenties milking pleasure from the mouth of the serpent. There were foreigners who'd been ravaged by this city and forgotten why they came here in the first place. Mona May went to the bathroom and came back to join us for the first round of shots. Then she met an old schoolmate and went over to chat with him at the bar. I sniffed under my armpit and realized how smelly I was. I'd spent the whole day at work in the street, amidst the scorching heat and choking humidity.

"I can't stand this heat!" shouted Kiko. "Moud! Why don't we go to the beach?"

Mona May started dancing with her old friend. She had the lower part of her shirt tied up in a knot just above her bellybutton, and her breasts tucked up into a white satin bra. She closed her eyes and let go.

At some point, she came back to sit next to me, and took one of my cigarettes. Smoking is harmful to your health and causes cancer. She took out her phone.

"Fuckin' A," she blurted out with a smile. "You know who's coming over?"

"Surprise me."

"Ihab!"

"Ihab who?"

"Our Ihab. Ihab Hassan."

"Who's Ihab?" Moud butted in.

"The guy I told you about," I said, giving Mona a light.

"Err . . . I don't remember."

We had just gotten started on the website. Mona had bought the domain name and server with Ihab's credit card, while Ihab himself had left town.

"I've got some errands to run," he had said. "We can stay in touch through email."

A tree of excitement sprouted up inside me. We were on the verge of something big. Mona got up to dance again, while I started telling Moud everything that had happened to me since Ihab took me to the bunker under Garden City. His mouth hung open in utter astonishment.

"Bassam," he said. "You taking some new kind of drugs?"

"No."

"You really believe what you're saying?"

The shock of reason. Reality is a slab of concrete that hits you right in the head and fractures your skull. Before I'd take exams in school, my father would always say, "Concentrate, my boy. Don't let your imagination run away with you." I used to get to the grocery store and forget what my mother had sent me for. Was it all some sort of prank? Was Ihab pranking me, or was I pranking myself? Maybe it was a little bit of both.

I didn't tell Mona too much about the idea behind the website, except that we wanted to publish some important documents. But I didn't know how far her relationship had gone with Ihab. Had he told her? Did she believe him?

Mona May is certainly capable of believing in a game like this. But you, Bassam. Would you waste your life on a delusion like this?

What do you really know about life, Bassam? I turned to look Moud straight in the eyes.

"Why're you acting like this is all just my imagination?"

"Suit yourself, man." He took a shot. No salt. No lemon.

Reem insisted that the filming should take place with as little crew as possible.

"The picture quality isn't the most important thing," she said. "It's Paprika's last concern. Actually, it would be better if the film had a less professional and more experimental feel to it."

The solution we came up with was that I would be director and producer at the same time. Tohamy objected at first, but he couldn't refuse the sum offered up by Madam Dolet. Still, this didn't stop him from trying his regular bullshit.

"You've been mixed up with these people for too long," he said. "We've got more important work to do."

"They also wanna translate this film into English and show it abroad."

"We've got more important work with Al Jazeera and the other satellite channels."

"Madam Dolet told you we could make it a series on the BBC."

"If you're serious, man, go right ahead."

I was dancing with the GUC girl when I turned around to see Ihab walk into the bar. He had on a pair of tight black jeans and a blue silk shirt unbuttoned around the chest. Every time we met, Ihab never failed to surprise me. I imagined he took pride in choosing all these fine little details with the intention of capturing people's attention, and especially my own. A gold metallic bull head hung from a brown cord around his neck. He had one arm around the Tarantino girl and a hemp canvas bag hung over the other shoulder. I ditched the GUC girl and went over to shake his hand. Moud got up too and tried to cover his astonishment with formality.

"How do you do, sir?"

"All fine and dandy, dude," Ihab replied, mixing several generations of slang.

He opened his bag and produced a bottle of whiskey. The band got livelier. The GUC girl moved closer to Ihab. The man seemed to have electrified the place. Even at nightclubs, among the cigarette smoke and booze and dancing roosters, Ihab managed to be the center of gravity.

He seemed able to shift shapes seamlessly, less like an actor putting on a mask than a man giving expression to a truly multifaceted interior. He could suck everything in and make it all one.

I agreed with Reem that the documentary should unfold as an interior dialogue between Reem and herself. There would be two Reems. To distinguish between them, one would be veiled, while the other wouldn't be. We started the filming in her house with a small camera.

"Reem, tell me about your current job at the Society."

"My work with the Society began a few months ago in Cairo," replies veiled Reem. "It was all a coincidence. I wasn't really interested in architecture. But then I discovered that, for the Society, architecture meant more than just construction, or mixing together some rocks and concrete. Architecture is about modifying and conditioning the natural resources of the city in order to better suit the needs of all living creatures, including humans. It also entails the engineering of human beings on three levels—physical, psychological, and spiritual—in order to better condition them to their habitat. This engineering will speed up the wheel of evolution, which, in turn, will help us live up to our most sublime purpose on this planet: to settle the earth, to spread civilization over the land.

"The fact that the Society's 'sublime purpose' coincided more or less with the central mission of the Islamic faith didn't faze me one bit. What I did find remarkable, however, was the manner in which the Society worked to achieve this. They cared about the minute details of things as much as they did the larger issues.

They cared as much about man's interior design as they did his exterior environment. They cared about the future."

"And what is your specific position at the Society?"

Unveiled Reem responds, "At first, I was supposed to act as the go-between for the Society's dealings with organizations that had similar philosophies. As you know, the Society of Urbanists has special protocols for collaborating with dozens of other societies and groups around the world. After the opening of our Cairo branch, we wanted to cultivate new relationships with sympathetic groups in the area. My official duties changed, however, with the arrival of Miss Paprika. She's the Society's director of Futurist Planning, and I'm now her assistant."

"Might you give us more details about the nature of the work carried out by the Society's Department of Futurist Planning?"

Unveiled Reem replies, "One might compare the Department of Futurist Planning to the shaman of an ancient tribe. Its mission is twofold. First, after gathering ecological and demographic data about the city, it runs this data through a series of mathematical equations—and magical formulas—in order to predict the future of the city. By 'the future of the city,' we mean everything for the next fifty years. In accordance with these predictions, the department seeks to prepare for the best, and the worst, to come.

"The department's second obligation is to devise immediate and totally unrealistic solutions to the city's current crises."

"Tell us about the nature of your work with Paprika. As an assistant to the Society's director of Futurist Planning, does your work involve rendering services of an emotional or sexual nature?"

Veiled Reem replies, "My work for the Society does not involve services of this kind. Quite the contrary. In the Society, the relationship between a manager and her assistant is one of companionship. The manager accompanies her assistant through the corridors of knowledge and architecture. She guides her on a path of personal edification, and helps her to partake in the never-ending project of settling and constructing.

"I consider myself lucky to work with Miss Paprika. She's something of a genius, with lots of fresh, new ideas about how to modernize and revolutionize architecture and the settling of the Earth."

"Can you clarify the nature of these ideas?"

Veiled Reem replies, "I believe that it is better for Paprika her-self to answer this question. However, speaking for myself, what impresses me the most is her passion for the data. Not just the use and application of this data, but its fabrication and synthe-sis. There's something revolutionary about the way she works. She lets us see things we never could before. She lets us see things that never existed, but which she can produce and set right before your eyes."

Four o'clock in the afternoon.

A small boat sets off along a stretch of the Nile adjacent to the Radio and Television Building. On board are Ihab Hassan and Paprika. The two sit facing each other.

Reem had rented the boat for two hours. The first hour had gone by without a word uttered between its two passengers. An-other boat passed by them, blasting a song by the hairy teenage heartthrob Tamer Hosny. On board, a girl in a hijab was danc-ing among a circle of guys. Another boat passed, carrying a fam-ily of Gulf Arabs. A line of stopped cars stretched along the 15th of May Bridge.

Ihab had with him the English translation of Khairy Shala-by's novel *The Lodging House*. Every few seconds, Paprika leaned back and glanced upward at the sky. Another half hour passed.

The young boatman looked at his phone.

"Should we head back, then?" he asked Ihab, the other male on board.

Ihab nodded in agreement. The young boatman revved up the motor and started to turn the rudder.

"The decision's been made," Paprika said suddenly. "It shall be carried through."

"I won't let you take such unfair advantage of everything we've built up over thousands of years."

"But I already have taken advantage, Ihab dear," Paprika re-plied with a smile.

They returned to the docks, where Reem had been waiting. She shook hands with Ihab, then took off with Paprika toward

Maadi. Ihab crossed Abdel Moneim Square headed in the direction of downtown, with Khairy Shalaby's novel under his arm. He had made up his mind to bring the temple down on everyone.

"This film," Reem said at the end of the first shooting. "It will be my last will and testament, Bassam."

He opened the door wearing a blue robe, his chest showing. This time the golden bull was gone. Yes, I felt excited. Walking through the crowded streets of downtown with all these secrets and mysteries in my head, I couldn't help but feel important. I wasn't thinking about the consequences of what we were doing, and I didn't know much about what Paprika was planning. I wasn't concerned about the fate of this city. Whatever was going to happen, Cairo couldn't get worse than it already was. If a giant egg dropped down on it from the heavens and drowned it in thick gobs of yellow yolk, this would certainly be an improvement on things.

I sat down in the same chair. The rage and roar of traffic billowed up to us from Adly Street below. Clouds of honking, hammering, hollering, and hawking. A faint light spilled out of a lone lamp in the kitchen. I noticed this time that his apartment had no ceiling lights. His purple bed had the chaotic look of a battle of some kind, or of someone having slept under it.

The royal lion's den. The alcove of postmodernism. A flower of pure purple.

"Anything to drink?" Ihab asked.

"Just water," I said, taking out my laptop.

My mother had phoned me this morning. "Bassam, we miss you. Your nieces and nephews ask about you every day. They wanna see you."

Even though my mother's house was only about two hours away from Cairo, her voice seemed like it was coming to me from a galaxy many light-years away. It sounded strange, carrying memories of everything that had happened before I met Ihab and got messed up in all of this. Memories of another person entirely.

My computer's background was a screenshot from Stanley Kubrick's *2001: A Space Odyssey*. Nothing of my past remained.

I glimpsed a hand poke out from under the purple sheets and turn on the bedside lamp. Ihab was in the kitchen making coffee. He took a bottle of water out of the fridge and put it on the table in front of me with an empty glass. I tried not to look in the direction of the bed, but to no avail. She tossed off the sheets and sat up straight. It was Mona May, in the nude. The bulb of a breast glowed in the lamplight, its nipple black and erect.

The voice of Hal 9000[1] rang in my head. "Dave, Dave, I'm afraid my mind is going."

She got up and picked up a t-shirt from the floor, then tiptoed over along the hardwood floor. Her legs glowed in the dark. She had nothing on but black panties and the t-shirt frankly showing her nipples.

"Bisou! Bonsoir!" She kissed me on both cheeks.

Over in the kitchen, a smile spread over Ihab's face. Only the devil, or the lost and fearful Hal 9000,[2] knew why.

"Why you drinking water, Bisou?" Mona asked, noticing my bottle. "Know this, darling: wine gives you truth, beer gives you strength, but water gives you only germs."

"My oh my," I replied, smiling and shaking my head.

She bent over and picked up a half-empty bottle of wine from under the table. She poured me a glass.

"So you people hide wine under the table now, do you?"

"No. We were having sex on top of the table," she replied with utter nonchalance. "We put the bottle underneath so it wouldn't break."

Later that day, Ihab showed us the first batch of documents he

---

1. Why did Arthur C. Clarke choose a name like this? He could have learned something from Edgar Allan Poe's only novel, *The Narrative of Arthur Gordon Pym of Nantucket*. Pym's name comes off the tongue like a stone gondola.

2. Contrast this to Poe's novel, published in New York in 1838, in which no one is fearful of solitude. The novel's protagonist stows away on a whaling boat for a long and, at first, seemingly normal journey. Soon, however, things take a turn for the worse, as the boat heads toward the South Pole. Sprung from his hiding place, Pym endures an endless series of life-threatening catastrophes: mutiny among the cabin crew, drownings and sinkings, murder, scalping, cannibalism, battles with primitive islanders.

wanted us to publish. Two days after that, a whole pack of ghosts and demons were chasing him around trying to kill him. The day after that, Paprika's plan to put an end to Cairo had started to come into effect, with sudden changes to the climate, alterations in the course of the Nile, and shifts below the surface of the earth.

I can still remember this meeting because of the strong flavor of the wine, the faint light, and the rancid smell of *mulukhiyyah* that drifted in from one of the neighbor's windows. There was also Mona's bare thighs, her attempts at foot play with me under the table, and the loneliness that so overwhelmed me I couldn't perceive the gravity of the battle to come.

I finished the meeting and called Lady Spoon. I paid a visit to her bed in Zamalek and made violent love to her. I gave it to her in the cunt, and from behind too. She collapsed from exhaustion and dozed off, while I went into the bathroom to masturbate. I calmly observed the sensual contortions of my face in the mirror. I could see the reflection of Hal 9000's red light behind me.

"I'm afraid, Dave. Afraid, Dave."

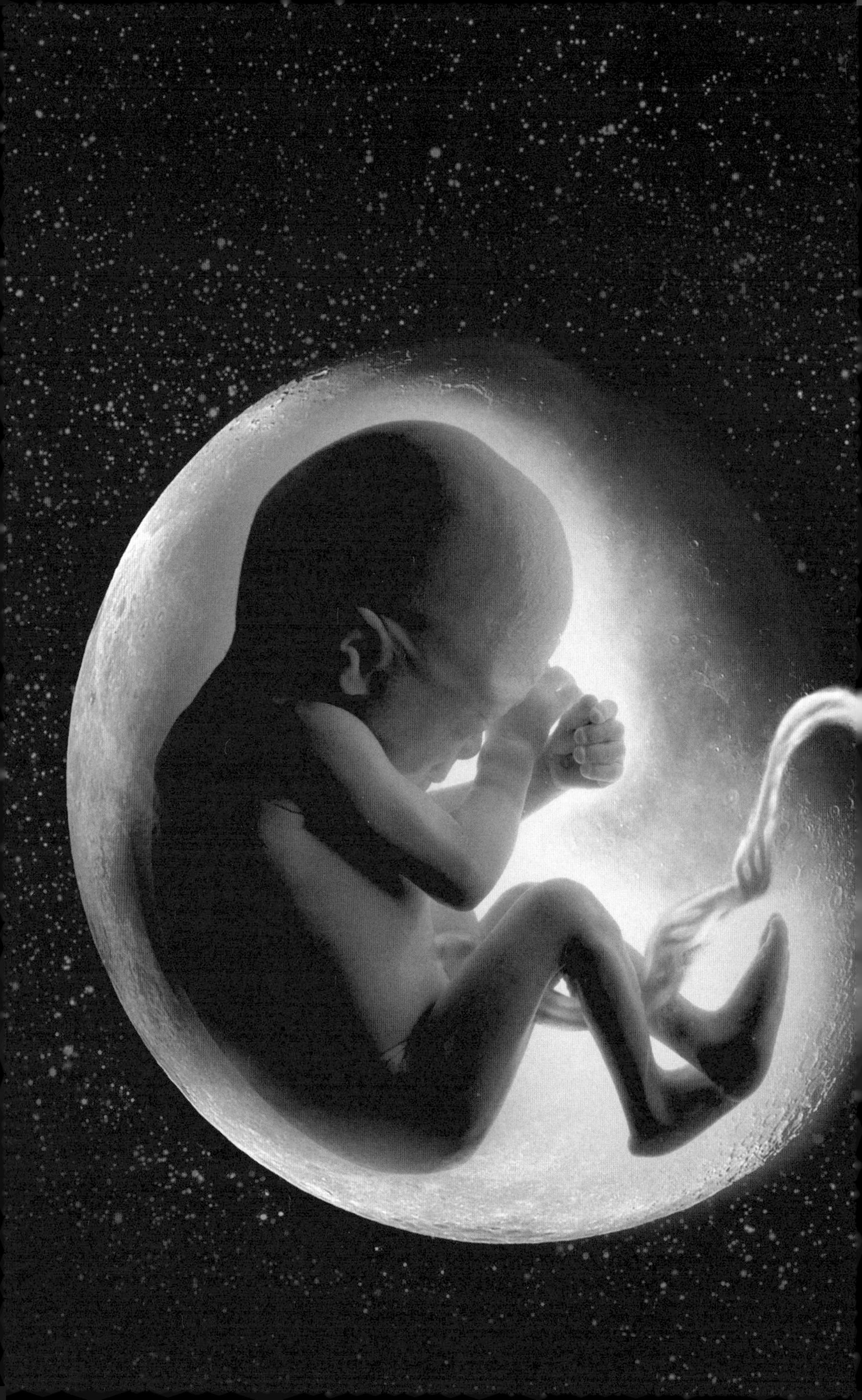

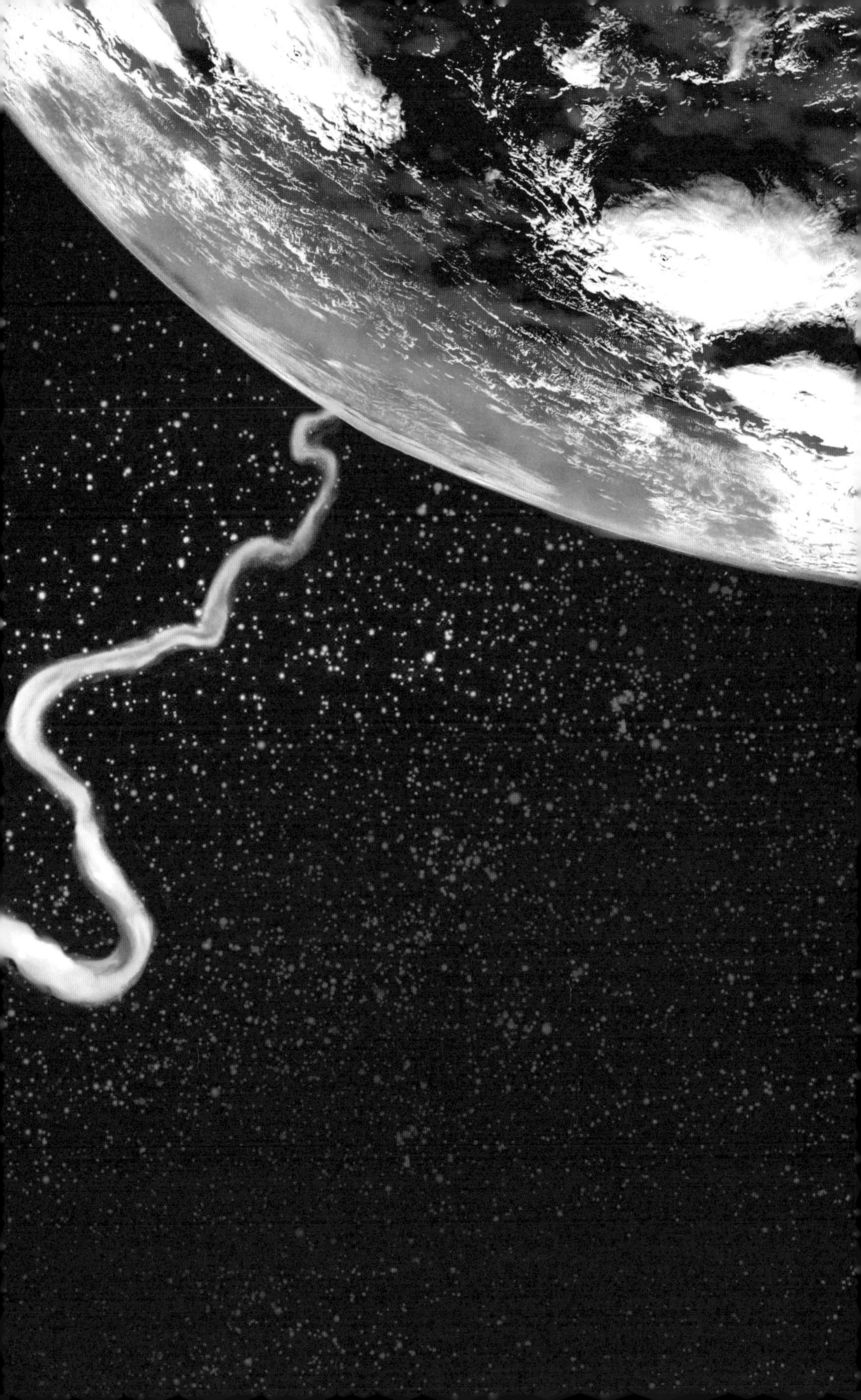

. . .

THE THIRD FLOWER . . . WHERE DO I
PUT THE THIRD FLOWER, REEM?

I was tired, Bassam, and lonely. My pain blinded me to the truth. But let me first ask you a question that takes us to the very heart and soul of the matter: If the forbidden fruit were your daily bread, how would you ever experience climax?

Reem didn't hate her family. She was their elder daughter. It was they who wanted to suck the life out of her.

While a student in the Faculty of Languages, she met the man with whom she would fall in love. Their secret romance unfolded between his family's apartment in Heliopolis and the bars of downtown Cairo. Her family wasn't particularly religious, but they were still conservative. Her parents didn't ask her to wear the hijab, but she wasn't allowed out past nine. There was a long list of things she was forbidden from doing.

"Why must I do this, while I'm forbidden from doing that?"

"Because we worry about you, Reem. Because we love you."

"Spare me your worries, spare me your love!"

College kids were fed up with a lot of things about their country. They forever dreamed of taking off abroad. "I just wanna be left by myself, to find myself." They would talk about politics with such rage, insulting everyone, but unable to make decisions. Any decision. There's nothing more difficult than making decisions in Cairo, since it's Cairo that usually makes decisions for you. How to live your life. Where you can have relationships, and when they can end. When you can eat, how many years of your life will be wasted stuck in traffic. Your chance of getting cancer, the precise timing of your getting hit by a car, the amount of filth in the food you're forced to eat from the street. The total number of dogs in your life that chase you during the nighttime. You are a slave to this city. The only way to win her over is to sell her your soul in a contract written with blood fresh from your veins.

Reem eventually gave up hope that her boyfriend would take the next step. He seemed ill. His illness infected her too, striking her in the heart and leaving a gaping wound in her soul. She talked to her parents about traveling. At the time, all she could find was a teaching job in Qatar. Her mother was terrified at the prospect that her daughter might live so far from home, surrounded by dangers she couldn't possibly imagine. Her father was concerned, but had more faith in his daughter. All Reem wanted was to get away from this city and everything it contained, away from this failed romance that made her cry for hours over the phone, and cut herself with a razor in the bathroom.

But travel only brought her more misery. Instead of saving her from hell, her journey threw her into solitary confinement. Doha was a wasteland. Its grand corniche stretched along miles of uninspiring shoreline. An underclass of imported labor vastly outnumbered the wealthy locals. On only her second day there, she collapsed from sunstroke while wandering through the empty city streets.

She could only stand it for three months. She was told that no one ever walks outside here. In beautiful Doha, we only walk inside our great international malls, where we shop at our international boutiques and eat at our international restaurants. Like the other cities of the Gulf, ours is an international city. Yet we aspire to become an intergalactic city like Dubai.

She came back worse than she'd left. She wasn't even able to taste freedom, or escape her family's love. Devastated by her leaving but unable to end the relationship, her boyfriend finally made up his mind.

At sunset, young men climb to the rooftops. They wave a great big red flag and whistle to bring the pigeons back to their nests. The greatest of Cairo's pastimes involve launching things into the air and waiting for them to come back. Some toss out paper planes tied to a string. Others unleash pigeons, whether as a hobby, or as a business, or as a private fantasy of flying.

Reem married her college sweetheart. Not for love, as she thought at the time, but because both of them had failed to escape. Cairo had determined their course in life. It set down the cornerstone for their home, and cemented it in place with suspicion and paranoia.

They lived together in an apartment he had inherited. It was the same apartment where I'd later accept her invitation to a bottle of whiskey. We would stay up talking and teasing 'til six in the morning, when we finally melted into bed like honey.

Her relationship with her college sweetheart—his name was Tamer, by the way—didn't go so well. Like all young intellectuals in Cairo, they suffered from what they call alienation, simply because their ideas about basic human dignity differed from those of everyone else. What's more, Cairo herself never gave them a single opportunity to forget who they were or what they needed. As a result, their personal problems would erupt into torrents of saltwater. They'd suffer periodic bouts of isolation, from which they would only return at the top of their lungs. And then alcohol, alcohol, and more alcohol. And finally, an assorted mix of chemical cocktails and illicit drugs.

During one such period of desolation, Tamer had an affair with an American girl who lived in Cairo. Most likely she was a student, almost certainly she was in love with Cairo. She was sad enough, and just the right amount of happy. They met five times, first at the party of a mutual friend. They spoke briefly about her research, which surely involved a doctoral dissertation on the comparative mating rituals of the drainpipe roaches of Cairo and the sewer rats of New York, and the influence of both on the rise of political Islam in the Middle East. He engaged her thrice in intercourse. On one of these occasions, he got annoyed with her insistence that he wear a condom, so he threw it away and came right inside her. "That's the best feeling I've had in my life," was what the girl said in English.

The affair ended with Tamer slamming the door in the girl's face after he had spun some made-up argument. He came back to Reem, only to get an email shortly thereafter from the American girl saying she was pregnant and had decided to go back to New York and keep the baby.

He came back and cried. His relationship with Reem fell apart.

He left her and followed the American girl to New York, only to return after six months, a few days after the baby was born.

He and Reem were officially divorced. They remained friends, however, occasionally sharing an early breakfast at one hotel or another overlooking the Nile in Garden City.

Is this the end of Reem's story?

Was I able to get it all down in less than two pages?

It's astonishing how I'm able to recount the whole story in just three minutes, yet when I try to remember the totality of its effect on me, I feel I'd need a lifetime to do it justice. Indeed, I can remember almost everything that happened back then, but can't remember what I did just yesterday. This is what they call old age.

Paprika can not only read your thoughts and predict what you're about to say, but she can also project new memories and sensations directly into your mind, altering your perception of yourself and the world around you. For example, she might fool around with the color receptors in your brain, making you see red instead of green or purple instead of pink.

Paprika has the power to be in more than one place at once. She has a total of seventy-seven companion spirits—the result, they say, of having lived seventy-seven lives. Each companion spirit is unique, with its own language, mind games, and supernatural tricks. The knowledge of each flows in mighty streams, which all deposit into the lake of Paprika's mind. They say the sum of her knowledge is seventy-seven times greater than that of any individual within the Society or without. Rumors of her powers echo across the dome of the sky. It is said that her true and complete story is preserved on a single rock among millions at the Machu Picchu[3] complex, and is protected by a special curse.

Some say she is the chosen one, the mother of all, the first female who decided to seek refuge in the cave. A special cult once surrounded her in ancient Syria; she fits the general description of

---

3. In the language of the Incas, Machu Picchu means "the ancient summit." It's what they call the city of the sky, the lost capital of the Incas. Amazingly, it was one of the only things to survive everything that happened.

the savior in the holy book of the Druze. All the Society's experts in the sciences of the soul confessed that Paprika, unlike all others, was a closed book.

And yet, never did she entertain such rumors herself. She detested the reverence of her followers and devotees, and spurned their pitiful beliefs and superstitions. Believers of any kind were a nuisance to her. Sounding like a cartoon character dubbed in formal Arabic, she would say, "The mind alone do I worship. Out of my way, you pious scum!" In her mind, all she was doing was using logic and reason to find radical solutions to the current state of things.

Reem was sitting at home wearing only a pair of white panties with red and orange flowers. She struggled to breathe under the heat and humidity, and gradually became drenched in salty layers of sweat. The dog paced back and forth between the office and the living room. Her mind tried to figure out when it would be appropriate to light the cigarette she held in her fingers. That's when she heard Paprika's voice cutting through the fog.

"Where do you want me to put the flower, Reem?"

Reem spread open her palm, revealing a white rose.

"And the other flower?"

Reem spread open her other palm, revealing another white rose.

"And the third flower? Where do I put the third flower, Reem?"

.   .   .

MUHAMMAD TAHA

I always loved Gawaboura. Only a few years younger than me, he was full of the patriotism and passion for change so typical of college kids. Not long after graduating, his tone began to change. "Fuck this country and her mother," he would say. "To hell with passion, to hell with change."

His relationship with Egypt became strained. So did mine. The country dumped me and broke my heart, and my relationship status on Facebook changed accordingly. The two of us began to lose passion. Gawaboura stopped going to demonstrations, and I stopped following them in the news.

Still, Gawaboura possessed such an endearing lightness of soul—or was it just his special smell—that I always felt the need to check in on him now and then. One day, we ran into each other at the office, where he'd come to take a position as a graphic designer.

"Where you been, man? What you been up to all this time?"

Sitting down to a computer, he looked like a serene little Buddha.

"Been workin'. And huntin'."

"Huntin' what?"

"Fish . . ."

"Just like ol' Muhammad Taha?"

"Muhammad who?"

"Taha . . . the singer."

"There's a singer named Muhammad Taha?"

"Shit, man, you ain't heard of Muhammad Taha?"

By the waters of the Nile we sat and fished. The voice of Muhammad Taha serenaded us from my phone. While working on our latest film—*The Disappearing Nile*—I decided to involve Gawaboura in shooting some scenes with amateur fishermen. Some of them were set up along the bridge, while others sat by their lonesome selves along the shore. They knew each other by name, and felt a certain intimacy even when hanging around together in silence. One was an old taxi driver who told me how he met his best friend, Hagg Muhammad, on his first outing here some twenty odd years ago. They would only ever meet when they fished.

"He was more than a brother to me. When my wife was about to give birth to our first daughter, I ran out here to the shore one night, with no more than one hundred Egyptian pounds in my pocket. I was frantic, not knowing how I'd be able to feed the girl or buy her clothes and whatnot. Hagg Muhammad patted me on the back and said, 'Cast out your line, my dear boy, and you'll do just fine.' So I cast out my line, and he came over and put one hundred bucks in my pocket!"

When we finished filming the next morning, this very same taxi driver offered me a lift downtown. He ended up charging me thirty bucks.

Amidst all the traffic, the road rage, the scorching heat and lingering clouds of smut, driving in Cairo for a living was a profession for the brave. "This isn't just a job," he told me. "We're out here fighting on the front lines."

Another taxi driver told me, "What I do each and every day on the streets of Cairo is more than anything I did in the '73 War."

Gawaboura laughed and said, "Really, man? What division did you fight in?"

Without taking his eye off the road, the older driver responded, "Civil defense."

We both fell silent. I looked over at the driver, noticing his awkwardly matched clothes and bitten fingernails. From the back seat, Gawaboura started talking to me like he'd forgotten our veteran of the road was still there.

"What I wanna know is what they're gonna do with that fish."

"That ain't no fish, dude."

"What is it, then?"

"I don't know. But I can try to find out."

Gawaboura had just appeared on the front pages of a number of tabloids and scandal magazines. He'd felt something heavy at the end of his line, and reeled it in to discover a creature with pink skin, roughly the size of a three-day-old child. Its feet and gangly arms ended in what looked like hooves. The fishhook was caught in its behind, which dripped blood as the creature squiggled and squirmed. Gawaboura was stricken with panic, thinking he'd just pulled out a newborn child that someone had cast away in the river. Yet unlike any human child, this creature had no face. Instead of a neck, it had a small protrusion at one end topped with two small antennas.

Gawaboura decided to take a picture of this godforsaken creature, which he still insisted was a fish, and called the police. (Why the police, for god's sake?) The police, in turn, called the para-medics. (Why, for god's sake, the paramedics??) And the whole thing exploded into an urban legend about an adulterous woman who'd given birth to a deformed child and tossed it away in the river.

Our veteran of the road dropped us off at Talaat Harb Square. Gawaboura went on his way to the Townhouse Gallery, and I headed over to Ihab's place on Adly Street.

I could never stand small children. Can't stand them now, won't stand them ever.

"These aren't just any children," Ihab said, looking over the pictures. "They're imported from abroad."

He zoomed in on Gawaboura's fish pictures. But this was no fish. It was one of a batch of children that had been imported from Japan.

At that point, there were three things we knew for certain:

- Paprika would never give up her plan to finish Cairo.
- Paprika had already begun to implement her plan.
- Paprika was in possession of tools and techniques the likes of which we couldn't begin to imagine.

In light of all this, Ihab was of the opinion that we should maintain a series of safety buttons, ranging in color from yellow to orange to red. Our "red button," pathetically enough, was to launch our website with a single click, thus publishing our trove of documents and statistics, which might very well bring about the end of the Society and lead to the exposure of all its secrets.

"She probably won't care about any of this," Ihab was saying. "In all likelihood, she's attached to the romantic notion that the Organization is protected by the very laws of the universe."

Ihab didn't know that the universe already was Paprika, and Paprika the universe, in all of its laws.

.   .   .

MEETING THE DOCTOR

Ihab first realized there was something missing in his life when he found himself standing for the second time in front of Arata Isozaki's Tsukuba City Center in Japan. As he silently contemplated the complex of buildings, a poisonous blue substance coagulated around his eyes before seeping into his ocular veins and settling into a small corner of his heart.

Another time, he was flipping through a book of photographs about modern architecture in Europe, when he came across Frank Gehry's Guggenheim Museum in Bilbao, Spain. An even greater quantity of this poisonous blue substance shot through his eyes and deposited itself in the tissues of his brain. In that moment, he sensed that something was not quite right. He had noticed a flaw in design, an ungoverned error. This was disturbing, since even errors—intentional or not—were always governed by certain rules and constraints.

He could only explain this with reference to the particular tendency of postmodernist architecture to avoid the abstractness of the Bauhaus School, preserving just enough detail to toy with our notions of history and aesthetics, and consistently blurring any line between the two. The effect was to make bad art appear to be no more than a matter of perspective.

Of course it's a matter of perspective. But what about the functional element of architecture and design? Where did he stand on all of this?

It's true that this museum's primary function was social and psychological. Its function was to make the residents of the city feel important, and to mediate their sense of collective identity. It's also true that museums, in the end, are a reflection of how particular artists view themselves and their relationship with the world around them. But what happens when these artists are "true" artists?

We've all heard that phrase. You might wear it like an advertisement, a fracture in your skull, an identity and an image all at once. You wear it in the street, at the bar, when you're cutting a deal or speaking at a conference. "I am a true artist," you say.

With his signature, the true artist will judge what counts as true art. Even if he's the kind of revolutionary artist that refuses to sell out to corporations, and violently attacks the powers that be. He'll still think that what he produces is genuine, pure, and deserving of attention. He'll call it art. *His* art, true to the touch.

And so, Ihab was struck with a dilemma. Might not the "truth" of art conflict with its duty? That is to say, the duty art has to be functional?

To be sure, Ihab's question reflects a certain critical self-confidence, and a laughably blind faith in the existence of absolute determiners of right and wrong. Moreover, his question betrays a belief in the "duty" of art and the obligation of the individual to his surroundings. All these notions are susceptible to doubt, even by Ihab himself.

But he was now advanced in age. He had become dispirited. His ties to the Organization made it difficult for him to express his true opinions about such matters. Indeed, his public face as a professor of comparative literature and cultural criticism was just the tip of a tremendous iceberg.

His questions about the functional duty of art, architecture in particular, led him back to the ideas of his grandfather, and then to the Bauhaus archive.

The glorious bastards had designed entire worlds. There were detailed drawings that had taken years to complete, depicting a world roughly the size of Earth, but rectangular instead of round. Humans would live inside it, rather than on the surface. Another group of glorious bastards made detailed conceptual drawings of the nerve networks inside the brain, modeled on the mind of a woman called Hazel Jelinek.

Ihab dug deeper. He traveled to New Zealand and Japan. He vacationed in Prague. His meetings with many of the older members led him to more questions, which led him in turn to investigate the Organization's true functionalist purpose. Along the way, his questions aroused the murmurings and suspicions of members around the world.

In the city of Arica, in Chile, there was a young man who specialized in the aeronautical mechanics of insects and microscopic creatures. He was having sex with a forty-something woman, a member of the Society's Administrative Council. The details here are important. This woman was a housewife with two children. She met her young lover through the Organization, when he asked her to help him find a way to travel to Uganda to complete one of his research projects. He went to Uganda, where he received word of Ihab Hassan's work. He returned to beautiful Arica and reconnected with the woman, who invited herself over to his house. The young man fucked her like a runaway train. He licked every inch of her body, then attempted to penetrate her from behind. This she found painful, so he went slower. Her face writhed with pleasure, encouraging him to take his time. He could see clearly now. He turned her head toward his and planted a kiss on her lips—the kind of pure, sensuous kiss that comes from being seized by the light of a fundamental truth.

He whispered in her ear, "Moving forward. Maybe that's all there is: moving forward without end."

The young man's words reached Ihab in a text message as he was strolling down Fifth Avenue in New York. He raised his head to the sky above.

Ihab's life would never be the same. Perhaps this was like one of those Chinese stories where the key to your salvation lies only a few feet in front of you, but you don't see it because you're looking behind.[4]

---

4. I sometimes like to imagine the moment of "enlightenment" that brought Ihab together with the young man from Chile. It must have been something similar to one of the many epiphanies experienced by the great founder of Saint-Simonianism, the spiritual father of all those demons and sons of the nineteenth century, the innovator of the Church of Industry. The dawning of Paprika, on the other hand, would be more akin to the rays of enlightenment that seized the movement's later disciples. I recall in particular the meeting that took place

On the dilapidated facade of an old building in Rod El Farag, there's a sign that reads: "Doctor Ahmad Mahmoud Hamed, MD in Internal Medicine." The sign is sun-bleached and covered in dust, its paint cracked in several places. The building's entrance is plastered over with flyers. "The International Weight-Loss and Fitness Center." "We treat baldness, sexual impotency, and all men's illnesses." "Treatment for hepatitis B and C. Diabetes cured for good, God willing." Each has a phone number written at the bottom.

You see these sorts of flyers spreading everywhere around Cairo. What's strange is that nobody can tell you when it all started. On public buses, for example, you'll find a flyer advertising phallic extension, breast enlargement, and breast reduction, all without the need for surgery. On lampposts and telephone poles you'll find flyers advertising treatments for hepatitis and diabetes. The addresses listed are usually vague, with only a telephone number to go by.

With a small camera in one hand and Ihab in the other, Bassam started up the building's stairs. They stopped in front of a wooden door. Smiling, Ihab rang the bell. Bassam, as usual, was equal parts confused and excited.

A bald, thirtysomething man opened the door. Uncut toenails stuck out from his leather sandals, his clothes were a simple arrangement of earth tones, his face was half shaved. A perfect specimen of the "wild rhinoceros," one of Cairo's most famous fauna.

"Peace be upon you."

"The center opens at eight o'clock."

"We have an appointment with the Doctor."

---

in 1846 in a modest apartment on the Rue de la Victoire in the 9th arrondissement of Paris. The disciples had gathered to launch the Société d'Études du Canal de Suez with a fund of 150,000 francs. The minutes of the session are available in the public domain; there's no need to go digging for them in the archive. The closing words of the "Enlightened One" still resonate: "Dear gentleman, the Suez Canal is no longer a philosophical theory or political issue. It is a commercial deal." The train had left the station, though the tracks had yet to be laid.

"You're Mr. Ihab."

"Yes."

"Please, come in."

In marked contrast to its exterior, the apartment was nicely kept and smelled of a mix of fresh perfumes, disinfectants, and incense. Everything was painted in shades of white or blue, even the chairs and bookcases, which were wrapped in plastic coverings to protect them from any pollutants the patients might have in their clothes. Some of those who came here had physical illnesses. Others suffered from obsessive-compulsive disorder. A number of the women and girls had come in search of a measure of self-confidence, or for a short thrill followed by an extended period of relaxation.

The wild rhinoceros disappeared behind one of the many doors that surrounded the waiting room. He came back out to open a different door, and gestured for us to enter.

"The Doctor is waiting for you."

To Ihab, the Doctor represented a potential ally. Maybe he could help him in his fight against Paprika, and maybe he couldn't. Ihab wasn't counting on him too much. But at the very least, he might serve as a sort of buffer or restraining device while he prepared his secret weapon: publishing the documents and bringing down the temple.

The Doctor's older than anyone Bassam's ever seen, but he's all in one piece. Nicely parted hair, like the actor Mahmoud Yassine, and no glasses. A large wooden pipe, engraved with strange markings, hangs from his mouth. Its smoke fills the room. In addition to the Doctor's desk, there's a bed and a glass cabinet full of medicine. An antique scale, alone in the corner, probably doesn't really work. Everything's a mix between the sublime and the decadent, between the noble and the debased.

The name on the sign outside the building isn't the Doctor's real name. It's one of many he hides behind. You see, his real age is approximately 174 years. In order to live that long, you have to change your address every now and then, and get used to carrying a fake ID. It's necessary, too, that you avoid the outside light as much as possible, and shield yourself with protective layers of insignificance. With more than one life, you'll be able to complete your true mission.

The Doctor does not concern himself with the Organization's internal power struggles. For decades, he's been occupied with his own research: hypnotherapy and its physical effects on both the therapist and the patient. The results have been rewarding. Some years ago, he found a way to treat certain forms of cancer in their incipient stage. By intervening in the pathways that connect mind and body, he was able to influence the arrangement of particular cells and tissues. Besides his scientific research, the Doctor is known in the Organization as the "Guardian of the City." Specifically, he is the guardian appointed to Cairo. It's the same position that Paprika would later offer to me, but for 6th of October City.

A pack of dogs barked in the distance. It was almost four o'clock, and the kids in the street would still be playing until the sun went down. The curtains let in only a faint glow of light. The Doctor stood up to greet us, without extending his hand.

"Please." He gestured for us to take a seat.

Ihab tossed the day's paper down on the Doctor's desk. The front page was covered in images of the fish-child. With the calm detachment of a man stirring his tea, Ihab said, "Have you seen this?"

The Doctor looked down at the pictures and said coldly, "Some new kind of fetal deformation?"

Like sugar dissolving in tea, Ihab replied, "What you see here is a *kappa*."[5]

---

5. The *kappa* is a creature known to the world of cryptozoology. In the Shinto religion of Japan, it's considered a water deity. It is mostly represented in Japanese art as a childlike creature with the face of a monkey or frog. Unfortunately, most accounts of the *kappa* do not clearly distinguish between the fanciful imaginations of the Japanese artists and the actual processes of genetic engineering that may very well give rise to such creatures. The truth of their provenance is among those many secrets held exclusively by Paprika.

The Doctor raised the paper to his eyes, took a long drag of his pipe, and said, "This here is no *kappa*."

Ihab sat down and said, "It's a genetically modified *kappa*. I have evidence that Paprika is responsible for it being here."

"However modified it might be, I doubt it would be able to survive in the Nile's water."

"Perhaps it was attempting to acquire further modifications."

The two men fell silent. They exchanged glances like sugar dissolving in tea.

. . .

THE GRAVEYARD OF MUSIC

No one would call what's happening now "chaos." They would use other terms and expressions with generally positive connotations.

The languages you hear in the streets—a mix of New English, Chinese, and French with traces of Arabic—testify to the energy and ambitiousness of the moment. People are finally proud of their diversity.

During my meeting with Paprika in the restaurant, she explained that one of the many positive outcomes of what happened was that humankind had now reached a point where it was ready to move beyond the narrow nationalisms imposed by modern states and their militaries. This could be achieved thanks to the new economy. Large corporations should be given freer rein to operate. The most powerful corporations will inevitably be in construction and real estate, thus it is necessary that the Society become one too. Perhaps it should become the only one, and competition could take place as a nice little game between its various subsidiaries.

"Look at them all, Bassam. For the first time, everyone loves each other. We've gotten rid of the past and created a future that, while not totally perfect, promises some real light at the end of the tunnel."

During the Storm, we lost thousands of artists here in Egypt. Humankind lost many times more in cities around the world that experienced similar devastation. So many were lost that I could no longer remember who was alive and who was dead. I stopped caring, until one day I heard two guys on the bus saying how Samira Said had died in the Storm. Death is inevitable, but at least there's light at the end of the tunnel.

Now, twenty years later, the memory of Samira Said is preserved at the Laboratory for Archiving and Documentation. Her data and works are displayed next to those of Umm Kulthum.

The younger generations often confuse the two artists. For these forward-looking children of the future, both women belong to the time before the Storm. The world was a whole different place.

Which brings us back to the exhibition called *Love Letter for Frogs*. Nine artists were involved, the oldest of whom was only five when the Storm struck. One of them had created a pastiche centered on a laughing Samira Said, her teeth sparkling in the flash of the camera. Above her, the phrase "It's too late" was rendered in Arabic calligraphy, alongside a green sun and a clock stopped at a quarter past nine. The image's frame was a string of colored light bulbs.

I stood back and watched as the exhibit's mostly young attendees passed by the picture. They would pause for a few seconds—sometimes even a few minutes—and pretend to be absorbed in contemplation. Or perhaps they really were absorbed in contemplation. I spoke with some of the attendees and shook hands with the work's artist. Not one of them seemed to notice the discrepancy between Samira Said and the words strung above her, which properly belonged to Umm Kulthum. This is assuming that they were able to read the Arabic script in the first place. Many in this new generation had never learned the Arabic alphabet, knowing only the Latin characters, which generations before had started to be used to write Arabic in online forums and social media.

After the Storm, new theories in psychology were devised that happened to dovetail with the policies of construction and real estate companies. They would be applied to the re-engineering of the individual, the re-engineering of the family, and eventually the re-engineering of society as a whole. Among the new clinical-scientific fads that swept the world was the idea of "exterminating nostalgia." This went beyond the treatment of the shock and agony suffered by many as a result of the loss of friends and loved ones. Even after such emotional disturbances had been corrected, it was still difficult to control the unexpected relapses that might occur when a patient happened to hear an old tune, or catch a clip of an old movie.

Numerous new studies warned of the dangers of listening to old music—that is, music from the pre-Storm era. This could result in unsafe levels of nostalgia, driving patients to tears or draining them of the energy that was so desperately needed for construction and development.

Look ahead, to the future.

"If pain prevents you from moving on, just tuck and tumble." "If there's a lump in your throat, swallow it down and keep on chewing." These were the slogans peddled by the latest schools of psychology, as well as by the new corporations for self-improvement and individual rehabilitation. I'd smile when hearing such propaganda, as I knew that "moving on" is an illusion and forgetting a matter of perspective. It tickled me more to see how they attempted to repaint the past, exaggerating the beauty and perfection of a Cairo that never existed. It was a circular process: implanting beautified memories, propagating them, and then asking that they be forgotten.

Such was the Society's new modus operandi under Paprika. Life was a circular process, pointless and without end.

. . .

MIND CONTROL AND MASTURBATION

Then one of the masked assassins stuck a short reed between his lips. Standing only three meters away, I could hear the air rush out of his lungs as he fired at me. For a split second I thought of trying to dodge the dart, but decided it was hopeless. It struck me in the shoulder, and I collapsed like Jell-O. Before my lights went out, I saw blood pouring out of Moud's chest, a dagger lodged right in his heart. The cold corpse of a masked ninja lay next to him. Moud had managed to crush his skull just before succumbing to the fatal blow. I didn't know if I was dying, or if this was just one of Paprika's sick jokes.

I woke up in my modest little apartment in 6th of October City. Everything seemed to be normal, except that the floor and furniture were all covered in a thick layer of dust. As I stretched out my legs I realized I was on the living room sofa, drowning in a pool of my own sweat.

It was all over now. I wasn't sure, but I could feel it. I opened my fridge, but found I was out of bottled water. I went over to the tap, but it was dry. I went back and stuck my head in the freezer, licking the ice off its walls.

I sometimes get asked, "You lived through the *naksa*, you were there for the dust storm and the quakes . . . Tell us, Bassam, how did you survive?"

In such instances I smile and pretend to be moved. I chew the sorrow I'm supposed to feel like a piece of gum, spit it out, and say, "I had an apartment in October. Never left the house."

My questioner nods his head in understanding. He won't want to ask anything further. Everyone's lost someone he loved in the Storm, everyone needs consolation. No one wants to open another man's wound.

For the first few years following the *nakba*, I felt that Paprika was right. I felt like a complete fool for putting so much faith in Ihab Hassan.

Paprika was right, I said to myself, as the supermarket attendant smiled and handed me my order. The city had been a terrible burden on its residents.

After the *nakba*, I felt incapacitated. I wandered aimlessly through the streets of October, and couldn't sleep at night. I was in a state of shock. My mother died a year and a half later. I abandoned my friends one after the other, despite their pleas that I should try to engage. I stuck to my apartment, to life in the ruins of the *nakba*.

I watched people change. I watched them undergo shock, only to regain consciousness amidst a world drowning in tears and nightmares. As the economy collapsed and famine began to spread, I watched the mounting of international humanitarian aid campaigns of historic proportions. Then I watched as the people of Egypt rose from the ashes—all this in the course of only five years. A new Egypt appeared. This wasn't the "Egypt" people had known before. It carried the same name and represented roughly the same geographic area, but was no longer bound by hand-drawn borders. The entire world had begun to change. What had happened in Cairo repeated itself along roughly the same lines in New York, Copenhagen, Fukushima, and a number of other major cities I'm not sure I can remember at the moment. Earthquakes, tsunamis, and strange, unexplained sandstorms.

To a large portion of the human race, it seemed that the Day of Resurrection had arrived. Others insisted that there was still light at the end of the tunnel.

The Society expanded its reach. It reinvented itself as a global alliance of nine corporations, which soon grew to include twelve, then twenty-one, then ninety-nine of the world's largest companies. Together, they ruled the world. Together, they were mere puppets in the hands of Paprika. The exposure that Ihab thought would spell the end of the Society had, in fact, only made it stronger.

The Society—let us now call it the Corporation—controls sixty percent of the world's agriculture. It manufactures everything from automobiles to medicine, has invented a second version of the Internet, and has expanded into the arms trade with record sales to some of the world's leading security firms (these were, in fact, merely subsidiaries of the larger "mother" corporation). It is involved in the recycling of seventy-five percent of the world's waste, and provides security for nuclear reactors. It has developed new communications technologies, including chips that can be implanted in your head and allow you to call and connect with others. For those who, like me, are troubled by such human-machine hybrids, the Corporation also manufactures smart devices in the shape of traditional telephones, wristwatches, and shirt buttons. And that's not all. The Corporation also runs the world's major media conglomerates. It owns hundreds of name brands in children's wear, in addition to special lines of clothing that include men's boxers, nightgowns, sparkling women's undergarments, and jeans for both men and women and everyone in between. It offers a diverse array of pornographic materials.

The whole world was changing. Finally, in the course of only about ten years, the era of nation-states was coming to an end. The involvement of national governments in politics and the economy became no more than a formality, reminiscent of the role played by the monarchs and figureheads of ages past.

The nightmarish cities that had been founded by the old nation-states were destroyed in the dust storms, earthquakes, floods, and hurricanes. Some were swallowed up by the sea. The cities that survived were reformatted and recolored by the Corporation. Borders were melting away, geography was getting a facelift.

All of this was taking place outside, while I sat inside my apartment. In the morning, I'd work on making documentary films about this new "settling of the earth" and the spread of civilization. At night, I'd curl up in a ball next to the window, or masturbate in bed while staring at the ceiling.

I wasn't oblivious to everything. I just wasn't on the winning team. Not much mattered to me here anymore—even Mona May had left the country. We'd decided to maintain a minimum of contact. She was able to live her life for a while, taking painkillers and training herself to forget. But she eventually got bored with life in the cold north. She returned to Cairo—or what remained of it in the area of 6th of October City—and withdrew like me into spiritual masturbation. In the meantime, I had managed to train myself to feel just enough sorrow to keep on living.

"Cairo shouldn't have to be like this. Life shouldn't have to be like this. Reality can be different. We can change things. We can intervene to stop all this bullshit." Thus spoke Paprika in an address to the Supreme Council of the Organization, whose members had assembled in Ihab's apartment on Adly Street.

"We let them get carried away with their own foolish ideas," she continued, after a digression on theories of mind control and masturbation. "We let them keep putting up more walls and barriers everywhere. They continue to suffer. In their midst, we suffer too. Why don't we do something instead of just sitting around philosophizing for our entire lives?"

"Sitting around and philosophizing is what we're supposed to do," Ihab interrupted. "We ask, we question, we push for ever greater understanding. That's the meaning of our existence as the Society. That's the meaning of life on Earth. We can't just say we know everything for certain and go on making judgments about right and wrong."

"But how can we know the value of our greater understanding," Paprika continued, unperturbed, "if we don't put it to the test? How can we trust our wisdom if we don't engage with reality? What I'm calling for is, in spite of its cruelty, an essential part of our quest for knowledge and understanding. And I'm quite confident that everyone in this room has many ideas for research that can only be pursued if the current reality is radically altered."

Reem was watching all of this. She was watching, and listening.

When she got naked for the first time with Paprika, and the bitch stuck her tongue in her pussy, she cried.

Out in the world, Reem was under siege by masked assassins carrying poison blow darts. They lingered in the shadows of her guilty conscience, and sought revenge for her rebellion against the dictates of family and religion. Their presence could be felt in the hypocrisies of society, in the infidelities of loved ones, in her rumbling storms of depression and anxiety. But in here, with Paprika, she was having her pussy licked.

Paprika suddenly raised her head and stood up to embrace the tearful Reem. She whispered in her ear, "All the pain you feel is an illusion. An evil illusion. Toss back your head and shake it all off, my little one."

But Reem had reached that point of despair where illusion was the only hope. Her entire life had been a series of impulsive love affairs and long flirtations with belief, interrupted by brief but potent revolutions of doubt and disappointment.

The first of these affairs was with God and religion. Wrapped in a veil, she would accompany her father to the Mosque of Sayyida Nafisa (may God honor her memory). Then came doubt. In college, she protested against the absence of social justice, and would cry on the shoulder of her boyfriend and future husband. Then again came doubt, this time in ideology. She would place her trust in love. Then love would wither like an unwatered plant, and so she would put her faith, at long last, in herself. It was during this phase that I began to love her, but she decided to leave in the middle of the night and sleep on the couch.

Paprika's voice again: "Throw your head back and shake it all off, my little one. All these wicked thoughts are like insects. We can exterminate them."

At home with her dog, Reem realized how lonely and weak she was without faith, without an illusion.

Paprika knew from the very first moment that Reem's disease had no cure, save for another illusion. She needed faith to ground her. If this was the case, then the illusion should at least be beneficial to other people as well. Let Reem be a new messiah, let her sacrifice herself, that the son of man may live a new life.

Paprika gave Reem this new illusion, only to suck it dry for her own purposes. She needed one more life, in addition to the seventy-seven she already had, in order to summon the spirits and unseen forces necessary for the completion of her project. She needed a body, and a soul, to sacrifice.

This is how she would destroy Cairo.

Reem became a part of Paprika, and Paprika became all of Reem. All through the power of suggestion, mind control, and masturbation.

. . .

ONE OF THESE DAYS I SHAN'T AWAKE

Every city has a guardian. His job is not to protect anyone, but to hold the keys to the city's secrets.

Every city has its secrets, some more than others. Every city has seven keys. Some say it's no more than an urban legend, while others believe it's true. As long as the guardians keep tight-lipped about their business, there's really no way to be certain.[6]

The Doctor was the Guardian of Cairo. When I asked him if he had any secrets to share, he looked out over the Nile, cast a yellow grin, and said, "What do you expect me to say, you fool?"

"Maybe you know how to get through all this traffic, for example."

He turned around to contemplate the cars passing over the bridge below. From where we were, it was easy to guess that there would be an endless line of cars stretching as far as the eye could see. In Cairo, stalled traffic and long waits were part of the normal pace of things.

---

6. This system doesn't apply to some of the older cities. Its origins can be traced to the nineteenth century and the spread of the Industrial Revolution— or what I prefer to call "The Brotherhood's First Dawn." Back then, those elements that refused to assimilate installed sentinels to keep one eye on the new world's sundry transgressions and another eye on the hidden corridors of the past. The success of this policy can be credited in large part to the Algerian prince Abd al-Qadir, who introduced an advanced mechanized system of guardianship whose members were all descended from the race of al-Khidr (peace be upon him).

"Unfortunately, I don't know how to fly."[7]

The Doctor requested to see all the films that I'd made for the Society,[8] and asked about the particular areas of the city in which Paprika had shown interest. One of these could be seen right outside the window: the bridge along the Ring Road that connects to al-Warraq.

"We haven't won this place over yet," Ihab said. "But neither do we want to lose it."[9]

---

7. With the defeat of his forces at the Battle of the Smala, Abd al-Qadir was urged by his disciples to convince his French brethren to stop their barbaric war. A document preserved in the archive records the plea of one of his disciples to use more advanced weaponry, as well as the prince's response: "Unfortunately, I don't know how to fly."

8. In 1842, the French army began its assault on the stronghold of Prince Abd al-Qadir. In Paris, members of the Brotherhood supported the campaign under the ostensible pretext of spreading modernity and combating barbarism. Their real aim, however, was to get Abd al-Qadir to join them, hoping he would give them access to his secret trove of ancient knowledge. If their efforts failed, they hoped at least to force him to surrender and give up his secrets under duress. The prince told them to stuff it. When the French stormed the capital at Tagdemt, they found it deserted. Abd al-Qadir had ordered all its weaponry, arms factories, goldsmiths, tanners, and paper mills removed. He then founded the Smala (or *zamala*; literally "fellowship"), the world's first full-spectrum city of magic. The Smala, whose residents numbered some 70,000, could move around and disappear in the middle of the desert. At its center was "the Circle," which contained the prince's tents, his family, advisers, horses, and personal security detail, which consisted of thirty black slaves. At the periphery of the Circle stood his cavalry, whose distinctive costume consisted of a red jacket, blue pants, and two cloaks, one white and one gray. The Circle was surrounded by concentric rings, each containing up to thirty tents. The Circle also contained the prince's library, as well as an eight-sided mosque designed by the prince himself in imitation of the Dome of the Rock in Jerusalem. The Smala would settle down a reasonable distance from a particular town or city, and stay for as long as a week. When the prince got word of an advance by the French, the Smala would pick up its tents and disappear into the sands, before settling down elsewhere by dawn.

9. As a result of the tragedy endured by Abd al-Qadir and his Smala, the city guardians developed a capricious and unstable nature. They would move about according to an inscrutable monastic ethos, which made their movements seem rash and unpredictable.

From here the Nile flows out of Cairo. From what I could tell him about Paprika and Reem, the Doctor was trying to understand what the two were thinking. They talked about the need to change reality, the need to put an end to this tragedy. But what was the plan, exactly? What were they going to do?

He didn't have to wait long to find out.

The dust storms began brewing the next day, and the chaos commenced. Ihab had been scheduled to depart for London, but the airport was closed due to the weather.

Soon, the bridge along the Ring Road collapsed—the very same bridge we had just been contemplating in an attempt to discern what was cooking in Paprika's mind.

I stayed inside for two whole days in order to avoid the sands. I called Reem to determine when we should resume filming, but she didn't pick up.

Then one day, at four in the morning, I got a short text from her that read, "One of these days I shan't awake."

I tried calling again, but her phone was out of service.

A story the Doctor told me made a lasting impression.

"Ever heard of Christopher Wren, my boy? He was a famous British architect, and a major figure in the Society. Behind the scenes, he helped pave the way for postmodernism. On the outside, he founded a school or institution of some sort to encourage nonmembers to pursue their quest for knowledge. But that's not why I bring him up . . . By the way, what were we talking about?"

"You were talking about someone named Christopher Wren," I suggested.

"Right. So, back in the seventeenth century or thereabouts, a tremendous fire broke out that destroyed half of London. Wren was one of the principal players—there were rumors, in fact, that he had started the fire. Afterward, he drew up new plans for the city that included broad avenues and parks that resembled those in other major European cities of the time. Wren was successful in implementing some of these, but his most important ideas did not come to fruition. For example, he had insisted on the use of limestone and cement in the construction of new buildings in order to prevent future fires; this was rejected by the city's residents. He also had designs to redraw the city's demographic map by eliminating the more traditional and impoverished neighborhoods; here, too, he was unsuccessful. Had his most basic ideas seen the light of day, London would have been transformed into a true city of the future.

"Drawing on his connections with a number of sister organizations—most importantly the Freemasons, who were then at the height of their power—Wren was able to convince the British government to adopt his plan. But the government wasn't everything. Having entered into negotiations with a number of players, Wren was forced to make compromises and lower his expectations. The city's major landowners decided, in the end, to rebuild their property as it had been, according to the general shape originally devised by the Romans in the first century. So Wren wasn't able to make the city's streets as logical and organized as they were in other European cities. He was, however, able to implement some of his ideas as they related to the city's churches and cathedrals. You following me?"

"You bet." I smiled, without knowing why. I could see the end approaching like a black hole swallowing everything up, starting with me.

Sometimes, to see the light at the end of the tunnel, you have to blast open a wall with dynamite.

We walked out to the Doctor's Korean-made car, which was driven by his personal assistant, the wild rhinoceros. The Doctor continued: "Ihab's philosophy is rather idealistic. He holds a great reverence for the past. He'd like to be able to walk forward as far as possible, and still be able to look back at his very first steps."

He took the front seat, and I the back.

"No, my boy, I can't fly. But I have confidence that, some day, we will be able to." He reached over to turn on the radio, his voice fading amidst a crackle of frequencies.

CHAPTER EIGHT

. . .

The lines flow between my fingers like water. When I open my hands, there's nothing there.

Memory is a garden of wild herbs.

The weather today is clear.

I leave my hat and put on my guard. I go outside. I stand in front of the car and play around with my keys. I decide to put them back in my pocket and go for a walk in the park. After only a few steps, I think this walk will just make me moody, and that I should probably call someone to hang out. But my throat is sore, and I have no real desire to spend any time with Mona May.

I look at the people passing me by in the street, and feel my alienation. Who are these people?

Who the hell do you think you are!

I take a seat on the steps and consider the view. No clouds in the sky, and the park is green, well kept, and unbound by any walls or fences. There's nothing to spoil the scene but all these staircases to nowhere. The park is full of them: a scattered bunch of stone steps that go up and down in the shape of a pyramid, the highest reaching a height of some sixty meters. I don't know much about this park, having only discovered it by chance during one of my long walks.

The city's parks and squares have started to witness the emergence of a number of artworks resembling ancient antiquities. I once saw a government building whose entrance was designed to resemble the Mosque of Sultan Hassan. The pyramids, for their part, are virtually everywhere. But I am still amused by these staircases that just go up and down, going nowhere. Going up is the same as going down. Apart from this, what distinguishes this particular park is its moderate size and fine, mathematically calculated design.

The city has been seized by an overwhelming obsession with green spaces, green walls, and green dams to prevent desertification and keep out the dangers of the great yellow expanse.

The moisture and makeup of the soil are monitored by the tentacles of a great computer, which sets the appropriate times for watering the plants, and dispatches little robots to pick up people's trash and leftover food when the parks are less crowded.

I give myself a light. As the first jolt of nicotine rushes through my spine, I hear her voice.

"Spare a cigarette?"

He gave her a light. She drew out a puff and retreated behind her lashes.

"Thanks," she said in English.

"You bet," he replied.

She glanced over at the statue of *The Seated Scribe*, which sat inside one of the pyramidal staircases in the middle of the park. She shifted her weight from one foot to the other and said, "Did you happen to attend the opening of *Love Letter for Frogs*?"

He smiled like a shy tortoise. "Yes."

The two of them fell silent. She had really needed a cigarette, but didn't want to leave the park. She'd spotted the old man sitting all lonesome on the staircase, and decided she'd try with him. He tried not to look her in the eyes, lacking the energy for this sort of contact. He cast his gaze down and saw she was wearing a pair of flip-flops, with a silver ring on one of her toes. *Some things never go out of fashion*, he thought.

He felt it was his turn to speak, and pretended to look up again. He only got as far as her knees.

"You'll have to forgive me. There are a lot of new artists out there now whose work I don't really know. Are you an artist?"

She smiled. Above her knees she wore a green summer dress, and further up she had slightly disheveled hair, as though she'd slept over somewhere uncomfortable.

"I'm trying to be, anyway. But I didn't have anything at the exhibit. What about you?"

"I'm not an artist."

"Ah. Then you're a lover of art," she said in English.

"I used to be a lover of art. But now it's part of my work."

"Really. What do you do, then?"

"I'm an artistic coordinator," he said in English, making her smile.

"Aha. Marvelous! So you work in some sort of foundation?"

"I work for a number of foundations, give lectures here and there. On occasion I find an excuse to be a dealer or a middleman."

"Aha."

This time, the silence was all hers. This old man, she thought, was just another one of those parasites that plague the city's artistic scene, selling ideas and turning works of art into commodities. The girl had a rebellious edge and a lot of personal rage. Life hadn't asked much of her, so she still had a clear sense of right and wrong. No need to negotiate or change her opinion: he's an art dealer, therefore he's a parasite.

For his part, he stopped caring long ago what people might think about him. The job's a good source of income and security. It keeps him comfortable.

She drew in another long puff before tossing her cigarette. Then she beat it down with her worn-out flip-flops.

"All right. Thanks for the smoke." And off she went.

I once read that "old age is when you remember things from years ago, but can't remember what you ate yesterday."[1]

I'm now in my midforties and find myself submersed in the past. I'm living part of what I dreamed of as a child, but I'm unable to blend in. Propulsion doesn't move me forward but some-

---

1. By now I hope you've all grown accustomed to my sudden bouts of inanity.

how holds me to the ground as people rush past me. I might guess that they don't feel as I do, not because they don't know what I do, but because they've forgotten how things used to be.

On a personal level, I can't identify with all these images being produced that supposedly represent the past. There's a false filter of veneration that gets added to everything, but I don't feel I have the chance to object. I usually just smile and nod, amused more by my ability to put on a good face than by anything else. Somehow, I'm able to fake polite conversation. That's something we never had, in the Cairo of the past.

CHAPTER NINE

· · ·

On TV there's a girl in a sparkling tie-dyed spacesuit. Moud and Ihab are arguing about something. Even though I wasn't really paying attention, I made sure to butt in with a sarcastic jab or an obnoxious retort, usually aimed at Moud.

For the first time, I noticed Ihab had an old scar on his neck. Meanwhile, the girl on TV was inviting viewers to call for a chance to win tens of thousands of dollars if they could correctly answer the question: What do we call the thing we put in our room and sleep on top of?

Moud went on talking about his favorite subject: politics, politics, and then some more politics. But I could tell he was just skirting around the real question he wanted to ask his new friend. It wasn't long before he turned to the topic of informal political alliances in the United States. Showing off his great knowledge of the subject, Moud expounded on the fraternal ties that bind together the sons of the middle and upper classes, from their college days to their graduation into business empires and political parties. The picture he drew of American society made it seem like a bunch of sorcerers, priests, and military men jockeying for control of the great tribe. Ihab nodded in agreement with most of what Moud was saying, which suggested he might know something about the subject.

"So, any of them got anything to do with this Society of yours?" Moud finally asked.

"Maybe, but I can't say for certain. When secrecy is the only language you speak, it's hard to know the truth."

At this point in the conversation, I suddenly recalled one of my visits to the Mosque of al-Hakim bi-Amrillah. I had noticed a sign in a corner of the great complex that read, "A gift from the Rotary Club." It was clear the sign was of some age, and pre-dated the renovations done by the government in the surrounding area. It struck me that there really are no secrets, that the signs and symbols are all around for us to see. The dung gives away the camel, and the tracks lead straight to the chase, but we just don't notice. We exhaust ourselves tearing things down and throwing them away, without stopping to reflect calmly on how to cultivate and build.

That's when the doorbell rang . . .

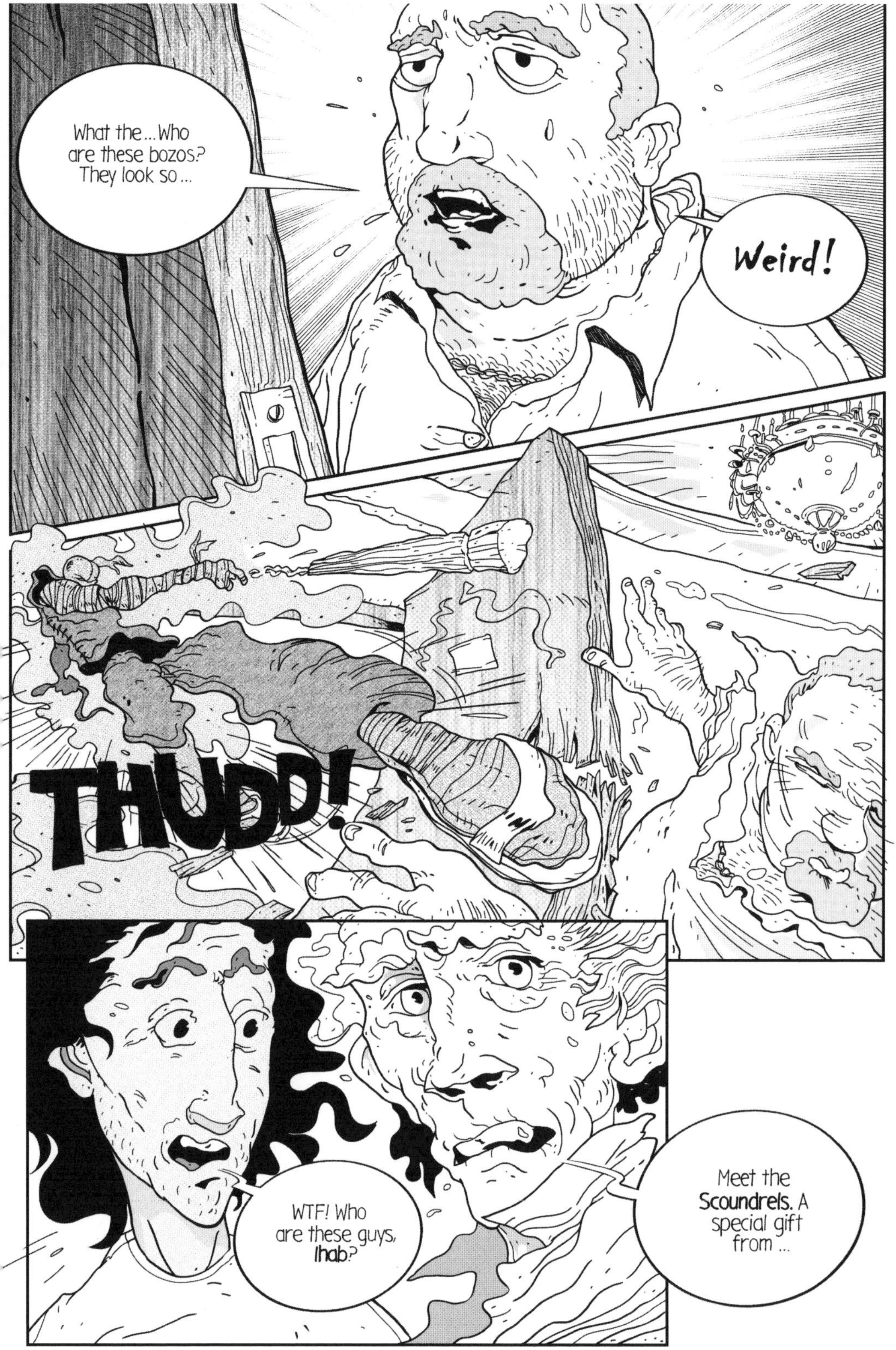
What the...Who are these bozos? They look so...
Weird!
THUDD!
WTF! Who are these guys, **Ihab**?
Meet the **Scoundrels.** A special gift from ...

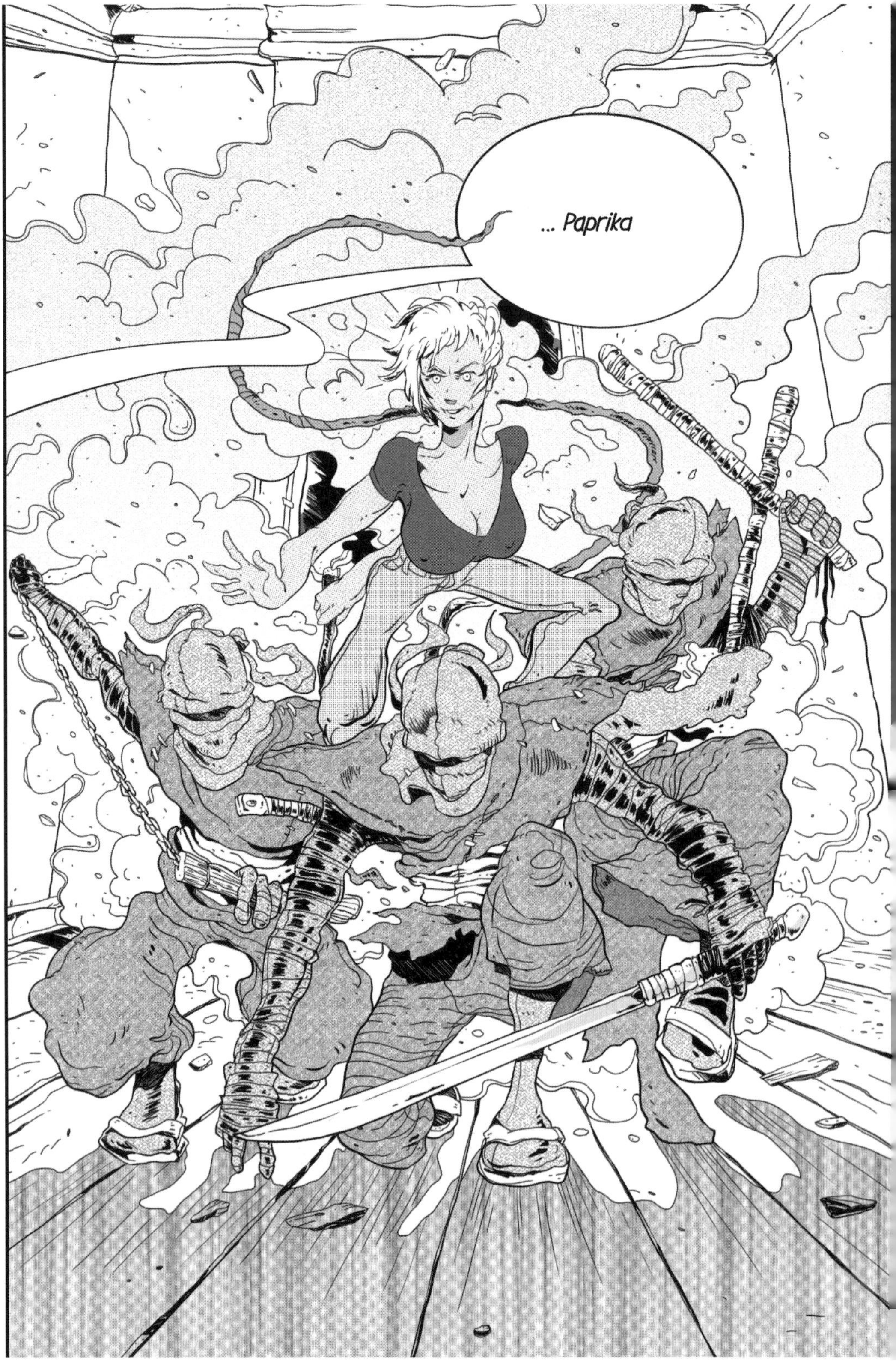
... Paprika

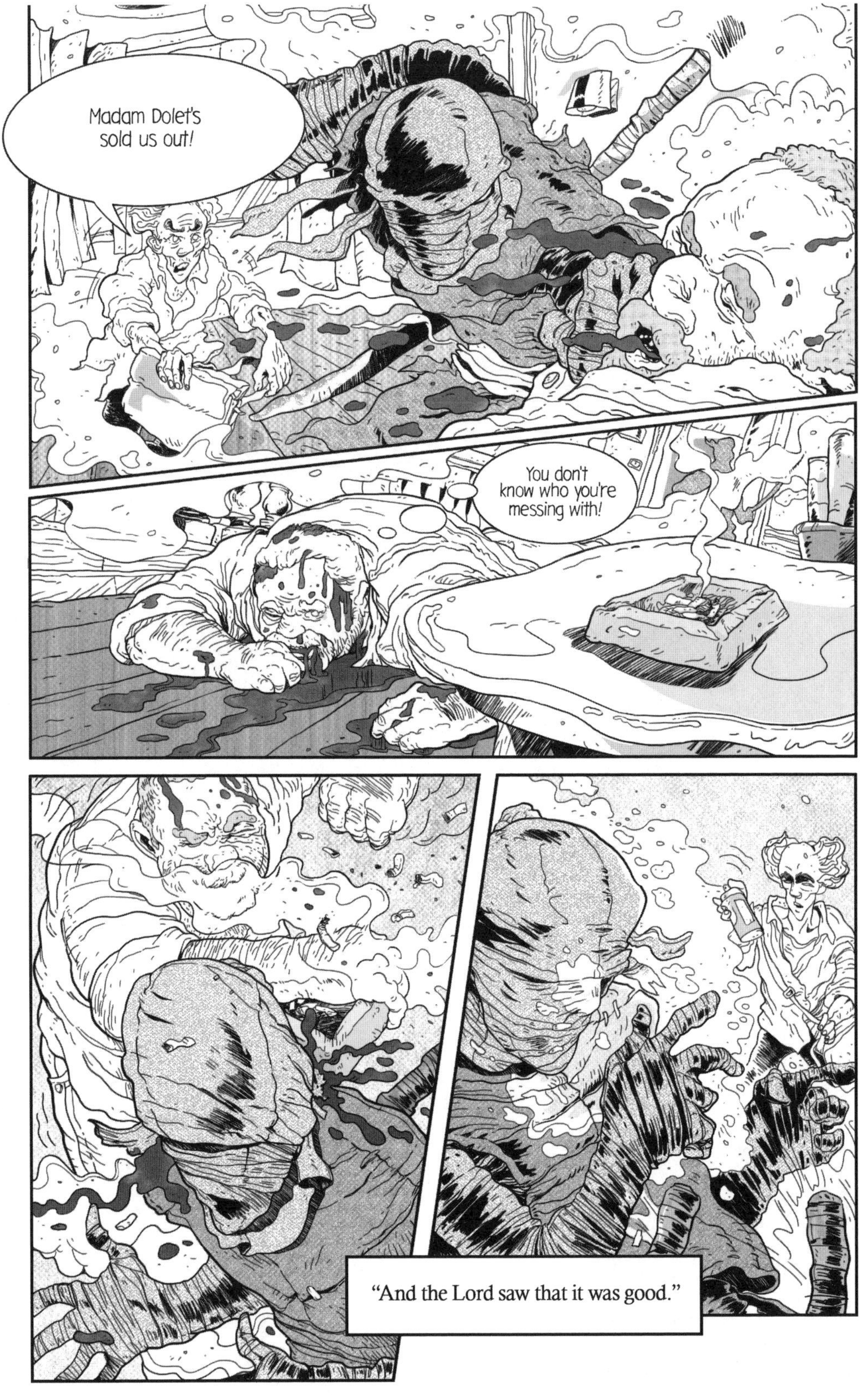
Madam Dolet's sold us out!
You don't know who you're messing with!
"And the Lord saw that it was good."

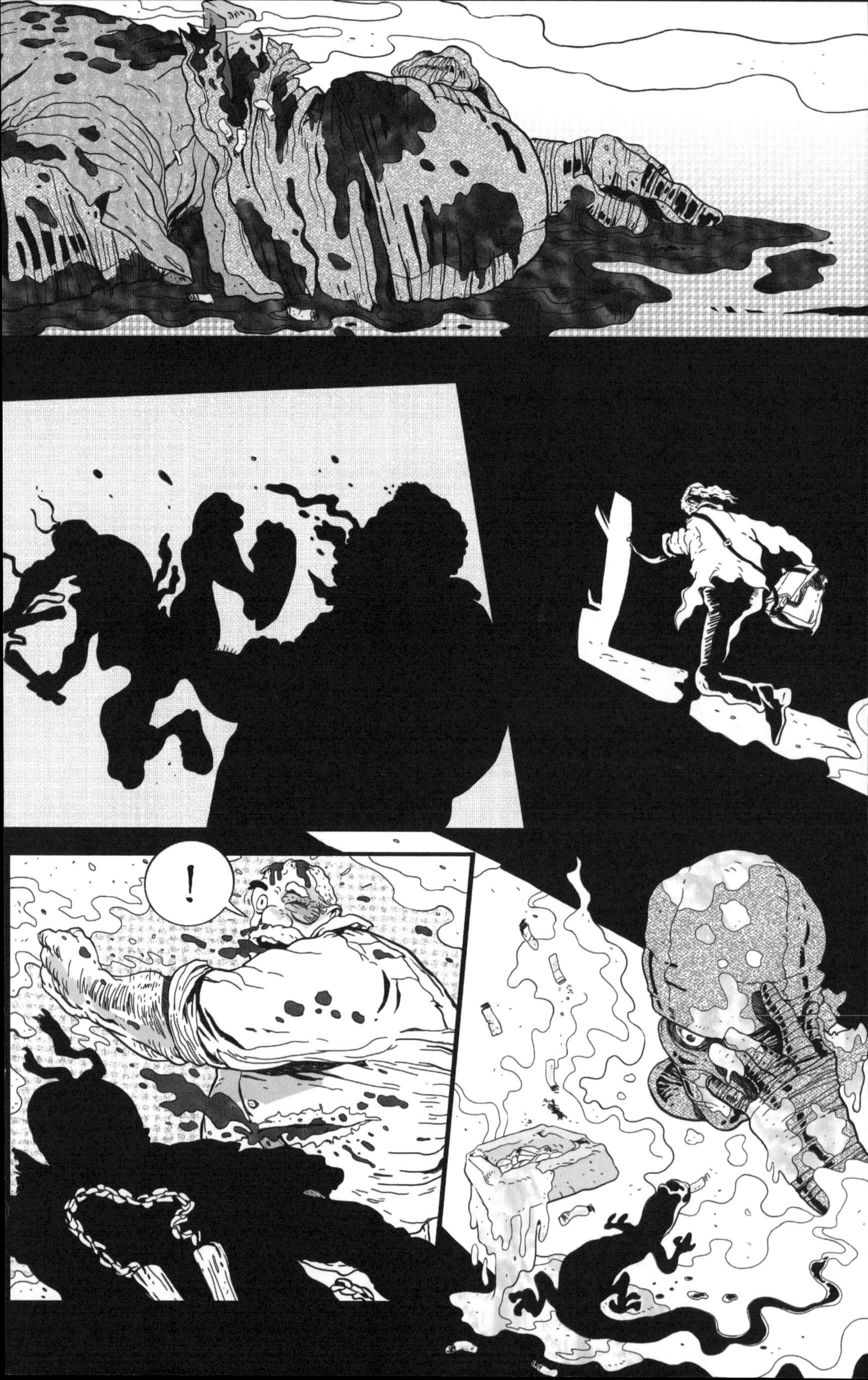
!

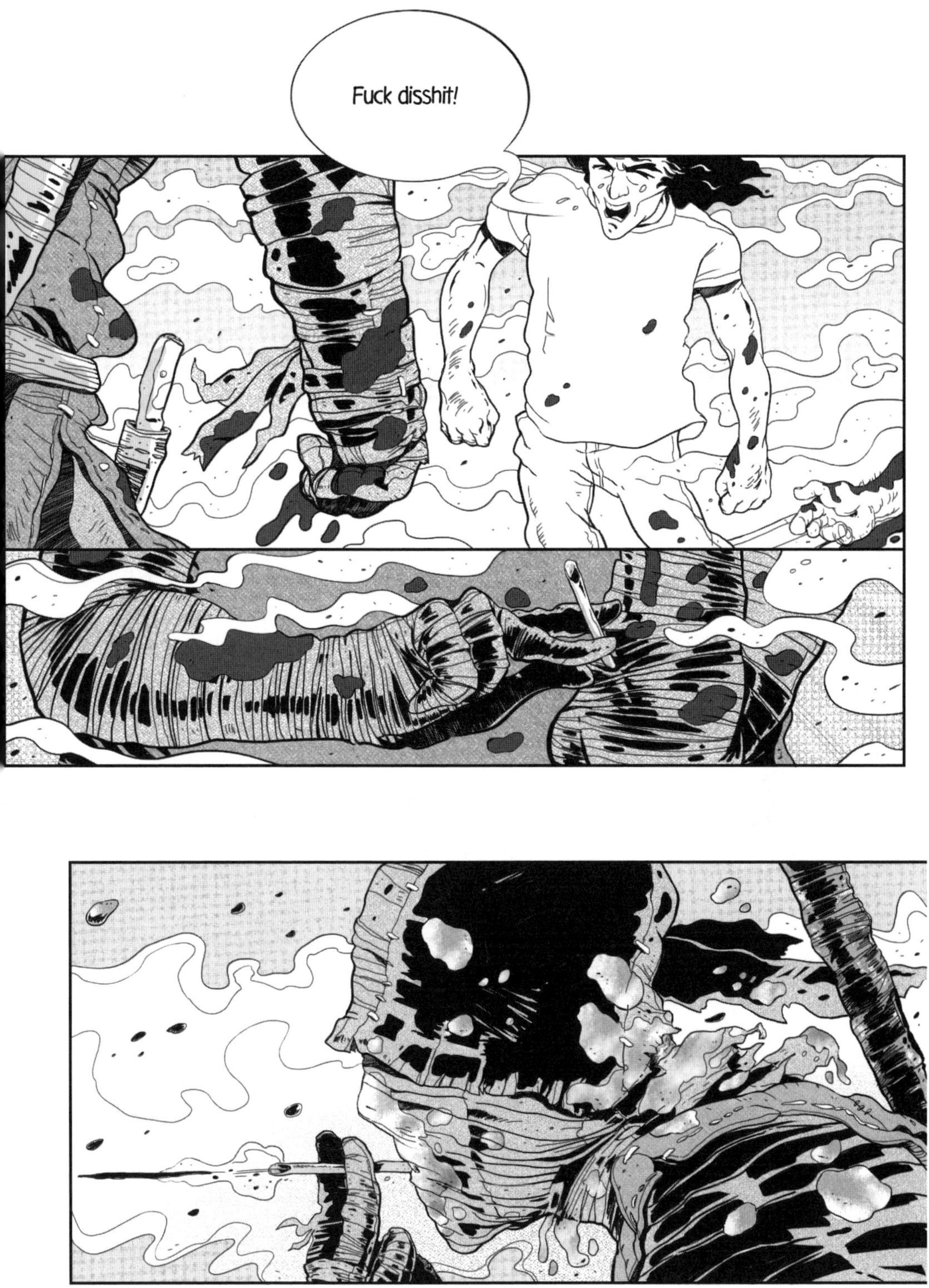
Fuck disshit!

. . .

THE TREE

I stick the side of my face against the wall of the freezer, wishing it were big enough for my entire body. I try to think, to remember. But memory's a dark room painted all black. How did I get back to my apartment?

The last thing I remember was the dagger stuck in Moud's life-less corpse. Was all that real? I switch to the other cheek. The tiles at my feet are warm. I leave the kitchen and search in vain for my phone.

Is this really my apartment?

I turn on my computer and go online. There's no news about anything. Everyone I should be worrying about is offline. Moud's offline, Mona's offline. I decide to text Ihab: "WHERE ARE YOU?"

Then I notice Samira's icon light up. "Online." I ask her for Mona's number, then rush out of the apartment without even tak-ing a shower.

The sky is orange. The humidity's the highest it could possibly be, and with every step I find it more and more difficult to breathe. The streets of October are almost empty. I continue nonetheless, and walk to the end of the street to catch a microbus to Cairo.

I don't know what's driving me. Why don't I stay home? I should consider this a humanitarian gesture by Paprika to keep me out of trouble. I should try to be normal and just go back, but there's a strange desire behind my persistence. Maybe it's just the pointlessness of life pushing me to the edge. Maybe it's my sense that the end is near, and I better make the most of it.

A number of microbuses pass by already full. Where are all these people headed?

I go over to a kiosk to call Mona. She picks up right away, let-ting loose a torrent of questions: "Bassam! Where've you been! Why's your phone off! Why don't you answer!"

"I . . . Errrr . . ."

I can't get the words out. My throat is dry but I don't feel thirsty. I can't stop the broken faucet: "And where's Ihab! He called me and he didn't sound right, then he disappeared!"

"Where . . . are you?" I utter with some difficulty.

"I'm headed over to his place on Adly Street."

Up goes the elevator. This time, it was me, Ihab, and Madam Dolet on board. It was my last visit to the chamber of secrets underneath Garden City. We got out and headed over to the car. Ihab turned to Dolet.

"Where are you planning on heading now?"

"I will go home and pack my suitcase. My flight leaves at six in the morning."

Ihab nodded in understanding. Madam Dolet drew closer and planted a single kiss on his left cheek.

"This isn't my fight, and neither is it yours, my dear Ihab." It was her good-bye.

I bought a bottle of water from a kiosk on the street, the last one in the owner's almost empty fridge. In the elevator on my way up to Ihab's apartment, I finished the whole thing, but still felt thirsty. My tongue was a dry clot of sand.

I rang the bell, and Mona opened the door. I was still thirsty. My vocal cords twitched. I couldn't breathe normally and had to open my mouth. Ihab wasn't there, and there was still no sign of him. Every attempt to call him would just give us, "The phone you've requested is currently unavailable. Press 'star' to leave a message." Beep.

Something inside my head suddenly lit up, like it had caught a current from the weird lamp in Ihab's apartment. I could visualize our last scene together. Moud: Would his corpse still be lying there? I looked over at Mona and said, half apathetically, "We have to go to Garden City."

"Why?"

I gave her the details of our last scene. She covered her mouth in horror when I told her what happened to Moud. More than once, she asked, "Are you certain Ihab was able to escape?"

"Yes," I said each time.

She sat down on the bed and pressed her palms against her face, caressing the spot on her nose with the tips of her fingers. I went to the fridge to look for a bottle of water.

"I can't go there," I said, opening the fridge. "The place is swarming with security officers. If they found out what happened, they'll arrest me. I'll be interrogated and tortured."

No water in here either. Only some queer-looking objects wrapped up in plastic bags. I took one out and opened it on the table. I could feel the bile rise from my stomach. In total disgust, all I could say was, "What is *this*?"

The digestion of food takes place in the stomach, with the help of an enzyme known as pepsin.

"What you've got there is meat," Mona said, as if not taking me seriously.

I leaned over to get a closer look at the stuff. Bright headlights from the opposite lane are a frequent irritation to drivers on the expressway.

"What *kind* of meat?"

"*Human*," she said.

I put it back in the fridge. I stuck my head under the faucet to wash off the thick layers of sand and sweat. That's when Mona's phone beeped. "You have one unread message."

"It's Ihab!" she shouted.

I took a roll of toilet paper and dried my face.

"Oh? What's he up to?"

The text read, "I'm in the asylum. I want to see you, my love, to say good-bye."

The sun was setting. The end of things to come swung backward toward the past. They say that nuclear war will wipe out all life on Earth, save for a certain species of desert lizard and wild boar. The streets of Cairo appeared as if they were in old movies, but instead of black and white, everything was covered in shades of yellow.

The asylum mentioned in the text turned out to be the old hospital of the medieval sultan Qalawun. Mona said that Ihab had shown a special interest in the place. On our way down in the elevator, she broke into tears. "He told me once it's the place where he hoped to die," she choked.

I patted her on the shoulder with caution, trying not to get emotional. I knew that the smallest spark of emotion, even something as simple as a brotherly hug, would be enough to send her into a fit of weeping and hallucinating. Madness was one of her proudest attributes.

We wouldn't be able to get a taxi on Adly Street, with all the cars coming out of the old city. We'd have to walk, and get a taxi somewhere else. You see, Cairo is arranged as a collection of historical circles, where it's easy to go to the future, but difficult to return to the past. This, too, I have learned.

Ihab was drenched in sweat. He clung nervously to his phone, its clock counting down to zero. Just thirty minutes and the poison would finish him. His body was crammed inside a small room that had been reconstructed to look like one of the asylum's old cells.

It's said that this place was originally made for soldiers returning from the shock of war. At dusk, a band of musicians would come to the courtyard and play. The cell doors would open and the inmates would listen, supposedly as a treatment for their madness.

There was no music here, and I wasn't sure which of the three of us was truly mad. Maybe the mad were only on the outside, while here between these walls stood the sane ones, impotent victims of a war that never took place.

"Go out from here in peace," Ihab chanted, concluding a melodramatic scene with Mona smiling and me smoking a last cigar.

CHAPTER TEN

· · ·

"I'm outside."

"Deal. Be there in five."

I hung up and had a smoke. The plan was to drive her out to the docks, where we'd go for a stroll. She showed up in black jeans and a white shirt, her hair let loose. When we arrived, traffic was light, with only a single boat still unloading its cargo. Most of the porters sat around on wooden crates, barnacled over in a purple haze. I stopped the car, and was just unbuckling my seat belt when I had an idea.

"Why don't we go in a bit?"

"In where?"

"Into the sea."

The October Sea is a vast expanse of orange sand, which differs in color from the normal yellow of the desert. It is sailed by dozens of boats whose movement depends on the ebb and flow of the sands, as well as the force of the winds. Cars and other land vehicles are unable to go out very far. At a certain point, the current would suck you into a vortex of sand, and carry you down into the deep orangy depths. Going by foot, you'd have to be careful too. Depending on the position of the moon and the movement of the celestial bodies, you might be able to walk on endlessly without a problem. Or, you could be swallowed up with your first step.

"Deal. Let's just hope no one's looking."

I shifted the accelerator and stepped on the gas, setting off from the docks. *Lo: The waves of the two seas split asunder, behold the isthmus betray'd there under.* Into the sea we went. It was smooth driving. She let down the window and stuck out her head, letting the sand and the wind blow gently through her hair. We passed by a slow-moving Gothic sailboat. When the sailors on board noticed us, they shouted out their greetings, and I honked in return.

The sands started to get rougher on the wheels. I wasn't comfortable with the sound of the engine, so I turned it off without pressing on the brakes. We got out of the car, and I made sure to lock the doors. She took two steps in my direction.

"That blue shirt's nice on you, by the way."

"Why thank you. God bless. Just got it yesterday."

We walked on, alone in the middle of the desert sea. Suddenly, without warning, she locked her fingers with mine. For a moment, I felt I had her back again, and nothing that happened really was. I looked at her, but her gaze was cast out over the dunes of orange.

I smiled to myself. *At least she's next to me now, holding my hand.* I pressed her fingers gently. I can't remember the last time we walked hand in hand. It was probably way before kitsch became camp.

Boats don't usually sail out in this direction. All you'll see out here is the occasional boney fish, which might surface for a second to take a breath before diving back beneath the waves of sand. From afar, you can see the sea elephants. Real big elephants with spindly legs some twenty meters in length, moving about in unison. We were now entering the Gulf of Dalí. The elephants lumbered together in herds, emitting the occasional trumpet blast. I could barely contain my excitement.

I guess she could tell. "This place sucks," she said, putting her hand on her stomach.

"All right, just a bit more, and we'll cross the Isthmus of Time over to the hill."

After five minutes of walking, we found ourselves among smoother streams of sand, trying to dodge Dalí's melting clocks.

We walked hand in hand, and climbed the hill of sand. When we got to the highest point, she gently withdrew her fingers. I looked out over the sand, before resting my gaze on a bunch of people in mismatched clothes standing on top of a giant rock. Prior to the bursting of the ozone layer, this portion of 6th of October had been sold to a real estate company that had no idea what to do with this rock the size of a mountain. They eventually decided to build a residential colony on top, like a garden nestled in the hills. After the ozone burst, the sands receded and the matter was settled.

We descended from the hill hand in hand, our legs covered in sand. Half way down, we stopped for a moment. She pulled her hand away to take out a pack of cigarettes.

"They're not working today or something?"

She looked over at the top of the rock. There weren't any balloons in the sky, or even any on the ground waiting to take off.

"I mean, it's been a while since anyone's gone up around here."

She took out her Zippo and lit up.

"But maybe they can launch one up just for me."

In moments like these, we'd deliberately shatter the melodrama with a stupid joke or a line pulled out of a trashy movie. But when my eyes met hers, I felt something strange. As if I were not me, and she were not her. Two strangers afraid to cry in front of each other, two idiots who'd lost their passports in the forest of solitude. I took a step closer to her and leaned in for a kiss. She pulled away and stuck a cigarette in my lips.

If it's true that pain is the strongest motive for writing, then perhaps it would have been better for me to start here. But out there in the middle of the October Sea, I decided to throw my heart overboard like a corpse with an ax in its head. And so I forgot the pain.

I looked down. She puffed some smoke in my direction, and I turned away.

"Anything you wanna do can be done, Mona."

The monkey tugged on the metal cord, kindling the flame and puffing up the balloon. He closed the wooden door and the balloon rose a few centimeters off the ground, but remained fastened to the docks.

Mona didn't wave, but she shook her head in delight as she shouted at me, "I'll see you there, then!"

The monkey untied the rope, and the balloon lifted off with him, his fez, and Mona.

A few clouds gathered in the sky. As soon as I got back to the car and turned on the engine, the rain had started coming down. A few minutes later, it picked up rather heavily. To distract myself from my loneliness I turned on the disc player. There was one of her discs. The window wipers brushing away the rain, I set my compass and headed south.

October 2007
January 2011

AUTHOR'S ACKNOWLEDGMENTS

This work would not have reached its final form without the support, review, and observations of the following: Sara el-Masri, Iman Mersal, Waiel Ashry, Hassan Abdel Mawgoud, Fadi Awad, Mariam Al Ferjani, Ben (our ambassador to the library archives of the West), Fawwaz Traboulsi, Marwan Imam, David Bowie, Ahmed Wael.